"Look, I know you hurt," he said softly. "And I know you're scared. It's going to be all right."

"Do you really think so?" Jordan asked, looking up at him.

He couldn't allow himself to answer her truthfully.

Instead, Beau found himself reaching toward the errant strands of hair that grazed her cheekbone. It wasn't a conscious gesture; it was as though his hand belonged to somebody else, as though he had no control over the movement.

He dared to let his hand linger there against her cheek, allowed his thumb to trace her jawline downward. When he tucked his thumb beneath her chin and lifted her face so that he could look into her eyes, he found something utterly unexpected in them.

A smoldering spark of attraction.

She was as drawn to him as he was to her.

He closed his eyes briefly, knowing that when he opened them it would be gone, that the shared passion would prove to have been his imagination.

But when he looked down at Jordan again, there was no denying the electricity that darted between her gaze and his. Before he knew what he was doing, Beau dipped his head and kissed her.

It was a fleeting, blazing kiss, one that told him all he needed to know.

Jordan Curry was dangerous.

BOOK YOUR PLACE ON OUR WEBSITE AND MAKE THE READING CONNECTION!

We've created a customized website just for our very special readers, where you can get the inside scoop on everything that's going on with Zebra, Pinnacle and Kensington books.

When you come online, you'll have the exciting opportunity to:

- View covers of upcoming books

- Read sample chapters

- Learn about our future publishing schedule (listed by publication month *and author*)

- Find out when your favorite authors will be visiting a city near you

- Search for and order backlist books from our online catalog

- Check out author bios and background information

- Send e-mail to your favorite authors

- Meet the Kensington staff online

- Join us in weekly chats with authors, readers and other guests

- Get writing guidelines

- AND MUCH MORE!

Visit our website at
http://www.kensingtonbooks.com

NIGHT MOVES

Janelle Taylor

ZEBRA BOOKS
KENSINGTON PUBLISHING CORP.
http://www.kensingtonbooks.com

ZEBRA BOOKS are published by

Kensington Publishing Corp.
850 Third Avenue
New York, NY 10022

All Kensington titles, imprints and distributed lines are available at special quantity discounts for bulk purchases for sales promotion, premiums, fund-raising, educational or institutional use.

Special book excerpts or customized printings can also be created to fit specific needs. For details, write or phone the office of the Kensington Special Sales Manager: Kensington Publishing Corp., 850 Third Avenue, New York, NY 10022. Attn. Special Sales Department. Phone: 1-800-221-2647.

Zebra and the Z logo Reg. U.S. Pat. & TM Off.

First Printing: July 2002
10 9 8 7 6 5 4 3 2 1

Printed in the United States of America

To my Native American friends Jana Nation, Ray Tracey, Jackie and Chuck Harris, Camille Gordon, and Pat Parker.

Chapter One

"Hi, this is Beau Somerville again, calling for Jordan. I got your message last Friday canceling Saturday night, and I hope you got mine rescheduling for tomorrow night. Unfortunately, I have to take a rain check on that. Give me a call and we'll reschedule again, hopefully before I leave on vacation next week. Sorry. 'Bye.''

Jordan Curry sighed as the Creole-accented male voice signed off and her answering machine beeped twice, signaling the end of today's second message.

The first had been a farewell call from her parents, reminding her that they were off on their Alaskan cruise for three weeks.

Newly retired from the social-studies teaching department of Jordan's hometown high school, Clark Curry had vowed to spend the rest of his life seeing the world. Naturally, her mother was gung-ho for the plan. After three blissful decades of marriage, she was gung-ho about just about everything Jordan's father did.

Jordan sat on the edge of the rose-and-cream-colored couch and bent over to remove her low-heeled navy leather pumps.

So Beau Somerville was postponing their blind date yet again, she thought, as she flexed her aching feet. Maybe he had a legitimate excuse.

Maybe not. Maybe he was as reluctant to go out with a total stranger as she was, despite his being newly relocated to Washington and not knowing a soul.

Jordan had done her best to resist Andrea MacDuff's efforts to fix her up. But the wife of Louisiana Senator Harlan MacDuff—and Jordan's most high profile client—wouldn't take no for an answer, basically assuming that her wish was Jordan's command.

With her conservative Deep-South upbringing and old-fashioned values, Andrea refused to accept that Jordan wasn't husband hunting, or that running a successful Washington catering business was as fulfilling as marriage would be.

So Beau wanted her to call him back to reschedule again?

Maybe she would—later. If she was in the mood to talk. Right now, she just wanted to trade the fitted navy business suit and pantyhose she had worn to meet a new client for a pair of shorts and a T-shirt suitable for lounging around with a Lean Cuisine and the latest issue of *Martha Stewart Living*.

Gathering her pumps in one hand and picking up her bulging leather briefcase in the other, Jordan rose and padded across the plush ivory carpet toward the stairway leading to the bedroom, flipping on lights as she went.

It wasn't yet dusk on this muggy June evening, but the sky outside had grown dark with the threat of an impending thunderstorm.

On the second floor, she paused in the hall to adjust the central air to a lower setting. When she had first stepped in from the ninety-five-degree humidity, the town house felt cool. Now it was bordering on stuffy.

This was her third steamy Georgetown summer, but Jordan still wasn't used to keeping the windows closed and the air on.

She had grown up in a leafy Pennsylvania town nestled on a hillside in the Allegheny foothills, where only the supermarkets and the local hospital had central air-conditioning. Jordan had always liked falling asleep on summer nights to the sound of crickets chirping, occasional breezes stirring the wind chimes, the hushed, distant chatter of her parents, and the front porch glider creaking gently under their weight.

There was something decidedly sterile about closed windows and the faint hum of the air conditioner—but it was a necessity in this part of the country.

In the bedroom, Jordan couldn't help admiring anew the pale yellow-on-white sponge-painted walls and white crown moldings. The redecorating job had been completed by her painting contractor only last week, replacing blue walls that made even this spacious room feel closed in.

She had chosen to redo everything in shades of springtime. Her new moss-green-and-yellow floral-sprigged Ralph Lauren comforter and imported Egyptian sheets were still in their zipped plastic packages on the floor beside the king-sized bed. A just-purchased area rug to cover a portion of the polished hardwood floor remained rolled up at the far end of the room.

Jordan yawned, wondering if she should get busy opening the packages, laundering her new purchases, and unrolling the carpet.

Nah.

She was too exhausted to finish the redecorating job tonight, as she had been every night this week. Maybe she would get to it tomorrow, now that Mr. Beau Somerville had canceled their date. Again.

It was just as well. She shouldn't be dating in the first place.

She reminded herself that she was perfectly content to spend her evenings solo right here at home. In fact, she would welcome the chance to indulge in the domestic hobbies she had loved since childhood: baking, decorating, gardening, needlework . . .

Then again, she had to admit that some of those hobbies might be better suited to a different lifestyle.

After all, one person could only eat so many home-made fudge brownies and cutout sugar cookies before wishing there were other mouths to feed.

Decorating the unspectacular rooms of a Georgetown duplex wasn't the same as redoing a real house—a lived-in house with a nursery, a playroom, children's bedrooms.

Although every available inch of Jordan's square brick patio and wrought-iron rails bloomed with colorful annuals in terra-cotta pots, and the railings were draped with fragrant boxes of potted herbs, container gardening on a small town-house terrace didn't compare to landscaping a backyard.

And after stitching countless needlepoint samplers as gifts for friends' weddings and babies, even the most content single gal could find herself growing a little wistful for what might have been.

After stripping off her suit, Jordan opened the double closet and deposited the jacket and skirt into a wicker hamper half filled with clothes that were bound for the dry cleaner. As she pushed the hamper in again, it caught on a plastic-draped garment hung in the very back of the closet.

Jordan frowned, moving aside the billowing length of plastic-shrouded white silk organza.

Her wedding dress.

Every time she tugged the hamper forward or pushed it back, it bumped into the garment, reminding her of a day she would much rather forget.

"Why don't you just get rid of the damn dress?" she grumbled to herself, firmly closing the double closet doors.

Because that would be even more painful. Then she would actually have to remove the wedding gown from the recesses of the closet and carry it downstairs, put it in the car, take it out again, and hand it over to . . .

Well, to whomever one presented wedding dresses that had been worn for exactly forty-five minutes.

Forty-five minutes.

That was how long it had taken for Jordan, the would-be bride, to ride in a limousine from her parents' house to the flower-bedecked country church nearby.

To pose for several pictures outside, alone, and with her parents, and with Phoebe, her maid of honor.

To stand, grasping her father's arm, at the foot of the aisle while the minister stood poised behind the pulpit and the organist played Pachelbel's Canon in D four times through, and the expectant gazes of the congregation volleyed from Jordan to the vacant spot by the altar.

Finally, Kevin's tuxedo-clad younger brother, David

Sanders, the best man, materialized in the doorway lead-ing back to the rectory and hurried over to whisper to the minister.

As Jordan watched, her heart pounding and her bou-quet of white lilies trembling, David hastily retreated.

The minister, now somber, walked slowly down the aisle toward Jordan.

Of course she knew, before he told her, what had happened. It was obvious. Maybe it was even expected, somewhere in the part of her mind obscured by denial.

Kevin, whom she had loved since they were seniors in high school, had changed his mind.

Kevin wasn't going to show up.

Kevin wasn't going to marry her after all.

Jordan winced even now, remembering the pain and humiliation that had coursed through her, remember-ing the pity clouding the familiar faces that filled the pews.

Phoebe had put her protective arms around Jordan, tears of sympathy shimmering in her eyes. Mother had bolted from her front row aisle seat and came scurrying down the aisle, determined to shield her jilted daughter from the curious gazes as Daddy ushered them all back out to the limousine.

Jordan's younger brother Andy and a couple of the other groomsmen had already tied old cans to the bumper and propped a big "Just Married" sign on the back window. The cans made a hollow, scraping sound on the asphalt as the limo transported the silent bridal party back home. There, Jordan discarded the white silk organza dress in a rumpled heap on her bedroom floor before collapsing in despair.

It was thrifty Phoebe, the product of a threadbare, impoverished household and newly married herself, who promptly rescued the dress, returning it to its padded hanger and covering it in plastic. "It cost hundreds of dollars and it's still brand-new. You can always sell it," Phoebe said, when Jordan informed her that she'd just as soon toss the gown into the nearest Dumpster.

Eventually, Jordan acknowledged that Phoebe was right. The dress *could* be sold. Sold, or thrown away.

But either scenario was just too much trouble. Either scenario meant looking at it, touching it, thinking about it, thinking about Kevin, thinking about the life they had carefully planned together only to have him carelessly toss it—and Jordan—aside.

She wasn't planning to bring the gown with her a year later when she left her parents' house and moved the rest of her belongings to Washington.

She had laid the dress, still wrapped and on its hanger, on top of an overflowing cardboard box she was using for garbage. She assumed the movers she'd hired had discarded it. It wasn't until she arrived in Georgetown and unpacked her belongings that she found that the movers had packed not only the dress, but the box of garbage as well.

She didn't know whether to laugh at the realization that she had paid to have her garbage, some of it smelly kitchen scraps, hauled three hundred miles, or to cry at the sight of the beaded, embroidered white gown that seemed bent on haunting her for the rest of her life.

So . . .

Here it hung, four years after the June wedding that wasn't.

She'd heard Kevin had gotten married not long after she moved away, to a local girl who had been several classes behind them in school. He and his wife didn't waste time starting a family, and already had two small children.

Pulling a T-shirt over her head, Jordan caught sight of her reflection in the mirrored closet door.

Strands of her long, dark hair tumbled from the casual updo she'd piled it into this morning. Her face was lightly but expertly made up, accentuating her large green eyes, high cheekbones, and full mouth.

She couldn't wait to scrub off all the goo. She wasn't big on makeup, but she had to look presentable on a daily basis, considering the caliber of her client list. She noticed that her face seemed paler than usual. Or maybe that was just because she had increasingly noticed the sun-kissed complexions of others now that summer was underway.

There was a time when summer, for Jordan, meant bare, golden skin. She and Phoebe actually used to lie out in the yard daily in bathing suits, coated in oil rather than sunscreen, too young and vain to worry about radiation and skin cancer.

Those were the days, she thought wryly.

When was the last time Jordan had even been in the sun? She grimly recalled pulling down the visor to block its rays through her car's windshield just yesterday.

You need a vacation.

Her business partner and old college pal, Jeremy Van Pragh, said that frequently. Weekly. Daily, even—especially lately.

Jordan never listened. Whenever Jeremy took advantage of their slow season during late winter by jetting off to the Caribbean, Jordan busied herself catching up on book work and trying new recipes.

Now, as she stared at her reflection, she contemplated her life.

All that she had . . . and all that suddenly seemed to be missing.

The catering business was successful beyond Jordan's and Jeremy's wildest dreams. Only three years into the venture, they counted among their regular clients some of the biggest names in the capital's high-profile political and social arena.

For the first time in her life, Jordan had plenty of cash, a nice-sized savings account, an IRA, and a growing investment and stock portfolio. She had a new car, a membership to an upscale gym, a complete business and casual wardrobe, and a newly renovated town house filled with custom-made furniture and draperies, top-notch appliances, and electronic equipment.

The trouble was, she was too busy to drive her black BMW convertible anywhere but to work—so busy that most of her casual clothing still had price tags attached, and she didn't know how to work half the appliances in her kitchen. She had never even watched a DVD or played a CD on her home entertainment system, surfed the Internet, or sent an E-mail from the home computer.

Poised, standing in the middle of the oversized master bedroom suite she shared with no one, Jordan thought about Andrea MacDuff, who seemed convinced that Jordan's lifestyle was bordering on tragic.

Andrea didn't even know that Jordan hadn't had physical contact with a man—not so much as a *kiss*, for Pete's sake—since Kevin left her at the altar.

It wasn't that Jordan agreed with Andrea's outdated views on women, careers, and marriage. But . . .

Maybe it *was* time to start dating again.

Even blind dating.

After pulling on a pair of shorts, Jordan made her

way back downstairs to look for Beau Somerville's phone number.

Beau didn't even look away from his computer screen when the cell phone in his pocket rang. He was intent on reconfiguring the kitchen island on the floor plan for the addition the MacDuffs were doing on their Virginia farmhouse. Andrea was insisting on an L-shaped island despite Beau's caution that it would mar the flow. She was a stubborn woman, whose honeyed drawl and delicate appearance were misleading. She reminded Beau of his mother. A real steel-magnolia type.

By the third ring, he absently reached for the phone as though swatting a pesky mosquito. He flipped it open, his eyes still fastened to the computer monitor. His head was beginning to throb and his shoulder blades ached from sitting in this position for hours. There were times when he missed the old-fashioned, more portable way of drafting architectural designs, on good old-fashioned paper instead of with CAD software.

"Beau Somerville," he murmured, electronically dragging a portion of island to a perpendicular position.

There was a slight pause. "Hi," an unfamiliar female voice said. "I'm surprised I got you and not your voice mail again."

"I don't have voice mail on this cell phone yet," he replied, his concentration broken, his hand poised on the mouse.

"Oh . . . this is your cell phone? I'm sorry, I called the wrong number. Andrea gave me both, but I thought this was your home number. . . ."

"Andrea?"

"MacDuff."

"Is there any other?" He found himself cracking a smile. "This is Jordan, right? Jordan Curry?"

"Is there any other?"

He chuckled, surprised at her snappy comeback. Maybe he shouldn't have broken tomorrow night's date with her after all. When he'd decided earlier to back out, it wasn't because he had a good excuse. It was more like . . .

A classic case of cold feet.

The last thing he wanted to do was get involved with someone. He had only been in Washington for a few months, freshly liberated from a relationship with Lisa, who had thought he was going to marry her, give her babies, and build her a dream house. And before Lisa, there was . . .

No.

He didn't want to think back that far. He dragged his thoughts to the present, but it was too late. The almost-memory had tossed a chill over his heart.

"Did you get my message?" he asked Jordan Curry, who was supposedly the most beautiful, intelligent, successful woman in the metro D.C. area. Oh, and she made "a praline pie that would do that Somerville N'Awlins heritage proud"—a direct quote from Andrea.

"I got your message," Jordan replied, sounding efficient, as though they were discussing a business proposition. "You wanted to reschedule?"

Not particularly. He had been hoping that after another round or two of phone tag, their telephone correspondence would fizzle and he'd be off the hook.

"Sure," he said, because that was, after all, the message he had left on her machine.

Irritated, he pressed some keys on his computer keyboard, hoping to sound busy so he'd have an excuse for cutting the conversation short. He asked, just as efficiently, "When do you want to meet?"

"It's up to you."

There was something sultry about the low pitch of her voice, he noted. And she didn't have a trace of any kind of accent. He was so used to Lisa's forced drawl that he welcomed Jordan's lack of one. Lisa had grown up in the Midwest but considered herself an adopted Southern belle. She'd gone to college at Tulane, which was apparently when she started dyeing her brown hair blond, got blue contact lenses, and learned to "y'all" in earnest. The mere memory of her syrupy inflections grated on his nerves.

"How about Saturday?" Beau heard himself suggest to Jordan Curry.

"Saturday, the day after tomorrow, or Saturday, next week?"

"I'll be gone on vacation next week, so the day after tomorrow," he clarified, wondering what the heck he was doing. Just because this woman didn't sound like Lisa didn't mean that he should date her. He shouldn't date anyone. Ever again.

"The day after tomorrow . . . ?" He could hear what sounded like datebook pages flipping. "I'm free that night," she said.

She didn't sound legitimately pleased about it, though.

Well, she was the one who had called him back. If she didn't want to go out with him, she shouldn't have returned the call.

"Great," he said with fake enthusiasm to match her own. "Do you want to meet for dinner, then?"

"That would be good."

"Good."

"Where do you want to meet?"

He named a restaurant.

She named a time.

They hung up.

Beau wondered if he should hunt down his Palm Pilot and mark the date and the details. Nah. He wouldn't forget. It was only two days away.

He scowled at the layout on his computer screen. A chunk of the kitchen island was now obstructing the mudroom doorway. How had that happened?

He had a date with Jordan Curry. How had *that* happened?

Beau shook his head. He honestly wanted to strangle Andrea MacDuff.

A little over twenty-four hours later, Jordan climbed out of her BMW and raced through a downpour toward her front door. What a day . . . and night. Her fingers ached like crazy from pitting cherries for the jelly she had made as favors for a bridal shower to be held on Sunday afternoon, and her shoulders were sore from bending over the painstaking task. She was sore all over, and now she was soaked, too.

The rain that had begun loudly in the middle of the night hadn't seemed to let up for a moment since. The world was a gray, humid, soggy mess.

All Jordan wanted was to get into her dry, air-conditioned townhouse, change out of her damp clothes, and curl up on the couch with that issue of *Martha Stewart Living*. When she had tried to read it last night, she had been so weary she'd dozed with her head on the page and finally gave up and went to bed. . . .

She stopped short now on the bottom step in front of her door.

Somebody was huddled beneath the overhang that sheltered the top step, which wasn't big enough to qualify as a stoop.

Not just one person, she realized, gaping at the figure in the dark-colored slicker. There were two. One was a third of the size of the other, also clad in rain gear.

"Jordan?"

"Oh my god!" Jordan recognized the voice, if not the sight of her best friend. "Phoebe!"

She raced up the steps and threw her arms around her friend.

"What are you doing here?" she asked, looking from the small section of Phoebe's face that was visible inside her hood, to the small child who stood with his arms wrapped around her leg.

"Waiting for you," Phoebe replied.

"For how long? Did I know you were coming?" Jordan was fairly certain it hadn't slipped her busy mind. A visit from Phoebe was monumental. She would never forget something like that.

"No, you didn't know," Phoebe said. "We haven't been here long. When you weren't home, I was trying to figure out where we should go next. We took a cab over from the train station. I should have told him to wait. . . ."

"Well, now it doesn't matter." Jordan fumbled with her keys, unlocking the door. "Let's get inside. Is this Spencer? Why didn't you call and tell me you were coming?"

Phoebe only said, "Yes, this is Spencer," as she and her son stepped past Jordan's beckoning arm and over the threshold.

Jordan followed them in, reeling.

Never in a million years would she expect her closest childhood friend to show up on her doorstep.

She hadn't seen Phoebe in . . . how long had it been? She backtracked mentally to their last meeting, in a hushed funeral parlor back in Glen Hills, their hometown. About eighteen months, Jordan realized. It had been eighteen months since Phoebe's father passed away. That was around the holidays.

She still recalled the late-night phone call that had preceded that unexpected trip home, and her surprise at hearing Phoebe's wavering voice on the other end of the line. Phone calls from Phoebe had been scarce for a few years, ever since she married Reno and moved to Philadelphia.

Yet whenever they talked, time and distance fell away.

"Jordan, Daddy's dead," Phoebe had said that night on a sob. Jordan had cried with her.

Of course, Jordan had gone home for the funeral. She flew into Erie on a tiny commuter plane in a blizzard and flew out the same day, thanks to a wedding she was in the midst of catering for the grand-niece of the Speaker of the House.

Now she recalled how fiercely Phoebe had clung to her when they embraced beside the casket—until Reno interrupted, drawing his wife away, saying the minister needed to speak to her.

Spencer wasn't even there, Jordan remembered. They had left him with a baby-sitter at Phoebe's older brother Curt's house.

"How old are you now, Spencer?" Jordan asked, crouching beside the godson she hadn't seen since he was a gap-toothed toddler.

"I'm thirty-one."

"No, Spence, *I'm* thirty-one," Phoebe said with a tight smile. "He's almost four," she told Jordan. "But he has an active imagination."

Phoebe was as pretty as ever, Jordan noted, watching her friend lower her hood, admiring her long blond hair caught smoothly back in a ponytail.

She was skinnier than ever, too. Her always-angular face looked almost gaunt. Her hazel eyes were trenched in shadows, as though she hadn't slept well lately.

"I can't believe you're really here!" Jordan straightened and shed her wet Burberry trench coat, tossing it carelessly over the back of a nearby chair. "This is an incredible surprise. Is Reno with you?"

"No. This is a nice place." Phoebe's gaze flicked around the entry hall with its maroon-and-ivory striped wallpaper and polished hardwood floor.

"Thanks. I just redecorated."

"I'm afraid we're dripping on your rug," Phoebe observed, gesturing at the woven welcome mat under her feet.

"That's why it's there." As she spoke, gazing at her friend, Jordan realized that something was wrong. Not just with Phoebe, but with her son, and with this whole scene.

Phoebe, always on the quiet side—and increasingly so following her marriage—seemed even more subdued than usual. Skittish, even. Jordan saw her friend fumbling with the buttons on her slicker, trying several times to unfasten each closure before succeeding.

And little Spencer just stood there, his wide brown eyes looking almost frightened beneath a sheaf of thick, straight brown bangs.

"What's wrong, Phoebe?" Jordan's thoughts were spinning. Had Phoebe left Reno? If so . . .

Well, it was about time. Jordan had never liked Phoebe's darkly handsome husband, who had swept her friend off her feet and married her after a whirlwind courtship. Jordan's feelings for him weren't based on anything he had ever said or done. After all, she hadn't spent enough time with him even to feel as though she knew him well enough to judge his character based on anything other than instinct. But sometimes instinct was sufficient.

"Phoebe?" Jordan prodded, watching her friend, who seemed reluctant to meet her gaze. "What happened?"

"I . . . I can't really explain it. Not . . . yet." Phoebe motioned slightly with her head, gesturing at her son.

Clearly, she didn't want Spencer to know about whatever it was that had brought them here.

Jordan didn't press her. She took Phoebe's coat and watched her remove Spencer's little slicker. Then she hung them both, along with her own trench, to drip-dry on hangers along the shower-curtain rod over the never-used tub in the full bath off the kitchen.

Jordan ushered her guests into the living room and offered them something to drink.

"Do you have any juice boxes?" Spencer asked.

"Juice boxes?" Jordan echoed the unfamiliar phrase. She crouched to be on the same level with the little boy. "I'm afraid I'm fresh out of juice boxes, but I have some nice oranges in the fridge, and I have a juicer that I've never even used. I'd love to give it a try."

"No, don't do that," Phoebe said quickly. "He can drink milk." Seeing Jordan's expression, she added, "or water."

"Water, I have." Jordan led the way to the kitchen, with its white ceramic-tile floor and backsplash with cornflower-blue accents, and cool slate-colored granite countertops. Several of the white cabinets had glass doors to display Jordan's collection of cobalt plates and stemware. She had replaced the existing appliances with a six-burner stainless-steel Viking stove and sub-zero refrigerator.

She walked over to the corner that held the spring-water cooler with its upended blue plastic bottle. "Sorry there's no milk," she said over her shoulder. "I haven't bought any in ages, ever since I stopped making coffee at home. Now I just get it from Starbucks on the way to work. It's so much easier. But . . . I can make some coffee now if you want some," she offered Phoebe. "Or wine. I have wine."

"No, thanks. I'll just have water, too." Phoebe helped Spencer climb onto one of the tall wooden stools at the breakfast bar island and sat beside him, watching Jordan take down three glasses.

With her back to them as she filled the pretty blue goblets, Jordan wanted to ask countless questions, finally settling on one that didn't seem overly nosy. "Are you staying overnight?"

There was a pause.

Jordan turned to see Phoebe wearing that same nervous, troubled expression. "Do you have room for guests?"

"I have nothing but room," Jordan said. "Look around. It's just me, and I've got plenty of space for company. You can stay as long as you want. I have a guest room upstairs next to mine, and the living room couch pulls out into a bed."

"Do you have cable TV?" Phoebe asked, glancing at Spencer, who was solemnly looking around the kitchen.

Jordan nodded, smiling. "Yep, I even have cable TV."

"Spencer likes to watch a program on the Disney Channel at around this time every night," Phoebe said. "Would you mind if I turned it on for him?"

"No problem. I'll do it. Come on, Spencer. You can bring your water into the living room, and I'll try to find some kind of snack for you to have with it."

"Do you have any plastic cups?" Spencer asked, eyeing the brimming goblet in her hand. "That looks too big. I might spill it."

"No plastic," Jordan said ruefully. "Not even paper cups. Don't worry. If it spills, it spills."

"It might break," Spencer told her worriedly.

"If it breaks, it breaks. I have lots of them. Come on. I'll set you up in front of the TV. I'll be right back, Phoebe."

It took her a few minutes to locate the Disney Channel. When she returned to the kitchen, Phoebe was still sitting at the counter, her water glass untouched, her elbow propped on the countertop, chin in one hand, fingers splayed broodingly across her face.

"Tell me what's going on, Phoebe," Jordan said quietly, sliding onto the stool Spencer had vacated. "Why are you here? Why isn't Reno? Did something happen?"

Phoebe nodded, running her hand distractedly through her hair as she met Jordan's gaze. Her expression was stark, haunted. "Reno's back at home, in Philadelphia."

Jordan knew then that her hunch was right. Phoebe had left him. Why? Was he abusive?

Jordan found it frighteningly easy to imagine her friend's moody husband lashing out at Phoebe, or even at his son. She had noticed, on the few occasions she had seen them together, that Reno frequently seemed to have a protective arm around his wife. Yet Jordan had witnessed little if any genuine affection in their marriage, let alone between father and son. It was Phoebe who held Spencer as an infant, who changed his diapers and fed him bottles and played with him. Reno seemed detached.

"It's going to be all right, Phoebe." Jordan laid a comforting hand on Phoebe's arm and noticed that it was terribly thin. She could feel the jutting bones beneath her fingers. "You must be a nervous wreck. I know how hard it is to go through something like this, but—"

"No, Jordan, it's not what you think," Phoebe said, casting a fretful glance toward the living room, where the television blared reassuringly.

"You and Reno aren't splitting up?"

"No."

Disappointment coursed through Jordan. On its heels came fresh concern. Something was obviously terribly wrong. If it wasn't Phoebe's marriage, and if Spencer was safely here and Reno back in Philadelphia, then what was it? Both Phoebe's parents were dead; the only family she had left was her older brother.

"Did something happen to Curt?" Jordan asked, doubting it even as she spoke.

Phoebe had never been close to her only sibling, the product of their father's brief first marriage and nearly a generation older than Phoebe. Even if Curt had met some tragedy, Jordan tried and failed to imagine that it would be shattering enough to send Phoebe to her doorstep out of the blue, looking like a nervous wreck.

"No, it's not Curt; it's . . ." Again Phoebe trailed off, looking anxious.

Oh, no. Jordan took in Phoebe's gaunt appearance,

her skin-and-bones figure, her distressed expression. Was it Phoebe? Was she seriously ill?

"Phoebe, you have to tell me," she pressed, her stomach flip-flopping in apprehension. "You're scaring me."

"I'm scared, too, Jordan." Phoebe's voice barely hovered above a whisper. "I'm so sorry to drag you into this, but you were the only person I could trust. . . ."

"Of course you can trust me," Jordan said automatically. Her mind flashed back to sunny summer days, to childhood promises.

How many times had she said those words? They had grown up next door to each other, had played together as soon as they were old enough to toddle back and forth across the yard between their houses. They had shared everything from girlhood confidences to eye makeup to double dates.

Though college had separated them long before Reno came along and Kevin ran off and Jordan moved to Washington, Jordan still considered Phoebe her most cherished friend. There was no secret she wouldn't entrust to her.

"I have to ask you to do something for me," Phoebe said, her voice edged with despair. "Something huge. Something you don't have to do, except . . . if you don't say yes, Jordan, I don't know what I'll do."

"I'll do anything for you, Phoebe. You know that. Believe me, no favor is too huge."

"I need you to take Spencer for me."

Jordan gaped at her. "*Take* Spencer? You mean . . ." She took a deep breath. "Are you sick, Phoebe? Are you—?"

"No, it's nothing like that. I'm not sick. And I don't mean forever. Just . . . take him. Please." Her voice wavered. "Keep him here, for as long as I need you to."

"But . . . why? It's not that I don't want to take him," Jordan added hastily, her mind cascading with frantic questions that mingled with apprehension and doubt.

Take a four-year-old boy? She had never even talked to a four-year-old boy, had she? No, not since she was a six-year-old girl with a kid brother.

"I can't really explain it, Jordan. All I can say is that nobody can know he's here. Nobody. Not your family, and not mine. Not even Reno."

"Not even Reno? Phoebe, what's going on?"

"Jordan, just say you'll do it. Please. It's . . ." Phoebe trailed off, wiping at the tears that spilled from her eyes.

"It's what, Phoebe?"

"It's a matter of life and death."

Chapter Two

"Jeremy? Did I wake you?"

"Wake me?" Jordan's partner's sleepy voice was barely audible on the other end of the line. "What time is it?"

"It's almost six," Jordan said, pouring her second cup of coffee from the stainless steel percolator. She had grown pleasantly accustomed to creamy Starbucks lattes, but today she was so exhausted that she didn't even mind this home-brewed black stuff.

"Six?" Jeremy echoed. "Not even six, but *almost* six? What the hell are you doing up? What the hell am *I* doing up?"

"You're preparing to do me a huge favor, Jeremy."

On the other end of the phone, she heard the rumble of a male voice and knew it belonged to Paul, who shared Jeremy's bed, his life, and four cats named Curly, Larry, Mo, and Joe—Joe being a recently adopted stray.

"No, it's Jordan," Jeremy told Paul around a yawn. "Go back to sleep. So what kind of favor do you need at this ungodly hour, Jordan?"

"It's an ongoing favor, actually. You don't have to do anything right at the moment—"

"Thank God for that."

"And before I tell you what's going on, I have to make it clear that I can't tell you everything, okay?"

"What do you mean by that? You can't tell me everything? What's going on? Did something happen?"

Did something happen?

You bet something happened. And I'm still not even sure what, she thought grimly.

Aloud she said, "Jeremy, I need to take some time off."

She heard him exhale audibly. "Is that all? You had me thinking the worst. It's about time you took time off. When, how long, and where are you going? I hope you've decided to check out that spa I told you about, because the massage therapist there is—"

"Jeremy, it's not like that. I'm not going on vacation. Something's come up and I need to take some time."

"What came up? And how much time?"

"I can't tell you, and I don't know."

There was a pause. "Did somebody die?"

"No!"

"Are you sick?"

"No. I can't—"

"Okay, I get it. You can't tell me. God knows you deserve time off, Jordan. Take all you need. I'll hold down the fort. When are you leaving?"

She hesitated, wondering whether she should let him know that she wasn't leaving. But maybe it was better if she didn't even tell him that much. The last thing she wanted was for him to give in to his curiosity, stop over to see her, and see Spencer. Then she'd have to offer some explanation—and Phoebe had made it clear that she wasn't to say a word to anybody.

"I'm leaving right away," she told Jeremy.

"As in . . . today?"

"As in, consider me gone."

"What about—"

"The Goff-Anderson wedding? The cold salads are already prepared, the lobsters are being delivered at noon, and the flowers at twelve-thirty. Make sure you're there by ten, though, because the tables and chairs—"

"I know." Jeremy yawned again. "The tables and chairs are coming at eleven. The paperwork is in the office, and considering your anal-retentive habit of writing everything down, I'm sure I won't have any questions. But if I do—"

"Then call me," Jordan said. "On my cell phone. I'll have it on."

"Fine."

"And the small jars of cherry jelly for the Clark shower favors are—"

"I know."

"I already tied the gingham fabric around the tops of the jars, so all you have to do is bring them with you. The shower is at—"

"I know, Jordan. I know what you've scheduled and when, I know where to go and believe it or not I know what to do and how to do it. For Christ's sake, just go away and forget about work for a while, okay?"

"Okay."

"And have a fabulous time."

"I will." Could he hear the hollow note in her voice? She sipped the acrid coffee. She'd made it too strong.

"Jordan?"

"Hmm?"

"I hope I get to meet him when you get back."

Meet him?

She almost choked on her coffee. "How did you know . . . ?"

"I figured it had to be a man. It's about time you met somebody."

A man? She smirked despite herself.

What would Jeremy say if he knew the "man" was three feet tall and wore Winnie the Pooh sneakers?

She sighed. "Jeremy . . ."

"I know. No details. But I'm filling them in myself. You met someone, you're wild about him, and he's whisking you off to some fabulously exotic romantic locale."

Well, okay. Let Jeremy think whatever he wanted.

"Bon voyage, Jordan," Jeremy said, making kiss-kiss noises into the phone.

"Good-bye, Jeremy."

She hung up, pressing a finger on the talk button and then lifting it again to hear the dial tone.

She had to look up the number. It wasn't one she knew off the top of her head, so seldom had she dialed it these past few years. Regret seeped into her at that realization. Growing up, she knew Phoebe's phone number better than her own, having called it at least a few times daily for more than a decade. There was a time, around fourth grade, when they went through an open-the-window-and-holler phase, but their parents swiftly nipped that in the bud.

Jordan's smile at that memory faded quickly as she punched in a Philadelphia area code and the unfamiliar number for Phoebe's home there.

The line rang four times before an answering machine picked up.

Reno's monotone announced, "We aren't here to take your call right now. Please leave a message at the tone."

Jordan hung up, staring into space.

There were so many things she needed to ask Phoebe. She would just have to try again later.

Beau got to the gym early for his morning racquetball game, which wasn't surprising. His mother had taught him that a gentleman was always punctual.

Ed wasn't there yet. That wasn't surprising, either.

Ed was late for everything. Beau had noticed long ago that his friend and partner seemed to spend a big chunk of his life on his cell phone, phoning in apologies and making excuses for delays.

He should be used to it by now. After all, he and Ed had known each other since their days as roommates at Rice University's school of architecture. Back then, Ed managed to go late to some classes and miss others and somehow come out with excellent grades. The guy was a bona fide genius.

After graduation, Beau drifted in Europe before marrying Jeanette, having Tyler, and settling back in his hometown of DeLisle, Louisiana.

His father wanted—no, expected—him to take over Somerville Industries, but Beau was content to work for a local architectural firm, relying less on his paychecks than on his sizable trust fund to support his family. His father, who considered architecture Beau's "hobby," always held out hope that Beau would come back to the fold—even now.

These days, Beau's cousin Redmond was being groomed by Beau's father to take over the company. But Geoff Somerville frequently let his son know that there was room for him, too. His sister's son might be willing and capable, but Geoff wanted Beau there, too.

Last winter, the ailing architect for whom Beau had worked for years was slowly running the firm into the ground. On the verge of breaking up with Lisa, Beau realized he needed a fresh start. But he knew that working for his father wasn't the answer.

There were too many memories in DeLisle. It was time to escape.

He and Ed had kept in touch sporadically over the years. He knew Ed had married a Richmond debutante, whose rich daddy funded the start-up of Ed's Washington-based firm. Several times, Ed had invited Beau to move up north and come on board. A few months ago, when Ed extended the offer again, Beau realized the time was right.

It was easier than he expected, leaving his family and DeLisle behind. Maybe easier than he wanted it to be.

He was no longer sure whether he had been clinging to the past, or truly longing to escape it.

Now life had settled into a rhythm of work, meals on the run, and working out at the gym.

Even at this early hour on a summer Saturday morning, Capital Fitness was already crowded.

Beau decided to wait for Ed in the exercise room. He found a vacant treadmill, got on, and worked his way up to a warm-up jog.

A few days from now, he thought, he'd be jogging on a sandy beach. He had rented an oceanfront home on North Carolina's Outer Banks. When he'd made the reservation last fall, he was living in New Orleans with

Lisa and had intended for the two of them to go together. It was her idea, in fact. By the time they broke up, he had already paid for the place, and it seemed a waste not to use it.

Anyway, a solo vacation was fine with him. He would welcome the solitude. So much had happened these past few months—the breakup, the move, the new job— he needed a chance to clear his head.

Actually, he thought, increasing his pace on the treadmill, it wasn't just this spring. He hadn't had a chance to get away and sort things through in years. It was as if his life had careened out of control in that one horrible instant that was forever imprinted in his mind, and ever since then, he had let the mad current sweep him along.

Well, he'd had enough. It was time to sort things out. To examine his life. To gain perspective on where he was now and where he wanted to be.

Hell, there's only one place I want to be, he thought grimly, closing his eyes, remembering . . .

He made himself stop. He forced his eyes to open before the tears could flood in.

As he glanced into the mirror in front of the row of machines, he locked gazes with an attractive woman with a blond ponytail and a workout leotard that bared her sculpted, tan abs.

She smiled at him. He smiled back briefly, then shifted his attention away. But he could feel her watching him as he moved through fifteen minutes of cardio, then checked his watch and stepped off the machine.

Ed must be here by now, he thought, wiping sweat from his brow with a towel.

"Hi, are you a new member?"

He looked down and saw Blond Ponytail standing at his elbow. She was petite, especially next to his six-foot-four frame. She couldn't be more than five feet, one or two, he found himself calculating.

Jeanette had only been five-one.

He used to call her Pip. As in Pipsqueak.

He swallowed hard, pushing back the intrusive memory, and focused on the question.

"Yes, pretty new here," he said. "I joined a few weeks ago."

"Where are you from? I love your accent."

"Louisiana."

"I knew it! I was in New Orleans for Mardi Gras once. It's such a great city."

"Yes, it is pretty great," he agreed.

And it was true. He did think New Orleans was a great city.

Suddenly, he missed home like crazy. But living there was too painful. Everywhere he turned, he saw Jeanette and Tyler. He just couldn't go on living like that.

"Well, D.C. is a great city, too," the woman said with a grin. "I should know. I was born and bred just a few blocks away from this very spot."

"You're the first person I've met here who can make that claim," Beau said. "Everybody around this town seems to have been transplanted from somewhere else."

It wasn't like that back home. In his small hometown, DeLisle, about halfway between New Orleans and Baton Rouge, most families could trace their local roots back for generations. The Somervilles had inhabited their sprawling antebellum plantation-style house for 150 years.

"Yeah, people come and go here. But you'll get used to it," the woman told him. He saw her glance down at his hand and realized what she was looking for.

A wedding ring.

He deliberately slid his fingers back beneath his towel, not wanting to see his ringless fourth finger.

He wasn't used to seeing it that way himself. He found it hard to believe that there was a time when he didn't think he wanted to wear a ring. He'd never been one to wear much jewelry, other than a watch and the occasional cufflinks. But when they established that they were getting married, Jeanette said she wanted him to wear a ring.

"Why? Don't you trust me?" he'd drawled, his eyes twinkling at her. They both knew she didn't have a thing to worry about.

"I trust you. But I'm an old-fashioned girl. I want an old-fashioned husband with an old-fashioned ring on his finger."

Funny, just when it seemed he'd finally gotten used to the gold band glinting there on his left hand, he had to try to get used to a bare finger again.

You can't wear that wedding band forever, Beau.

Those were Lisa's words, about a month into their relationship.

The truth was, he had believed he *could* wear it forever, even after Jeanette was gone. . . .

Just as he had believed he'd be married to her forever.

Forever.

Nothing was forever, he thought bitterly. Nothing but pain.

"So what's your name?" Blond Ponytail asked in a sultry tone.

He had forgotten all about her.

"Beau," he said. "Beau Somerville."

"Nice to meet you, Beau. I'm Suzanne Lancaster. I was just going over to the weight room to lift . . . Maybe you can spot me?"

"Sorry," he said, but his tone wasn't the least bit apologetic. "I have to meet someone on the raquetball court."

"Maybe another time," she said with a shrug. "Listen, maybe this is bold, but—maybe we can get together later and I can show you around a little bit. You know, show you some of the local sights that are off the beaten path. There's more to D.C. than the White House and the Smithsonian."

"I'm sure there is," Beau said. "But I'm not . . ." He hesitated.

"Not interested? Not available?" She was watching him closely. "Maybe a little of both, huh?"

He nodded. "Sorry."

"It's okay. It was worth a shot. My divorce was final last week, and I'm feeling kind of lonely."

"I'm sorry," he said again.

She shrugged. "I wasn't the one who wanted it."

"That must be hard."

"Yeah, divorce is hard."

He nodded. "I'm sure it is."

"How about you? Let me guess. Happily married?"

He felt the old familiar sick churning in his stomach. "Not anymore."

"You're divorced, too, huh?"

Beau looked down at his watch. "Sorry, I'm late for my game."

"See you around," she said with a wave.

He was already halfway to the door.

"Where's Mommy?"

Jordan blinked. The little boy lying in her guest-room bed didn't. No, Phoebe's son was staring right up at her with his big brown worried eyes, waiting. He looked as though he had been lying awake there for quite some time, pondering the very question he had just asked.

"Mommy is . . ." Jordan hesitated.

Damn Phoebe!

Damn her for leaving so quickly last night.

As soon as Jordan had agreed to take Spencer for her, she had said she wanted to catch the last train back to Philadelphia and asked Jordan to call her a cab. Jordan obliged, never expecting a driver to materialize at the door within minutes. She had thought it would take at least a half hour. That she would have time to talk more to Phoebe, to find out more about . . .

Well, about everything.

About her life, and her marriage, and her son—and about what could possibly have been earth-shattering enough to propel her back into Jordan's life with such a bizarre proposition.

But there was no time.

The cab was waiting, and the train was leaving.

Phoebe had to go.

Spencer had fallen asleep on the couch watching television while Jordan and Phoebe talked in the kitchen. With tear-flooded eyes, Phoebe kissed him gently on the forehead. He didn't even stir as she made her way to the door, with Jordan trailing along behind, asking every question she could think of—except the one Phoebe had already refused to answer directly:

Why are you leaving him here?

After she had disappeared into the rain-shrouded darkness, leaving a bewildered Jordan alone with her child, Jordan cried. She couldn't help it. She cried out of exhaustion, and frustration. She cried because seeing Phoebe again only reminded her of how much she missed her friend, and because her heart hurt for the abandoned little boy on the sofa, and because, quite frankly, she had no idea how to care for a small child.

She had watched Spencer sleep for more than an hour before deciding to move him upstairs to the bed. She decided that if he woke up, she would explain that his mommy had to go away for a short time but would be back for him soon. She even rehearsed the exact words she would use.

But he didn't wake up.

Not then.

Now, he was fully awake, waiting for an explanation.

Now in the grim light of Saturday, after Jordan's own sleepless night and her early-morning call to Jeremy, the previously rehearsed words had evaporated and an explanation refused to come as easily.

She took a deep breath and began again. "Mommy had to go back to . . . um, go back home."

But *was* that where she had gone? Was she back in Philly? The answering machine had picked up every time Jordan dialed the number since early this morning, wanting to ask Phoebe how she should explain her absence, and whether Spencer had any food allergies, and what kind of toothpaste he used. . . .

"Back home?" Spencer echoed. Jordan heard the sob in his voice before the first tear trickled down his cheek. "Without me? But—"

"Don't worry, sweetie," she said, hurriedly sitting on the bed and reaching out to take him into her arms. She stopped only when she saw him flinch and recoil.

She didn't blame him. She might be his godmother, but she was a virtual stranger to him. Phoebe—no, more likely Reno—had seen to that.

Jordan settled for a pat on the small, round arm that

extended above the pale blue sheet. "Your mom had to take care of something in Philadelphia, and then she'll be back for you. I'm going to take good care of you until she returns. Anything you want or need, just tell Auntie Jordan and I'll see that you have it. Okay?"

He didn't nod. He didn't do or say anything, except lie there staring at her with tears spilling down his cheeks.

Oh, Lord. Her heart was breaking all over again.

Where the hell was Phoebe? Why had she left?

And whose life, Jordan wondered, remembering her friend's chilling, cryptic statement, was in danger?

Was it Phoebe's?

Or was it Spencer's?

Chapter Three

Drumming the fingertips of his right hand on the cotton tablecloth, Beau checked the Rolex on his left wrist. Again.

"Sir? Would you like to order a drink, perhaps?"

Beau looked up at the waiter who once again materialized beside the choice table for two—a table that was currently occupied by one, and soliciting aggravated stares from the waiting patrons clustered across the room by the hostess podium.

Beau cleared his throat and contemplated the question.

Would he like a drink?

Yes. He certainly *would* like a drink. A good, stiff bourbon. But he had learned the hard way that intoxication tended to hamper his efforts to avoid temptation of the feminine variety. After all, he had met Lisa while drowning his sorrows in a French Quarter bar, and the next thing he knew, they were living together.

Yes, but he had long since successfully extracted himself from his relationships with Lisa *and* with bourbon. He now considered himself past seeking the brand of comfort that both had provided in his time of need.

His time of need.

He didn't want to go there.

No, he never wanted to go there.

Anyway . . .

He would be wise to conduct this evening's social engagement with a clear head and chaste intentions—especially if Jordan Curry was as bewitching as Andrea MacDuff claimed.

"Nothing to drink yet, thank you," Beau told the waiter. "At least, not until the lady arrives. I'm sure she'll be here in a few minutes."

But the lady *didn't* arrive. Not in a few minutes, and not in fifteen. Nor in twenty.

When nearly a half hour had gone by, Beau reached into the pocket of his navy Brooks Brothers blazer and checked his cell phone to make sure it was on, just in case she was trying to reach him. Maybe she had called and he hadn't heard it ring over the John Coltrane CD that was playing on the restaurant's sound system. . . .

The phone wasn't even turned on. Darn.

He still wasn't used to carrying one of these things around. His partner, Ed, had insisted that it would be good for business. It would make him more accessible to Ed, and to clients.

Well, it sure as hell isn't doin' me any good—for business or *pleasure—if I don't turn the damn thing on,* Beau chided himself, shoving the phone back into his pocket in disgust.

Now what?

Jordan might have been trying to reach him.

Or they might have gotten their signals crossed. Maybe he had the wrong date. Or time. Or place.

Beau reached into his jacket pocket and took out his Palm Pilot—another electronic gizmo Ed insisted was indispensable. Flipping it open, he scrolled to today's date to check the details. Nothing was written there.

He frowned. He was fairly certain this was the right date. He distinctly remembered Jordan asking him whether he meant this Saturday or next.

It wasn't unusual that he hadn't entered the date in his electronic organizer. As far as he was concerned, that was yet another device that was far more trouble than it was worth. The truth was, Beau happened to be an old-fashioned paper-and-pencil kind of guy, whether he was making a date or drafting a floor plan.

Shoot. If only he had grabbed paper and pencil and jotted down exactly when and where he was supposed to meet Jordan Curry. For all he knew, he was supposed to have picked her up at her place two hours ago.

Beau sighed and summoned the hovering, watchful waiter, who promptly rushed over.

"I'm afraid my date won't be able to make it," Beau said, pointing at the pocket that held the cell phone as though he'd just received the unfortunate news. He pushed back his chair, pulled several ten-dollar bills from his wallet, and handed them to the waiter. "I'm sorry I took up your table and your time. Have a good night."

"You too, sir. Come back again."

"I will."

And he probably would, he thought, as he left the large dining room. The exposed brick walls and spinning paddle fans overhead, along with the delectable savory aromas and piped jazz, reminded him of restaurants back home.

But Beau doubted he'd be back with Jordan Curry. She probably thought he'd stood her up.

After retrieving his sleek black SUV from the valet attendant, he headed out onto M Street. Stopped at a light, he wondered if he should find a place to pull over and call her from his cell phone.

Or you could just go over to her place, he reminded himself. After all, he knew exactly where she lived. Andrea had casually mentioned that Jordan resided in an upscale, relatively new townhouse development, and it turned out to be one of the few local places with which Beau was familiar. He had visited a potential client who was temporarily relocated in the same complex after losing his home in a fire. The client, who ended up hiring Beau to design his new home, knew who Jordan was when Beau inquired about her, and pointed out her place just a few doors down from his own.

Small world.

So what would Beau say if he did decide to show up on her doorstep late, or possibly early, or perhaps not expected there at all?

After all, maybe Jordan really had stood him up just now. Maybe he had all the details straight and was in the right place at the right time, and she had simply blown him off.

But what if she was all dressed up and waiting for him, pacing her living room, thinking he had forgotten her?

It wasn't as if a stranger's perception of him mattered so much to Beau in the grand scheme of things. No, it wasn't as though Jordan Curry's concluding that he was a rude cad would preclude what might have been a lifelong romance. He had no intention of getting involved with her either way.

But the old-fashioned Southern gentleman part of Beau simply wouldn't let it rest. He couldn't drive home and forget about Jordan. He couldn't let her think he was the no-show.

If it turned out that this was her fault, consciously or unconsciously—if she didn't want to meet him for whatever reason—well, he could deal with that. But he had to find out.

But if it turned out she was all dressed up and merely thinking he was late—or early—well, he would come up with a fitting excuse and never mention having waited at the restaurant at all. They would go to dinner—someplace other than the restaurant he had just left—and his obligation to Jordan Curry and to Andrea Mac-Duff would be fulfilled. End of topic.

It was a terrific plan.

His mind was made up.

Whistling, he drove the few short blocks to the familiar brick town houses on a quiet side street.

Jordan sat on a stool beside Spencer's, her chin in her hand, watching him push his food around on the cobalt blue plate.

"What's the matter?" she asked. "Aren't you hungry?"

"I am, but . . ."

"But what?"

He didn't look at her. In fact, she couldn't recall his looking directly at her since this morning, when she told him his mother was gone. He went out of his way to avoid her gaze—sort of the way Kevin had the one time they saw each other after the wedding that wasn't. They had bumped into each other in the supermarket back home around Thanksgiving, and it had been one of those superficial conversations about the weather and the Steelers and the recent election.

Jordan had been having superficial conversations like that with Spencer all day. Only they talked about butter-flies and chocolate and cartoons.

Rather, she talked while he listened. Or didn't listen. She couldn't tell. She wanted to know what was going on inside that poor little boy's head, but she didn't have a clue.

He mumbled something now as he dragged his fork through a pile of mashed potatoes.

"What was that, Spencer? I didn't hear you."

She bent closer to him.

He visibly moved back an inch. "I said, I don't really like this stuff."

She looked at his plate. "But when I asked you, you said you liked mashed potatoes."

"Not like this. This has little green things in it."

"Those are scallions," she explained. "To give it flavor. Scallions are kind of like onions—"

"I don't like onions, either."

"Oh." She looked at his plate. "How about the chicken? You said you like chicken."

"I meant McNuggets."

"Oh," she said again. "Well if you try this—"

"It looks yucky."

Yucky. Huh. Who would guess that somebody would call her cordon bleu yucky? It had taken her three years to perfect the recipe.

"Maybe if you try the greens," she offered.

He made a face.

"Look, I know you probably think you don't like it, but this isn't just regular spinach or something. I sautéed . . ." She trailed off, watching his face. He probably didn't even know what *sauté* meant. He was just a kid.

Well, she wasn't used to kids. She didn't know any kids. She might have been one once, but that didn't mean—

Her thoughts were interrupted by the ringing doorbell.

Jordan's heart leaped.

"Do you think that's my mom?" Spencer asked, brightening for the first time.

Please God, I hope so, Jordan thought, hurrying to answer it. "Maybe it is," she called over her shoulder, which was enough to send Spencer careering after her.

But when she opened the door, she didn't find Phoebe standing on the step.

She found a lanky, sandy-haired stranger wearing what was practically a business-casual weekend uniform: pressed khakis, a chambray shirt, a navy blazer, and polished loafers. He was so put-together—and so good-looking—that Jordan was instantly aware of her own appearance.

She had on a plain white Gap T-shirt tucked into her oldest pair of jeans, her feet were bare, and her pedicure was a week old. She had skipped her standing Saturday morning appointment at the salon in favor of watching cartoons with Spencer. Come to think of it, she hadn't combed her hair since pulling it back with a rubber band while brushing her teeth at five-thirty A.M. Oh, and she must have big, dark circles under her eyes. Lovely.

"Are you Jordan Curry?"

She recognized his voice as soon as he spoke.

She also remembered something.

It was as though a thunderbolt struck her from above.

"Oh, my god!" She clasped a hand to her mouth. "I completely forgot."

He looked mildly amused. "You forgot who you were? Glad I could be of service, ma'am."

Caught off guard by his quip, she found herself looking into a pair of green eyes—eyes that were precisely the shade of her own, she noticed. In fact, there were circles under his, too, but they were better concealed by a tan. There was an outdoorsy look about him, as though he belonged on the range or splitting wood rather than on this Georgetown doorstep in dressed-up clothes.

"You're Beau Somerville," she said.

"Thanks, but I knew all along who *I* was. I thought *you* were the one who had the problem."

She laughed. She couldn't help it. The man was charming. And for a split second, looking into those moss-colored eyes, she forgot all about Spencer.

Until Beau Somerville glanced at something over her shoulder, and she followed his gaze right to the child who stood in the doorway of the kitchen, disappointment written all over his round little face.

"How about you, fella? You know who you are?" Beau asked.

Spencer nodded.

"You sure? What's your name?"

"Spencer," the little boy said in a near-whisper.

"Hey, how's it goin', fella?" Beau asked gently, as though sensing something was wrong.

Spencer hung his head. "Okay."

"Nah, something's buggin' you. I can tell," Beau said, with a wink at Jordan.

Her heart melted despite the surge of worry that rose within her at the realization that somebody now knew about Spencer's presence. Not just somebody—a total stranger.

"Let me guess what the problem is. Hmm ... You just stepped in dog doo?"

Jordan was shocked when a sudden giggle erupted, and she realized by process of elimination that it had come from Spencer.

"No!" he said, looking up shyly at Beau. "I didn't step in dog doo!"

"Then what can it be? Oh, I know! You accidentally ate a caterpillar? Because it happens to the best of us, you know."

Another giggle. Another emphatic "No!"

"How did you do that?" she murmured to Beau under her breath. "He hasn't laughed all day."

"Kids love gross stuff," he muttered back. "Works every time." To Spencer he said, "Well, if it's not a caterpillar and it's not dog doo, I can't imagine what's got you so down."

"Guess!" Spencer commanded.

"Let's see ... oh, I know what it is. Your mom's making you eat eyeball soup, right?"

This time, there was no laughter.

Spencer's face fell.

Jordan realized why.

It was the mention of his mom.

Beau must think Spencer was her son. He couldn't possibly realize that the little boy was pining for a mother who had brought him to a strange place, vanished into the dead of night, and hadn't been heard from since.

"Listen, Beau," she said hastily, to change the subject, "I'm so sorry I stood you up. Were you waiting for me at the restaurant?"

He paused, then shifted his attention from Spencer back to her. "Actually, I was. I presume you forgot all about it?"

"I'm so sorry. I can't believe I did something like this. I never do things like this. I'm usually so organized, but . . ." She gave a helpless shrug.

"It happens to the best of us," he said. "But look, why don't you guys get your shoes on and come out with me to grab a bite to eat now? I'm starved, and it looks like there are lots of good restaurants right in your neighborhood."

"There are, but I just ate," she confessed.

"How about you, fella? Did you just eat, too?"

"Nope," Spencer said morosely.

"How come? I smell something good coming from that room behind you, and I'm thinkin' it must be the kitchen."

"It is," he said. "You want my chicken? You can have it."

"What's the matter? You don't like chicken?"

"Not the blue kind," Spencer said.

Beau chuckled. "Well, I don't imagine many people like blue chicken."

"It's *cordon* bleu," Jordan inserted. "And it happens to be my specialty."

"Chicken cordon bleu? That happens to be my favorite."

"There's plenty left," Jordan said. Having no idea how much little boys ate, she had doubled the recipe. "Would you like some?"

Beau Somerville nodded. "That sounds good to me."

"Come on in." Jordan couldn't believe she was doing this—inviting a strange man into her kitchen and volunteering to feed him. But it was such a relief not to be alone with Spencer for the first time today, and Beau seemed to know how to interact with the little boy in a way she did not.

Belatedly, she remembered Phoebe's warning. She wasn't supposed to let anyone know Spencer was here.

But after this, she would never see this man again. Now that he was here, face to face, she could explain that she wasn't really actively dating these days because . . .

Well, why wasn't she?

As she led the way to the kitchen, with Spencer trailing behind alongside the ruggedly handsome Beau Somerville, Jordan couldn't seem to remember *why* she wasn't dating. Or why she had thought dinner with this man was something to dread.

"Have a seat," she said, gesturing at the breakfast bar as she walked over to the stove, where the serving platters waited.

He sat. So did Spencer. Right next to Beau, she noticed.

When she'd invited him earlier to sit down to eat, with her, he had left a stool between them.

Obviously, the little boy felt a kinship with this stranger that he didn't feel with his own godmother.

Jordan tried not to let that bother her. After all, Beau was incredibly charismatic. He seemed to know just what to say to Spencer, and how to say it.

Come to think of it, he knew just what to say to her, too.

Warning bells went off in her head.

Don't let him charm you, Jordan. You fell for a charmer once before, and look what happened.

Well, she was on guard. She would never fall for a good-looking, smooth-talking man again. Period.

"Nice place," Beau said, looking around Jordan's kitchen. He surveyed the three big foil-covered casserole dishes on the stove. "You always cook like this for just the two of you?"

"Actually, I never cook like this here at home," she said, her back to him as she took down a plate from the glass-fronted white cabinet.

"Oh, yeah, that's right, you're a caterer. I almost forgot. Guess that means I'm in for a treat." He leaned forward and peered at the contents of Spencer's abandoned plate. "What's this, mashed potatoes with chives?"

"Scallions."

"And—hey, are those sautéed greens?"

"Yes!" She turned to look at him, obviously pleased at his culinary detective work.

"I *love* greens," he said. "My grammy used to make them in one of those big old white enamel pots. She would let it simmer for hours, with bacon and onions and vinegar and molasses and her secret ingredient."

"Secret ingredient?"

"She never would tell my mama what it was," Beau said, smiling at the memory. "She said that as long as she could stand at the stove and make her greens, nobody else was going to have her recipe. She said she would give the recipe to Mama when the day finally came that she couldn't do the cooking herself anymore."

"But she wouldn't tell her the secret ingredient when

the day came?" Jordan asked, taking flatware from a drawer.

"It wasn't that. She died suddenly one day when she was only in her early sixties. Just keeled over and had a massive stroke. None of us saw it coming. We all thought she had years of cooking left."

"That's terrible. I'm sorry about your loss."

"Tragedies happen." His eyes were shadowed. "It was a long time ago. I just wish she had told us her secret ingredient."

"Well, I'll tell you one thing. Her recipe sounds an awful lot like mine. You named every ingredient I use, except one."

"What's that?"

"Beer. I use a whole bottle. It gives the greens a nice flavor."

He shook his head, smiling. "Nope. Mama wouldn't allow liquor in the house. She was a strict Southern Baptist. It must've been something else."

"Maybe it was hot pepper flakes," she said conversationally. "I've seen recipes that call for that."

"I don't think so. Grammy's greens weren't spicy. They just had a very distinct flavor that I've never tasted since, and believe me, I've had lots of greens. I'm a Southern boy at heart."

He watched Jordan heap his plate with golden chicken, mashed potatoes, and greens. As she carried it over to him, he looked down at the little boy seated beside him.

"So what's up, Spence?" he asked. "You don't like blue chicken, but what about the rest of this stuff?"

"Guess," Spencer invited.

"Well, I'd say you don't like those little green things in the mashed potatoes."

"She said they're like onions," Spencer said, with unpleasant emphasis on the *she*.

"Most kids don't like onions," Beau agreed. "Especially green ones. Because most kids don't like anything that's green. Least of all something that's called 'greens.' Right?"

"Right!" Spencer nodded, and the expression on his face officially ordained Beau a superhero.

"When I was a kid, I liked onions, and green vegetables, and greens," Jordan said, setting the heaping plate down in front of Beau.

"Yeah, but you were a girl," Beau said, as though that explained everything. To Spencer he said, "I bet you would'a rather had a peanut-butter-and-jelly sandwich, huh?"

Spencer nodded emphatically.

Jordan seemed to consider that. "I have peanut butter," she volunteered. "And I think there's a jar of marmalade in the pantry cupboard . . ."

"Marmalade?" Beau and Spencer echoed in unison.

"What's marmalade?" Spencer asked, wrinkling his nose.

"You don't have regular jelly?" Beau studied Jordan as though she had just whipped up a batch of eyeball soup.

Didn't all moms keep jelly on hand? Didn't all moms know that marmalade didn't qualify as jelly? Jelly was purple and sticky, and these days, it came in a plastic squeeze bottle.

"How about honey?" Beau asked. "Got any of that?"

"Yes! I have honey!" She looked as though she had successfully answered a $32,000 question on *Who Wants to Be a Millionaire*.

"Ever have a peanut-butter-and-honey sandwich, Spence?"

"Nope."

"Want to try one?"

"Yup," the little boy told Beau, who promptly pushed back his stool.

"I'll make it for you," he said.

"I can do it," Jordan said. "You eat."

"Nah, I have a special way of making peanut-butter-and-honey sandwiches. You got any pretzel rods?"

"Pretzel rods?"

"I didn't think you did. Well, got anything that looks like a pretzel rod?"

"I have sesame-garlic bread sticks," she said from the pantry cabinet, from which she removed peanut butter and a jar of honey. Not the plastic bear-shaped kind of honey jar, Beau noticed. A pricey glass jar with a fancy brand name.

Well, better that it wasn't the familiar bear jar, Beau told himself. The bear jar would have brought back memories that were better left buried.

The trouble was, they refused to stay buried.

He distracted himself by saying to Jordan, "Sesame-garlic bread sticks? Can I see them?"

She held up the package. He peered at the contents, then shrugged. "That'll do it."

"You're going to make a sandwich on bread sticks?"

"I'm going to make the sandwich on bread," he said, draping his blazer over a nearby doorknob and rolling up his shirtsleeves. "The bread sticks are for something else. Stand aside."

She threw up her hands in a whatever-you-say gesture, then took a seat beside Spencer.

"Where's the bread?" Beau asked.

"Top drawer on your left."

"Knives and spoons?"

"Top drawer on your right."

He retrieved the bread—a fancy whole-grain kind, of course, but it would do—from the metal-lined bin and took two butter knives and a teaspoon from the drawer. He used one to spread the bread with peanut butter, then drizzled honey over it with a spoon.

As he worked, he forced his thoughts not to stray from the project at hand. Not to venture away from the here and now—from this Georgetown kitchen and this little boy, a world and so many years away from another kitchen, another little boy, another peanut-butter sandwich. . . .

"What do you think he's going to do with the bread sticks, Jordan?" he heard Spencer ask.

"I have no idea. Let's wait and see," she replied.

Jordan? Beau was surprised to hear the child call his mother by her first name. Some families did that, he knew. Maybe that was "in" up north here, but the old-fashioned Southerner in Beau found it disrespectful.

He found himself wondering about the little boy's dad. Andrea hadn't mentioned whether Jordan was divorced, or a widow. Nor had she mentioned that Jordan had a son. Beau figured that she must have assumed it would turn him off to date a woman who came with that kind of baggage.

Truth be told, if he had known about Spencer, he probably wouldn't have gone along with the date in the first place. It was hard enough to see little boys in his everyday life—playing on swings when he drove by the park, eating fast food when he picked up his lunch, clinging to their parents' hands in crosswalks when he stopped at lights.

It seemed that there were children everywhere he looked, and all those little boys were reminders of the one who had left an aching void in Beau's heart that could never be filled.

He was caught off guard when he'd spotted Spencer standing in the doorway tonight behind Jordan. But something about the child drew him in. There was a desolate aura about him that touched Beau's heart, made him want to help. Instead of turning and fleeing, he'd found himself reaching out, venturing inside.

And now, here he was.

And here was the sandwich. He carried the plate over to Spencer and set it in front of him.

"Whoa! A sailboat!"

"Like it?"

"It's great!"

"It *is* great," Jordan said with a smile, studying his handiwork.

He had cut the square sandwich diagonally in half, then cut the point off one of the halves, which gave him a large and small triangle, which he arranged side-to-side on the plate as a sail, with the bread stick in between as the mast. The remaining piece of bread was shaped like a boat, and he positioned it beneath the sails.

"How'd you learn to do that?" Spencer asked, taking a big bite of the mast.

He shrugged, a lump in his throat.

"Beau's an architect," Jordan told the little boy. "I bet he knows how to design all kinds of neat things. Now let's let him eat his dinner. I hope it hasn't grown cold."

"I'm sure it's fine." He sat down again, his appetite diminished by the wave of emotion that had washed over him. How well he remembered those days of peanut-butter sandwich sculptures, and shared jokes, and being part of a cozy threesome. . . .

"I can warm it in the microwave for you," Jordan offered.

"That's okay." He raised a forkfull of greens to his mouth and chewed mechanically at first.

Then his eyes widened in surprise. "I can't believe it. This tastes just like Grammy's recipe."

"Are you sure?"

"I'm positive. The flavor is identical. Delicious. I haven't had anything this good since she passed away."

Jordan grinned. "I think she was holding out on your Southern Baptist mama, Beau."

He considered that. It wouldn't be so far-fetched for Grammy to have had a stash of beer somewhere. Come to think of it, he half remembered Mama accusing her of spiking the Christmas eggnog with bourbon one year.

Beau gobbled down the food, the best he'd tasted in years. Well, how long had it been since he'd had a home-cooked meal? Lisa didn't cook. Mama did, but she sure didn't have a flair for it.

Only Jeanette had cooked for him in the years since Grammy died. She made all his favorite foods: fried catfish, sausage gravy over biscuits, cornbread. She teased him that she was going to make him fat, and he was well on his way. . . .

And then she was gone, and there were no more home-cooked meals, and even if there had been, Beau had lost his appetite. Permanently, it seemed. For food, anyway. Liquor went down easy. It dulled the pain. The booze and lack of food had whittled his once-expanding waistline until none of his clothes fit and he was a shadow of the man he used to be.

It was Lisa who turned him around. Got him off the booze, and into salads and sprouts—and a gym. Lisa was a health nut.

Well, at least one of her healthy habits had stayed with him. He didn't care if he never saw another sprout or tasted tofu ice cream again, but he was hooked on his daily workouts.

"My dad has a boat on the river," Spencer commented, munching on one of the sandwich-sails. "But it's not this kind. It's a yacht."

Startled back to the present, Beau glanced down at the little boy, then at Jordan. "Is that so?"

She shrugged, her eyes clouded, expression veiled. It didn't take a genius to figure out why. Spencer had referred to his dad in the present tense, so clearly his parents were divorced. Maybe Jordan's ex was one of those playboy types with a yacht—and a female first mate in every port.

"Does he take you sailing on his yacht?" Beau asked, setting his fork down and pushing away his empty plate.

"Yup. But my mom doesn't like it when we do that. She says I should learn how to swim first."

"That's probably a good idea." Again he looked at Jordan. "I'm sure your dad makes sure you have a life jacket on when you're out on the water."

"Uh-huh."

"That's good."

"Do you have a boat?" Spencer asked.

"Actually, I do." Truth be told, he had a few boats. But he wasn't about to elaborate. Knowing Andrea, who was from Louisiana and had to be well aware of the vast Somerville fortune, Jordan had been duly informed that Beau was a wealthy man. That didn't mean he had to go into detail about his sailboats, speedboats, his yacht—

or any of the other trappings that no longer meant anything to him. He would trade all of it . . .

No. He had to stop thinking that way. What was done was done. There was no turning back, no bargaining, no chance that he would wake up tomorrow and find that it had all been the cruelest of nightmares.

"Where is your boat?" Spencer was asking.

"It's down in Louisiana, where I used to live."

"Oh. My dad's boat is in Philadelphia, where we live."

"You live with your dad?" He was surprised. He had assumed that Jordan had custody.

Spencer nodded. "And my mom."

"You share custody?" Beau asked Jordan.

She looked flustered. Maybe it was too forward a question for him to have asked.

"What's custody?" Spencer asked.

Now Beau was flustered.

"Your mom can explain it," he said.

"I'll ask her . . . when I see her again."

That was when it hit him. No wonder she didn't have jelly in her cabinet. No wonder he didn't sense any natural, easygoing warmth between Jordan and Spencer. No wonder Spencer called her by her first name.

They weren't mother and son.

Spencer didn't belong to her after all.

Beau didn't know whether he was relieved at the simple explanation, or disappointed.

Disappointed? Why would you be disappointed? an accusing inner voice demanded.

He knew the answer, and he didn't like it.

He was disappointed because, just for a fleeting moment, he had allowed himself to indulge in a fantasy. About himself, and Jordan, and Spencer. He had mentally inserted himself into what he thought was their little family—a family that was missing a husband, a daddy.

He had just for a moment imagined himself stepping into those roles again. . . .

But it was wrong.

They were wrong.

Jordan was the wrong woman.

Spencer was the wrong child.

His fantasy shattered, Beau looked from the child to the woman who wasn't his mother.

"I thought he was yours," he said simply.

Jordan shook her head. She didn't offer an explanation. Spencer was intent on his sandwich, unaware of the look that passed between the adults.

That was when Beau realized that the tension wasn't just on his end. He had his baggage, yes. But clearly, something was going on with Jordan. There was something about the way she nervously twisted one hand around the fingertips of the other; about the way she checked her watch—almost as though she was waiting for something.

Waiting for him to leave, maybe, Beau decided, when he saw her look across the room at the jacket he'd draped over the doorknob.

"You probably have things to do," he said, standing.

"You probably do, too," she agreed, also getting to her feet.

Disappointment was blatant in Spencer's eyes. "Do you have to leave?"

"I do," Beau said, conscious of a painful twinge somewhere deep inside him. "So . . . I'll be seeing you guys."

"You will?"

Beau was startled by the flicker of interest in the little boy's expression.

He hadn't meant it literally. It was just something you said when you left. *I'll be seeing you.*

He had no intention of seeing either of them again.

"Sure," he said, with a glance at Jordan. He couldn't read her expression. "I mean, I guess I will."

"When? Because I'll be going back home soon," Spencer said.

"When are you going back home?"

"When my mom comes back for me. She's—"

"She'll be back for him soon," Jordan cut in. "But maybe before Spencer leaves, we'll run into you again. Right, Spencer?"

He knew she didn't mean it. He recognized her tone. It was the manner an adult used to pacify a child making an unrealistic request.

He found himself annoyed by Jordan's attitude. Maybe he was being irrational, since he was the one who didn't want to extend this relationship. But she seemed to assume that they wouldn't be getting together again. That if they saw him again, it would be purely by accident. By "running into" each other. For some reason, that bothered him.

"Maybe, before you leave and after I get back from my vacation next week, we can go to the zoo or something," Beau heard himself tell Spencer.

"All of us?" he sounded disappointed.

Beau glanced at Jordan. "Or just the two of us, if Jordan is busy," he said.

She shook her head. "I don't think that would be a good idea. I mean . . ." She faltered. "You know what? Why don't you just give me a call and we'll see?"

He had clearly been dismissed. "That's fine," he said, picking up his plate and carrying it over to the sink.

"Oh, you don't have to do that," she said hastily. "Just set it there and I'll put it into the dishwasher."

It seemed as though she wanted him out of here as soon as possible. Well, okay, he was going. But he found himself wondering why she suddenly seemed so cagey. The way she was acting, you'd think she thought he was going to kidnap the kid or something.

"I'll let myself out. Good-bye, fella," Beau said, chucking Spencer under the chin on his way to the door. To Jordan, he said merely, "Thanks for the meal."

Whatever she murmured in reply was lost as he firmly closed the door behind him.

"Oh, well, you don't have to do that," she said faintly. "Just sit here and I'll get it into the dishwasher."

It seemed as though she wanted him out of here as soon as possible. Well okay, he was ready. But Dr. Pond probably wondering why she suddenly seemed so edgy. The way she was acting, you'd think she thought he was going to harm the kid or something.

"I like my coffee. Good bye, baby," Brad said, looking at Steven under the edge of his arm. "In fact, I'm its Jordan," he said sincerely. "Thanks for the meal."

She gave no indication in reply. Brad smiled briefly closed the door behind him.

Chapter Four

On Sunday afternoon, Jordan ventured out into the world with Spencer for the first time. She had to. They had run out of bread and eggs. Besides, she thought she'd better pick up some kid-friendly groceries. Juice boxes, jelly . . .

Oh, and macaroni-and-cheese mix.

To think she had been so relieved when Spencer asked her for macaroni and cheese for lunch! That she could make. She even happened to have all the ingredients on hand.

She should have known better.

Her recipe called for tricolor shell pasta, gruyere and mascarpone cheeses, and crushed toasted walnuts.

Apparently, Spencer's recipe called for a familiar blue-and-orange box containing elbow macaroni and a powdery orange substance.

"How come we have to drive so far to go to a grocery

store?" Spencer asked from the backseat as she headed out to the Virginia suburbs.

Because I don't want to run into anybody I know while you're with me, she thought grimly, steering into an unfamiliar neighborhood filled with familiar stores and restaurants. Target, Wal-Mart, Applebee's, Burger King. There had to be a supermarket around here somewhere.

Sure enough, she found a sprawling grocery superstore and pulled into the parking lot. It was crowded, but most likely every car here belonged to a stranger, unlike in her Georgetown neighborhood, where she recognized the store clerks and often bumped into clients and neighbors.

They climbed out of the car. The sun beamed onto the blacktop, so hot that it shimmered in waves. Jordan wiped a trickle of sweat from her brow and wished she dared to take Spencer over to her health club to go swimming.

Nobody can know he's here.

Phoebe's words came back to haunt her yet again, bringing with them an increasingly familiar chill.

What was going on? Why hadn't Jordan been able to reach her friend since she left Friday night?

She had tried Pheobe's number again several times last night and today, but each time there was only an answering machine.

Wouldn't Phoebe want to check on her son? Wouldn't she want to talk to him, to reassure him that she would be back?

What else had she said?

Jordan had gone over everything repeatedly in her mind, searching for some clue.

I'm so sorry to drag you into this . . .

Into what? Phoebe's words made it sound as though

there were something huge going on. Something scary. Dangerous. Life-threatening.

Jordan glanced warily around the parking lot, almost expecting to see strangers' eyes probing her.

But there was nothing disconcerting about the scene.

Nobody in this supermarket parking lot on this sunny Sunday afternoon was paying the least bit of attention to her and Spencer. They must look like just another mother and small child out getting groceries.

She reached down for his hand, but he pulled it away. She tried not to be hurt, yet she couldn't help remembering how quickly Spencer had warmed up to Beau last night.

Jordan had to remind herself to walk slowly through the parking lot so that Spencer's short little legs wouldn't have to run to keep up. Her usual pace was briskly efficient, and when she shopped, she was usually buying ingredients for her catering business, or staple items for her own cupboards. This, she decided, should be an interesting—and enlightening—experience.

"Now, if you see something you like, you have to tell me," she told Spencer as she pushed a cart through the electronic doors and into a refreshing blast of arctic air.

"I like that," he said promptly, pointing at a display of chocolate bars as Jordan plucked two bags of gourmet coffee from a large sale bin.

She grinned. "You like chocolate? Who doesn't? Okay, sweetie, go ahead. Grab a couple."

He grabbed enough to hand out to a horde of trick-or-treaters on Halloween night and deposited them in a heap beside the two bags of coffee. Jordan looked dubiously at the contents of her cart. "Does your mom let you eat chocolate?"

"Sure. All the time. Sometimes I have candy bars for breakfast," he said, looking her in the eye.

She fought back another smile. Smart kid. "Okay, whatever you say, Spencer. Let's move on."

As they moved through the store, she learned that a four-year-old's diet consists mainly of prepackaged, preservative-filled convenience foods. At least, if Spencer was telling the truth about his usual diet.

He probably wasn't, she conceded as he tried to convince her that he always had an ice-cream sundae topped with M&M's and a can of cream soda as a bedtime snack.

But she bought the ice cream, the M&M's, the cream soda.

She bought the boxed, kid-targeted kits containing miniature rounds of dough and packets of tomato sauce, cheese, and pepperoni, even though she could make delicious homemade pizza with fresh tomatoes and basil.

She bought the canned franks and beans, casting a wistful glance at the packages of navy beans that she could soak overnight and simmer all day with molasses and mustard and thick slabs of bacon.

She bought the boxed macaroni and cheese, the grape jelly, the juice boxes whose ingredients seemed to be all sugar and water and very little, if any, actual fruit juice.

In the checkout line, she allowed Spencer to choose several kinds of Pez and packages of bubble gum from the conveniently placed display. He told her that his mom always let him do that.

When she and Phoebe were little girls, they always talked about the kind of parents they would be. They decided they would let their kids eat candy for dinner and pizza for breakfast, wear shorts in March if the weather was freakishly warm, and stay up as late as they wanted. They wouldn't make the mistakes their parents did, and they wouldn't have a bunch of meaningless rules.

Well, Jordan thought, placing the groceries on the conveyer belt, either Spencer was lying about what his mom let him eat, or Phoebe really had followed through on their plan.

Jordan suspected the latter was too far-fetched to be true. But she had to admit, it was fun to spoil the kid a little. This was the first time he hadn't been sad or sulking since . . .

Well, since Beau Somerville left yesterday.

She felt her face grow flushed at the mere thought of the man. When he left, she was annoyed with herself for having invited him to stay in the first place. But when she finally climbed into bed, exhausted from lack of sleep the night before, she was transported swiftly off to dreamland—and Beau was waiting there.

In her dreams, they were alone together, making love. When she awakened abruptly, it was as though she could still taste his kisses, still feel his warm hands on her bare flesh.

Then reality crashed back in—and she realized what had awakened her.

It was Spencer, and he was screaming in the guest bedroom across the hall. Apparently he was having some kind of nightmare. By the time she rushed in, he was already sinking back into a fitful sleep. She sat by his bed in the dark for a long time, not sure whether her heart was pounding because she was haunted by his screams—or by her dream about Beau.

"Jordan, can I have one of those comic books?" Spencer asked, interrupting her thoughts. "Please?"

She glanced up to see the little boy gesturing at the display of newspapers and magazines, also conveniently placed beside the register.

"Does your mom—" she started to ask, but he was already nodding vehemently, and anyway, what was the point?

It didn't matter what Phoebe let him read, or eat, or do, because Phoebe wasn't here. Jordan was in charge. She had to find something for the kid to do for the rest of the day, since they couldn't go anywhere or see anyone.

"Go ahead," she told Spencer. "Get a couple. We can go back home and read."

She picked up a couple of papers for herself: the hefty *Washington Post,* the heftier *New York Times.*

She used to have the Sunday paper delivered, but finally realized that she never had time to read it. She worked weekends, after all, and by the time she dragged herself in the door in the evening, the last thing she wanted to do was face a newspaper thicker than the metro phone book. She would keep the thing around all week, telling herself that she would get around to reading it, but invariably tossed it into the recycling bin on Saturday, just in time for a new paper to arrive.

Well, today she would certainly have time to read. Heck, she could probably get through both papers word for word while Spencer leafed his way through the pile of comic books he had just dumped into the brimming cart.

After she had paid for their purchases, they left the store.

"It feels like a furnace out here," Spencer complained, shading his eyes against the sun's dazzle.

"I know, sweetie. We'll turn on the air in the car. And the house is cool, too."

"We're just going back to your place?" he asked, sounding disappointed.

"What else did you have in mind?"

"The zoo. Beau said—"

"But Beau isn't here today," Jordan pointed out. "And he's going away on vacation, I think. Didn't he say something about that?"

"He said he would take me to the zoo."

"Maybe I can take you to the zoo," Jordan offered.

"Today?"

She glanced at the cart full of groceries, newspapers, and comic books. "I thought we could go home and read today."

"Read?" he echoed, as though she had suggested that they go home and scrub the floor with a toothbrush.

"Don't you want to read your new comic books?"

"No. I want to go to the zoo."

"But Spencer—"

"With Beau."

"Spencer . . ." She sighed.

He was just a little boy. He was bored out of his mind. She had to get his mind off Beau and the zoo—and off his missing mother, too. He had frequently asked about Phoebe this morning, wanting to know when she was coming back and why she had left him here.

"How about the movies?" Jordan said suddenly, on a whim.

"The movies?"

"Sure. We can bring the groceries home—we have to put the cold stuff away—and then we'll go see something."

"What?"

"We'll check and see what's playing."

"I don't want to see anything with pirates," he said quickly.

"That's okay. I'm not crazy about pirate movies, either. You can pick."

He seemed to be mulling it over.

She did the same.

It would be dark inside a movie theater. Dark enough so that they wouldn't be seen.

Again with the secret agent stuff. Why did she feel this unnerving sense that danger was dogging their every move?

Because Phoebe made it sound that way, she reminded herself.

Or had she?

Had Jordan read too much into her friend's words?

Had Phoebe literally meant that Jordan's taking Spencer was a matter of life and death?

Remembering Phoebe's haggard appearance and the haunted expression in her eyes, Jordan was able to answer her own questions.

No, and yes—in that order.

Late Sunday afternoon, Beau settled in front of the television on the burgundy leather couch in his living room. The air conditioner was running full blast, but it still felt warm in here. Maybe he should call the building super.

He was renting a furnished two-bedroom apartment in a four-story brick building not far from DuPont Circle. The place was perfectly functional—clean, roomy, and efficient.

Everything about it was rectangular, Beau had

noticed. The rooms, the windows, the furniture—even the draperies in every window fell in geometric precision, with nary a ruffle or tieback in sight.

There was a lot of chrome and glass, mirrors, and lacquer in the modern decor. Beau couldn't help contrasting the look to his collection of antiques back home, with their flowing, graceful, curved lines and rich, polished finishes. The upholstered pieces he had were overstuffed and warm in color, rather than the navy-and-maroon color scheme in this place.

No, this certainly wasn't his kind of apartment—but then, the situation was only temporary. Sooner or later, he would buy a place of his own and move all his stuff up from Louisiana. He just hadn't had the time or energy to go house hunting yet.

Beau leaned back against the couch cushions, his neck muscles aching from working in front of the computer screen at his office all day. Now all he wanted was to relax. In one hand was the television remote; in the other, a sandwich he'd picked up at a minimart on the way home when he'd stopped for the Sunday papers.

Taking a bite, he channel-surfed past a wrestling match, a home improvement show, and a couple of tearjerker movies. Coming across a golf game, he watched for a few minutes. He hadn't played in a while, he realized. Maybe he should bring his clubs along on his vacation. The beach house he was renting wasn't far from one of the finest golf courses on the East Coast.

Taking another bite of the sandwich, he decided that he should have got the ham instead of the turkey. This was pretty flavorless.

Then again, everything he had eaten today tasted flavorless compared to that amazing meal Jordan had whipped up last night. Andrea MacDuff was right about one thing: the lady was some cook.

Andrea. That reminded him. He had promised to call her today and let her know whether he'd be able to have her plans ready to file for a building permit before he left for North Carolina.

He had worked exclusively on her project all day, and it looked as though the plans would be ready to go to the zoning board by Tuesday morning. Thank goodness. Andrea MacDuff wasn't the kind of woman who tolerated delays very well.

After finishing his sandwich, Beau reached for the cordless telephone on the rectangular—of course—glass coffee table beside the couch. Might as well call Andrea now, since the news he had for her was good.

He dialed her number, wondering whether she would even be home, but she picked up on the first ring.

"Beau! How wonderful to hear from you," she drawled. "How is every little thing?"

"Every little thing is great, Andrea, and so is the big thing," he said easily. "Meaning, I'll have everything ready to file for the building permit before I go away this week."

"Why, Beau, bless your heart!"

They chatted for a few minutes about the changes that she had requested and he had incorporated into the plan. He promised to have the paperwork to her for a signature by tomorrow afternoon at the latest.

About to hang up, he was startled when she slyly said, "So where is it that you and Jordan are headed on this little romantic getaway, Beau? Or can't you tell me?"

"Jordan!" he sputtered. "What makes you think I'm going on vacation with her?"

"I called her office this morning to see about ordering

some of her cold lemon-spinach soup and tomato tartlets for a little garden luncheon I'm having this week, and her partner told me that she was away. He hinted she had met somebody and that it was about time."

"Well, she may have met somebody, but it isn't me. And she isn't away," Beau added.

The moment he said it, he wished he could take that last part back.

Sure enough: "How do you know she isn't away?" Andrea asked.

"Because I saw her just last night," he said. Rather than going into the complicated details of how he had come to be at Jordan's apartment, he said—because Andrea seemed to be waiting for further explanation— "We had dinner together."

"How wonderful! What did you think of her?"

"She was very sweet, Andrea, and I appreciate your introducing me to her, but—"

"But what? Don't tell me you aren't interested. She's beautiful, intelligent, charming—"

"She is all of those things," Beau agreed.

Yes, Jordan was all of those things, and more. He had found himself recounting her various charms ever since he left her last night—along with all the reasons he could never get involved with her.

"So what can possibly be the problem?" Andrea asked.

"It's just that she seems to have her hands full right now, with her nephew, and—"

"Her nephew?"

"Spencer. The little boy who's staying with her. At least, I got the impression that he was her nephew. Maybe he wasn't." Beau frowned, trying to remember exactly what Jordan had said about Spencer when Beau finally figured out that they weren't mother and son. He thought he recalled the little boy calling her Auntie Jordan. . . .

No, wait. That was what she called herself when she was talking with him. Spencer only called her by her first name.

"And will her nephew be traveling with you on your trip, Beau?" Andrea asked.

"No! Why would he be coming along?"

"I thought maybe it was a threesome, and maybe you had hoped it would be a twosome instead. After all—"

"Andrea, as I said, I'm not going on vacation with Jordan Curry or her nephew. I'm going by myself, to the Outer Banks."

"All right, Beau," Andrea said in an infuriating *sure, whatever you say* tone. Obviously, she didn't believe him.

He thought about Jordan's business partner. He had said she was out of town with a man. Spencer was no man, and they seemed to be settled in at Jordan's town house with no plans to leave. Was she taking time off to baby-sit the child? Had she lied at the office about it? If so, why?

With some effort, Beau extracted himself from the conversation with Andrea.

After hanging up, he sat pondering Jordan Curry and her nephew—if Spencer was her nephew.

There was very little affection between them, and it was clear that Jordan wasn't used to being around children.

Not only that, but she had seemed tense. Not the whole time, because if she were, then he could assume that she was just nervous by nature. She was, after all, a stranger.

But looking back on their encounter, he realized that

she had seemed to alternate between being a laid-back, casual person and an uptight, wary one. It was almost as if every time she forgot whatever was troubling her, she allowed herself to relax. But there was no denying her cagey answers to some of his questions, and her skittishness when she thought he was getting too close.

What the heck was up with her? What was going on over there? Whatever it was revolved around the boy; that much was clear.

Maybe he was Jordan's foster child.

Maybe he was her own child, and she had never told anyone she was a single mom.

No—you couldn't hide a thing like that. Besides, she had said he wasn't hers, Beau reminded himself. And Spencer had talked about his parents and his home in Philadelphia.

Well, whatever the case, something told Beau that there was more to the situation with Spencer than Jordan had told him—or her business partner.

Oh, well. None of this had anything to do with Beau. He planned on keeping his distance from Jordan Curry . . . no matter what he had promised Spencer when he left.

Spencer . . .

No.

Maybe you can tell a woman you'll call when you have no intention of doing so, but you can't do that to a little kid, he scolded himself. *You told him you'd take him to the zoo. You can't just vanish off the face of the earth.*

He still didn't know why he had blurted out the invitation as he was leaving. Now he was stuck.

Well, maybe he could call over there before he left for North Carolina. He would make up some excuse about why he couldn't go to the zoo after all.

A prickle of guilt threatened to push its way forward, but he shoved it away from his consciousness.

By the time he got back from vacation, Spencer would no doubt be back home in Philadelphia, and Beau would have put Jordan Curry's charms out of his mind for good.

He *hoped.*

The movie was actually enjoyable, to Jordan's surprise. Naturally, on her own she would never have chosen an animated G-rated comedy about a talking piano's journey to another galaxy, but she found herself laughing at the slapstick mishaps along with a genuinely amused Spencer.

They sat in the back row of the crowded theater and shared a big tub of buttered popcorn and a box of Snowcaps. She timed it so that they would arrive during the previews of coming attractions—meaning the lights were down in the theater—and she made sure they were the first ones out of their seats when the credits started rolling. That was fine with Spencer—he had to go to the bathroom so badly that he was practically doubled over.

Which presented a problem.

Should she let him go into the men's room alone? Or take him into the ladies' room with her? Jordan pondered the dilemma as she led him hurriedly toward the rest rooms over by the exit door. She had no idea what the mom of a young son did in a situation like this, but realized she really had no alternative. She couldn't let him out of her sight.

She hurried him into the ladies' room and parked herself outside the stall, wanting to hustle him in and out of here before the throng from the theater flooded the place. She had chosen a suburban Cineplex that was a good twenty-minute drive from Georgetown, and she doubted that she'd run into anyone she knew at a kiddie matinee, but she didn't want to take any chances.

If only she knew what was going on with Phoebe.

"Spencer? Are you okay in there?" she called, rapping on the door as a line formed in front of the three stalls.

"Uh-huh. I'm coming out."

She heard him fumble with the lock.

The door didn't open.

"Uh-oh," his voice said. The lock rattled again.

"Spencer? Can't you open the door?"

"I'm trying."

"How old is your son?" one of the women in line asked her.

She opened her mouth to correct the mistake, then realized that would only draw more attention to them. "He's four," she said simply, and put her mouth close to the crack in the stall. "Spencer, slide the metal bar to the side, okay?"

"I'm trying. It's hard to move it."

Jordan looked down, figuring that she could probably crawl under the space beneath the stall door. She was about to do so when she heard a click and the door opened.

"Thank goodness. I was just about to rescue you." She bent toward Spencer to hug him, but he flinched.

The woman who had asked about his age said in a confidential tone as Jordan led Spencer past, "My son is four, too, and he doesn't like it when I hug him in public lately, either."

Jordan smiled politely.

"I'm not her son," Spencer informed the woman and the roomful of strangers.

Her stomach turning over, Jordan steered him straight to the door, bypassing the sinks despite his protest that his mother always made him wash after using the rest room.

As she led him out to the car, Jordan told herself to stop being so paranoid. It wasn't as though she was harboring a fugitive. For Pete's sake, she was simply baby-sitting her godson for a few days.

But no matter how hard she tried, she couldn't shake the feeling of apprehension.

Why hadn't Phoebe called?

What if she *never* called?

What if she had abandoned Spencer with Jordan and run off forever?

What then?

Chapter Five

As Andy Rooney wrapped up his *Sixty Minutes* report and the show's closing music began to play, Beau clicked off the television set and stretched. He hadn't moved from this spot since this afternoon, and it had felt good to kick back and watch some television. But he'd had enough relaxation. He wasn't cut out to be a couch potato.

He stood and wandered into the kitchen, opening the sleek, black refrigerator and surveying the contents. Ketchup, mustard, mayo, butter, a few bottles of beer, and a white cardboard takeout Chinese container so far past its prime that he could no longer recall what was inside.

He removed the container and, without opening it, deposited it in the garbage can. What he wouldn't give for leftovers from that meal Jordan Curry had served last night!

Thinking about her chicken cordon bleu made him hungry.

Thinking about *her* made him hungry, too, he reluctantly admitted to himself. She hadn't been far from his thoughts all day, and try as he might, he hadn't been able to talk himself out of calling her.

Calling Spencer, he amended.

But of course, Jordan would answer the phone. They would have to have some kind of conversation. Perhaps she would be friendlier today than she had been when he left last night. Maybe something would click between the two of them and . . .

What the heck are you thinking, Beau?

He didn't want something to flare up between them. He didn't want another romantic entanglement. Look what had happened with Lisa. In the end, he had realized he was only using her. It wasn't fair to her. That was what he had tried to make her see when they broke up. That she deserved better than him. She deserved a man who was willing to build a future. Not one who was shattered by the past.

His mouth set grimly, Beau strode back to the living room, ignoring the cordless telephone receiver. He reached past it for the newspaper and settled back on the couch.

He would not call Jordan Curry's house. At least, not right now. He was feeling too frustrated, too vulnerable.

For now, he would just sit here and read the paper to take his mind off Jordan and Spencer.

And it worked.

Until he stumbled across the photo accompanying an article on the last page of the national news section.

* * *

"Do I have to take a bath?" Spencer mumbled sleepily as Jordan escorted him into the guest bathroom, where she had already started running the tub.

Did he have to take a bath? Frankly, Jordan had no idea. Phoebe hadn't said anything about it, and it wasn't as if he had been rolling around in the mud. But there were faint orange stains around the corners of his mouth from the canned spaghetti he'd had for dinner, and he must have splashed soda or something on a clump of his hair, because it felt like broom bristles.

"Yes, you have to take a bath," Jordan said firmly.

"But I'm too tired."

He *did* look exhausted. And his head had been drooping dangerously close to his bowl of spaghetti earlier at the table.

Jordan had heated up leftover chicken and greens from last night for herself, but every bite reminded her of the man she'd just as soon forget. It didn't help that Spencer brought up the topic of Beau and the zoo every chance he got.

"It'll just be a short bath," she promised. "As soon as you're done, you can go right to bed."

"I don't want to go to bed," he protested.

"But you're exhausted."

"No, I'm not," he said, stifling a yawn as she pulled off his T-shirt. It, too, was stained with orange sauce. She would have to wash it later. She might as well throw in the rest of his dirty laundry, too, while she was at it. It seemed that Phoebe had packed Spencer enough clothes to last another couple of days. Jordan wondered if that was any indication of how long she expected to be gone.

This was really beginning to wear on her. Not the fact of having Spencer around—that part was surprisingly pleasant, now that he had gotten over his tendency to scowl at her every time she glanced in his direction. It wasn't as if he were chatty and relaxed in her presence, but they had actually had a lively conversation on the way home from the movies.

It had lasted until Spencer had brought up the topic of Phoebe again. When Jordan couldn't tell him any more than she already had, he grew silent and moody.

She felt the same way inside. How much longer could she go on taking care of this little boy without word from his mother?

She reached out to unfasten his shorts.

He pulled away. "I can do it myself," he said.

"Are you sure?"

He nodded, looking embarrassed. "Can you leave?"

"But . . ."

"I can give myself a bath."

She hesitated. "Can you wash your own hair, and rinse all the soap out?"

"Yes."

"Okay. But call me if you need help," Jordan said, noticing the tub was almost full. She reached toward the flowing tap.

As she turned off the water, she heard it.

The phone was ringing.

Jordan bolted from the bathroom, rushing toward the nearest phone, which was in the master bedroom. She knew the answering machine would pick up after the fourth ring, but if it was Phoebe, she might not leave a message.

Before she even reached the bedroom doorway, Jordan heard the machine turning on downstairs. She had only heard the phone ring once. The sound of the tub might have drowned out earlier rings.

She snatched up the receiver with a frantic "Hello?" just as her own recorded voice was asking the caller to leave a message.

A click, followed by a dial tone, greeted her ears.

Whoever it was had hung up.

"Damn it!" Frustrated, Jordan banged the receiver back into its cradle.

She was halfway back to the bathroom when she remembered two things.

That Spencer didn't want her in there with him . . .

And that she had recently installed a caller ID device on the kitchen telephone.

Tossing aside the cordless phone, Beau paced across the living room floor to the window with its view of the Washington Monument. He gazed at the distinct white obelisk, particularly striking this evening against a backdrop of pink-streaked dusk. But he didn't even see it. His heart was pounding furiously.

Just now, in the instant before he had hung up, he had heard Jordan's voice. But as if of its own accord, his finger stayed on the "talk" button, pressing it to disconnect the call.

He hadn't known what he was going to say if she answered—let alone what he might say into an answering machine.

But now he knew that she was home.

Great. Next step?

His mind raced again through the only options he had been able to come up with earlier.

He could confront her directly about the little boy in her care . . .

Or he could go to the police.

Common sense told him not to get involved—to turn the situation over to the authorities.

But moments ago, when he lifted the receiver to dial the number for local law enforcement, something stopped him.

Something made him dial Jordan's number instead.

That same impulse kept him from calling the police now, even though everything he had seen in her townhouse last night indicated that the little boy didn't belong there, that he wasn't comfortable there. And everything he had read in the newspaper told him that the little boy's life hung perilously in the balance.

But somehow, deep in his gut, he couldn't believe that Jordan represented any kind of threat to the child. Beau had no idea how Spencer had come to be in her care. And yes, the woman was a complete stranger to him—and, for all he knew, to Spencer as well.

Yet he found himself wanting to believe in her. Based on nothing other than pure, illogical instinct.

So . . .

If he wasn't going to call the police, he would have to confront Jordan. If he did it over the phone—and if by chance his instincts about her were completely off base—there was no telling how she might react. She could take off with Spencer, or . . .

Or worse.

No. Beau shook his head.

Jordan wouldn't hurt Spencer. He had no idea what

she was up to, or even who she was, but he knew that much.

Grammy used to say he was a good judge of character. She said it whenever she recounted the tale of how Beau, as a toddler, inexplicably bit the new bank clerk, Mr. Cheever, on the finger so hard it drew blood. Not long after, the man was arrested for embezzling. The incident shocked the town, but not Grammy. She told everyone who would listen that she knew something wasn't right about Cheever when the normally affable Beau took such a violent dislike to him.

Grammy also liked to tell people how Beau stubbornly refused to pose for pictures with the bride or even kiss her when he was the ring bearer at his Uncle Cal's wedding. The marriage lasted only long enough for Cal's new wife to run up a mountain of debt before running off with a married man.

"That Beau," Grammy always said. "He doesn't put on any pretenses. If he likes you, he shows you. If he doesn't, he shows you. And if he doesn't like you, there's usually a good reason."

Well, Beau liked Jordan Curry.

He might not want to get involved with her, and he might not entirely trust her, but he couldn't go reporting her to the police just yet, no matter what the newspaper said. He would just have to check things out for himself.

In person.

At last, her hair damp from a long hot shower, Jordan settled into the comfortable recliner in one corner of the living room with the newspapers she had bought that afternoon. Spencer was tucked into bed and had been sound asleep before she even finished emptying the laundry hamper in one corner of the guest room.

She had thrown a load of clothes into the washer, then turned on the television and tried to lose herself in an old Frank Capra movie.

But she couldn't concentrate. She realized she was waiting for the phone to ring again.

So far, it hadn't.

Why hadn't Beau left a message when he called?

When she'd run downstairs to check the caller ID display, she had truly expected to see a Philadelphia phone number and perhaps Phoebe's last name, not Beau Somerville's. Obviously, he didn't want to talk to a machine. Fine. He would probably call back, and when he did, she would come up with some excuse for why she—and Spencer—couldn't see him again.

The problem was, she *wanted* to see him again.

Just knowing that he had called—just seeing his name on the small digital screen—had sent a quiver of anticipation through Jordan. She could almost convince herself that she was on his mind today as much as he had been on hers.

Almost.

The truth was, he wasn't calling her. She knew this had to do with Spencer. He was following through on his promise to the little boy.

Jordan shook her head and opened the paper, trying to focus her attention on the news. The house was hushed, except for the hum of the refrigerator and the ticking of the clock on the mantel.

She read an article about the president's upcoming trip to the Middle East twice without digesting a word of it. She was halfway through a third attempt when a shrill scream suddenly pierced the silence.

Jordan leapt from her chair and raced for the stairs.
Spencer.

Spencer was screaming.

Spencer was in trouble.

Terrible thoughts raced through her mind. What
would she do if there was an intruder in the house?
What if somebody was trying to kidnap him? What if
somebody had hurt him?

She had promised Phoebe she would keep the little
boy safe. That was Jordan's all-consuming mission when
she burst into his room, prepared for anything . . .

Except what she found.

Spencer lay on his back, sound asleep.

Puzzled, Jordan took several steps closer to the bed,
wondering if the scream could have had another source.
But the television wasn't on downstairs, and all the windows were closed.

Besides, she had recognized the sound. She'd heard
the same terrified shriek last night, when a nightmare
had awakened Spencer.

He must have been having another one just now.

As she watched, he tossed his head restlessly on the
pillow. He muttered something.

Jordan leaned closer.

He spoke again, saying something about a pilot.

Or was it a pirate?

His next word was much clearer.

It was "no," and it came out in an eerie, high-pitched
plea.

"Spencer . . ." She reached out to stroke his head.
"It's okay. Shh . . ."

The little boy whimpered and turned fitfully away.

"No . . . please . . . no . . ."

"Spencer, wake up," Jordan whispered. "You're having a nightmare."

His eyes slowly opened wide, filled with stark terror.

"It was just a dream," Jordan said in a soothing tone, resting her hand on his cheek. "Everything's all right. It wasn't real."

"Yes, it was." He was trembling.

"What were you dreaming about?"

"The pirate," he said without hesitation.

"Well, he wasn't real, sweetie. Pirates aren't real."

"Yes, they are. This one is really real. He's scary and bad and mean, and he has a black eye patch."

A black eye patch. Okay, the classic image of a pirate could be scary. Black eye patch, black hat with skull and crossbones, peg leg or hook arm.

Jordan remembered Spencer's earlier mention of not wanting to choose a movie about pirates. She recalled seeing the animated movie *Peter Pan* when she was little, and being so frightened of Captain Hook that she had to sleep with the light on.

"Pirates are only in movies and on TV, Spencer," she began, but he cut her off with another vehement protest.

"They are *not*. They're real!"

"Well, they used to be real," she conceded. "Years ago, pirates used to sail the seas, and bury treasures, and that sort of thing. But not anymore." That wasn't entirely the truth, but she assumed he was talking about eighteenth-century buccaneers and not modern-day pirates.

"I saw a real pirate with my mom and dad. And he's a bad guy. Really bad!"

"Spencer . . ."

He cowered into his pillow. "He's coming to get me!

I want my mommy." His words dissolved into a shuddering sob.

"Oh, Spencer." Jordan pulled him close. He stiffened, but she didn't let go.

Eventually, she felt his little body relax. She held him and stroked him and crooned to him until his eyes began to flutter closed again. When he lay back on his pillow, she pulled the covers up to his chin and began to tiptoe out of the room.

"Stay," he said softly, and she turned to see his sleepy gaze on her. "Please?"

Warmth pooled within her, and she smiled. It was a small victory, but an important one. He wanted her here with him. For once, he wasn't pushing her away.

"I'll stay," she whispered.

And she did, sitting on his bed long after he'd drifted off to a peaceful sleep at last.

As he walked up the steps to Jordan's town house, Beau told himself that he was prepared for anything. But he knew that wasn't true.

He wasn't prepared to learn that there was a criminal side to Jordan Curry. That seemed as unlikely as a blizzard blowing into town tonight.

Beau hesitated in front of the door and wiped a trickle of sweat from his forehead. According to the televised weather forecast he'd seen earlier, the relative humidity tonight was almost a hundred percent, and he could feel every bit of it. He longed to be on the beach in the Outer Banks, with cool saltwater lapping his toes and a fresh ocean breeze in his face.

Well, it wouldn't be long now. In no time, he would be leaving on vacation. Then he could put everything behind him: the unbearably steamy weather, stewing about the breakup with Lisa, his work . . .

Jordan Curry.

Spencer.

And the newspaper article he'd just read.

Hell. No wonder she'd been so tense last night. No wonder she hadn't volunteered any information about the boy.

Beau took a deep breath. It was now or never, and never was out of the question. He couldn't just go off on vacation knowing what he knew without doing something about it.

He looked at his watch. It was nearly ten o'clock. The porch lights were off, but he could see lamplight inside, filtering through the drawn draperies. She must still be awake in there.

He knocked.

He waited, but only a few seconds.

The door was thrown open more quickly than he expected. Either she had happened to be in the hallway, or she had rushed in from the other room.

Jordan stood framed in the doorway, the anticipatory expression on her face quickly changing to surprise— and then disappointment.

"I take it you were expecting somebody else," Beau said dryly, hoping she couldn't see his hands shaking as he jammed them into the pockets of his jeans with what he hoped was a casual gesture.

"Actually, I wasn't expecting anyone, but when I heard the knock I thought maybe . . . well, I didn't think it was you," she finished awkwardly.

"Sorry, but it is me."

"I see that." She made no move to step aside or invite him in, just regarded him warily with her big green eyes.

She was wearing a pair of cotton boxer shorts and a sleeveless white cotton top that revealed more of her than he had seen yesterday . . . and more than he wanted to see now.

Damn it. He wanted to forget that she was a desirable woman. He wanted to forget that he was a lonely man.

No, what he really wanted to forget right now was that Jordan might be involved in an unimaginable crime. He wanted to forget that he had ever laid eyes on Spencer and that he had ever read that article in the paper. He wanted to forget that he had sworn off women and romance and passion.

But he couldn't forget.

He couldn't take her into his arms and kiss her. He couldn't release the years' worth of pent-up longing or the man he had once been.

So he did what he had come here to do. He said, fighting to keep his voice nonchalant, "Mind if I come in?"

She was clearly taken aback. "Now?" She looked down at herself, as if realizing for the first time that her attire wasn't meant for a virtual stranger's eyes.

"You know, you shouldn't go opening your door at this hour of the night without knowing who's there," he pointed out.

"I know that. But I told you. I was expecting someone. *Else,*" she added purposefully.

"Actually, you didn't tell me that. What you said was—"

"I know what I said."

"Who were you expecting?"

"A friend." She lifted her chin and looked him in the eye, as if daring him to ask her for more information.

Fully aware that he could ask and that she wouldn't

tell, he took a step forward. She held her ground, not stepping back to allow him access. He was aware of her nearness. She was so close that he could smell honeysuckle wafting from her hair.

He was overcome by the completely irrational urge to move closer still, close enough to touch her. Close enough to bury his face in her neck, in her hair, to breathe her heavenly scent . . .

He found himself taking another step forward.

Still, she didn't move.

He was in the doorway now, but he didn't dare cross the threshold. Not yet. He needed to win her trust.

"I just wanted to talk to you about something, Jordan. Can I come in? Please?"

She narrowed her eyes, folding her arms across her chest as if to conceal herself. "I was just getting ready to go to bed. . . ."

"Where's Spencer?"

The mention of the child's name brought a flicker of apprehension to her eyes before she shifted her gaze away from his. "He's sleeping."

"Look, we really need to talk, and it'll only take a minute. Please?"

She shook her head and reached for the doorknob. "I just . . . I don't think that's a good idea."

She's afraid, he realized, caught off guard by her shaking hand, and by her sudden vulnerability. *She's thinking that I might be here to harm her.*

A wave of emotion swept through him. He recognized it—recognized an overwhelming protective instinct he hadn't experienced in years. Not since . . .

Not since he'd met Jeanette.

He pushed the thought aside. Jeanette was part of

the past. For now, for this moment, it was crucial that he focus on the present. On Jordan.

Because suddenly, as he comprehended that his instincts were telling him to keep this woman safe, to trust her and to win her trust, Beau knew that she was innocent. There was no longer a shred of doubt.

Whatever had happened in Philadelphia, and whatever the child was doing in her care . . .

He was sure there was a logical explanation.

"Jordan, I want to help you," he said in a low voice. "I'm not here to hurt you. You can trust me. Just let me in so that we can talk."

Still, she didn't move. Still, her guarded expression didn't falter.

"What do you mean, you want to help me?" she asked nervously. "Help me with what?"

"Whatever you need," he said simply.

"I have no idea what you're talking about." She put her hand on the doorknob, pulling it toward her a fraction of an inch.

He reached out and put his hand on the door, stopping it. "Don't close it," he said. "Please. Just tell me what's going on. Maybe I can help."

"What are you talking about?" She sounded bewildered, but the shadowed expression on her face told him that she somehow suspected what he meant. That she knew he was referring to Spencer.

"Look, I saw the paper tonight. I saw his name, and Philadelphia, and I figured . . ."

She just stared at him, shaking her head slowly, her brow furrowed as if she was searching for meaning in his words.

"But it wasn't just that," Beau pressed on, watching

her carefully. "It was the picture—he wasn't in it, but I could see him in their faces."

She genuinely looked confused. Again, she pulled the door toward her. Again, he stopped it.

"Beau, I don't know what you're saying. You're not making sense."

He had to say it straight out. What else could he do? He sensed that she was on the verge of slamming the door in his face.

He took a deep breath. "Jordan, I know. I know that kid upstairs is Spencer Averill. And I know what happened to his parents. What I don't know is why he's here and whether you were involved in their murder."

It was as though Jordan had toppled into a bottomless sea, floundering, then sinking quickly.

Everything around her was suddenly blurry, distorted, distant. She couldn't breathe, and when she tried to move, her limbs seemed to accept her command in slow motion only.

She took a leaden step back, away from Beau, away from the horror of what he had just said.

She felt her legs give way beneath her. She sensed herself beginning to fall, saw Beau reaching for her.

As he steadied her, she managed to come up for air, sputtering, struggling to grab hold of something that made sense.

"Jordan, are you all right?"

She couldn't speak.

"You didn't know. My God. You didn't know." Both his hands were on her upper arms, and he was holding her so that she couldn't move. Through the roar of incomprehensible thoughts swirling in her mind came one coherent one: that she should feel threatened by this stranger's presence—yet somehow, she didn't.

"No," she managed to say. "I didn't know."

"It's him, right? He's Spencer Averill?"

She nodded mutely.

"And his parents were Reno and Phoebe Averill?"

Were.

The word slammed into her, just as *murder* had.

"What happened?" she asked him, her voice little more than a croak.

"According to the paper, they were probably killed on their boat. Execution-style murders, the paper said. Their bodies were found floating near the scene, but their son's was missing."

Killed. Execution. Bodies. Missing.

She grappled with what he was telling her, but none of it made sense.

"The police are assuming Spencer was killed with them and that his body hasn't surfaced yet, Jordan. You need to tell me how he came to be here, and what you know."

"I don't—I don't know anything—" She faltered. Again she felt his grasp steadying her.

"Let's go sit down," he suggested.

She was aware of Beau closing the door behind them. He locked all the locks, then ushered her into the living room, where he helped her into a chair. The whole time, she felt as though she were watching the scene from a great distance rather than living it.

Her best friend was dead.

Phoebe was dead.

Somebody had killed her.

It was impossible, and yet it wasn't. Jordan buried her face in her hands, remembering Phoebe's palpable dread that night. Had it only been forty-eight hours earlier?

"She told me it was life and death," Jordan murmured over the lump in her throat. "But I didn't realize . . ."

"You didn't know she was in trouble?" Beau's voice asked. She looked up to see him crouched before her. He was still touching her, his hands reassuring on her shoulders.

"I thought she might be in trouble, but I never . . ." Jordan shook her head, wondering what she could have done differently.

"Was she a friend of yours?" Beau asked.

A friend? The lump rose to choke her words. "A friend. Yes. We grew up together. Then she got married, and I moved. . . ." She took a deep breath, trying to get hold of her errant emotions.

"When was the last time you saw her?"

"Friday night. She showed up here out of the blue with Spencer, and she said she had to leave him."

"For how long?"

"She wouldn't say. She wouldn't say anything except that I couldn't tell a soul that he was here." Jordan's gaze locked on Beau's. "And then you showed up."

"I'm the only one who knows?"

"That he's here? Yes. As far as I know." Jordan wiped hot tears from her eyes. Her mind was awash in memories of Phoebe. Swinging on the old metal play set in the backyard. Baking Christmas cookies for the Girl Scout caroling party. Passing notes in social studies class . . .

Gone. How could she be gone?

The irony was, Phoebe was the person to whom she would normally turn if paralyzing grief struck her. Now

Phoebe's loss was the cause of the grief, and there was no one Jordan could lean on. Even her parents were a world away, on a ship somewhere off the coast of Alaska. She felt utterly overwhelmed—and alone.

"Are you okay?" Beau's gentle voice startled her.

She looked at him, not seeing him, blinded by streaming tears.

"No." The word was little more than a whimper, and then she found herself sobbing in his arms.

He held her and comforted her just as she had held and comforted Spencer upstairs, and Jordan, like Spencer, resisted at first, then found solace in the human contact. She didn't know this man; she didn't *want* to know him, yet in this moment she needed him more desperately than she had ever needed another living soul. He was all she had.

Finally, her torment subsided. She was left feeling queasy, weak, shaken, as though she had been violently ill.

Beau produced a clean handkerchief. A handkerchief? Some part of her was startled by the gesture. She recalled Andrea MacDuff calling him an old-fashioned Southern gentleman.

The handkerchief was crisp and felt expensive. It smelled like clean linen, and like him. She buried her face in its musky masculine aroma, hiding in it, really, lest he somehow sense the inappropriate thoughts that suddenly rippled through her. How could she be thinking of him in that way at a time like this?

"We have to go to the police," she said into the handkerchief, forcing herself back to grim reality.

"I don't think that's a good idea, Jordan."

Startled, she lifted her face and looked at him. "Why not?"

"Phoebe didn't go to the police. She came to you. She knew her family's lives were in danger, but she only trusted you. Not the authorities. She must have had a reason."

Jordan nodded slowly. He was right. Yet . . . "But the police are looking for Spencer. Isn't that what you said?"

"They think he might have been murdered along with his parents and that his body wasn't found yet. But Jordan, whoever killed Phoebe and Reno knows that their son wasn't on the boat with them. They know he's still out there somewhere."

"You think they might come looking for him?"

"Phoebe must have thought so. Why else would she have left him here? She must have thought nobody would think to look for him here with you."

"It's true," Jordan agreed. "We haven't been close in years. I mean, we haven't seen each other much, but I still always felt close to her in my heart, and Phoebe must have felt the same way." Her voice broke. Beau squeezed her hand.

"So even after all these years, she trusted you," he said quietly.

"She knew she could trust me. That I would do anything for her. I promised I would keep Spencer safe."

"Until we know more about what happened, Jordan, I think keeping Spencer safe means staying quiet about the whole thing. Nobody should know that he's here."

"*You* know," she said simply, and the expression on his face told her that he knew what she was getting at without the need for further discussion.

"You can trust me, Jordan," he promised. "You and I might not have known each other for years the way you and Phoebe did, but you have my word that I won't tell a soul about this little boy."

Again, she quelled the urge to reach out to her usual support system—Phoebe, or her parents. They were the ones who had gotten her through her shattered wedding day when Kevin jilted her.

This time, she had nowhere to turn. This time, she had nobody.

Nobody but the man in front of her.

"I need more than your word, Beau," she heard herself say. The next words spilled recklessly from her, raw and honest. "I need your help."

As he drove away from Jordan's town house an hour later, Beau saw on the dashboard clock that it was nearly midnight. He fought back a twinge of guilt, telling himself that he couldn't have stayed any longer. She and Spencer would be all right—at least, for tonight.

Tomorrow he would go back.

He had promised her that.

Jordan's asking for his help had caught him off guard. Struck by her blatant plea and her desperate vulnerability, he had of course said yes, not knowing or caring what, exactly, she needed from him.

"Can you come back tomorrow?" she had asked him. "Please . . . I can't leave the house with him, and I'm afraid to be here alone with him."

He had nodded. He was afraid for her, too. So afraid that he'd volunteered to spend the night on her couch. She had turned that down. He was secretly relieved. After all that had transpired, he needed to get away, if only to clear his head.

This was big. This was huge. A child had been orphaned, and now his life might be at stake. Keeping Spencer safe and caring for him in this traumatic time was an overwhelming responsibility for one shell-shocked woman.

"I'll come back tomorrow," he had promised Jordan.

"Thanks. You're the only one who knows—the only one I can talk to about this. I need to figure out what to do—and I'm probably going to need some advice."

Advice? From him? He had no idea where to start, beyond telling her not to go to the authorities.

They agreed that they would talk more in the morning. He hoped his head would be clearer then.

Beau was yawning by the time he reached home. But when he climbed into bed, exhausted, the tension refused to leave his body.

He couldn't stop thinking about the child who had lost his parents, and about Jordan Curry's dilemma.

At one point he even sat up in the darkened room, swinging his legs over the edge of the bed, instinctively needing to get back into his car and return to her town house.

All that stopped him was the realization that a knock on the door in the wee hours would scare the hell out of Jordan after what she had been through. With any luck, she was sleeping, and he should be, too.

Tomorrow was going to be a tough day.

As night marched toward dawn, Beau tossed restlessly on the pillow, working through details in his mind. He would have to go to the office first thing to take care of a few details, such as Andrea MacDuff's plans. As for Tuesday . . . perhaps his long-awaited vacation would have to be put off a while longer. He wasn't sure that he could leave now. He couldn't abandon Jordan and Spencer if she needed him here.

Beau was drawn to both woman and child in the most primal way, realizing, in the last fuzzy moments before sleep overtook him at last, that he had designated himself their protector long before he had shown up on the doorstep tonight.

With trembling fingers, Jordan dialed the long-distance telephone number.

It had been surprisingly easy to get it. She simply dialed Information, gave the operator the name and city she needed, and *voila*—she no longer had to cope with this mess alone.

The phone rang several times on the other end.

It was what she expected.

After all, it was long past midnight.

Finally, a sleepy voice answered with a mumbled, fearful "Hello?"

It didn't sound familiar. For a second, she feared she had the wrong number. But she reminded herself that it had been years since she had spoken to him.

She cleared her throat. "Is this Curt?"

"Yes?"

There was a clicking sound on the line.

Had he hung up?

"Curt?" she said again.

"Yes?" he sounded impatient now.

"It's Jordan Curry."

Silence.

"Phoebe's friend," she clarified, just as he said, with sudden recollection, *"Jordan!"*

She paused.

She heard another clicking sound on the line. He must be fumbling with the receiver.

"I heard about Phoebe," she said, and then her voice broke.

"I know. It's a nightmare." His voice was hoarse, weary, as though he had been through all this before.

"Who could have done this to her and Reno, Curt?" Jordan asked.

"To all three of them," he said. "It was all three of them. They haven't found Spencer's body yet, but—"

"Curt, that's why I'm—"

She broke off, realizing she had just heard another click.

That was when it hit her. The phone line. It might be tapped.

Why the hell had she called? She shouldn't have. She hadn't intended to. But the anguish and worry had gotten to her after Beau left her alone. She wasn't thinking straight when she dialed Curt's number.

"Did you hear that click?" she asked Curt warily.

"It's just my phone. It's been doing that all day. We've had electrical storms in all this heat, and it screws up the lines." He sighed, sounding exhausted.

"I'm so sorry I woke you," Jordan said. "I just . . . I'm feeling so alone, and I didn't know who to turn to. My parents are traveling, and my brother is stationed overseas, and . . . there's just no one to talk to about this."

No one except a man I barely know.

But even Beau was gone now, leaving her alone with her grief and her fear.

"It's okay," Curt said. "I was going to track you down and tell you tomorrow anyway. How did you find out?"

"It was in the paper."

"Down there?"

"It was an AP story," she said over another click on the line.

"I guess it would be. Reno is pretty high profile."

"Do the police have any suspects?"

"Not really. I think they're assuming it was somebody with ties to one of Reno's cases. I told him he should be more careful with who he represented. I always worried about the lowlifes he was tangled up with. Apparently, he wasn't. And now look," Curt said bitterly.

"Are there funeral plans yet?" she asked.

"Not yet. Not till they find Spencer." He cleared his throat, and she could tell he was trying not to let emotion fog his voice.

She longed to tell Curt that his nephew was alive, and safe here with her.

But something wouldn't let her.

What if the clicks weren't from the thunderstorms after all? What if they meant the line had been tapped? Hadn't she read somewhere that if there was a bug on the line, the caller would hear some kind of click or tone?

Common sense told her that her imagination was getting the best of her. But she didn't dare take a chance. At least, not yet. Not tonight. Not when the pain and fear were still raw and her thoughts were hopelessly scrambled.

"I'll let you get back to sleep," she said.

"Fine. I'll call you as soon as arrangements are made for some kind of service. Are you still living in Georgetown? Is your number listed?"

"It's listed," she said heavily, wishing for all the world that it wasn't.

It had been so easy for her to get Curt's telephone number through directory assistance. She probably could have gotten it over the Internet as well.

If anybody was listening in . . .

Well, she had said her name when Curt first picked

up the phone. Anyone could use it to get her number and her address.

You're just paranoid, she told herself as she hung up.

Of course Curt's telephone wasn't tapped. This wasn't an episode of one of those detective television dramas her father used to love to watch.

This was real life.

Her best friend was dead.

Tears overtook Jordan once again as she flung the cordless phone across the room.

Chapter Six

The gourmet coffee Jordan bought yesterday at the supermarket had come in handy. It wasn't even nine o'clock Monday morning yet, and she was on her third strong pot of the brew.

Maybe it was the caffeine, or maybe it was shock and grief, but she still wasn't feeling the effects of her utterly sleepless night. She felt wide awake, and fully aware of the grim day that lay ahead. There was nothing to do but face it head-on.

After hanging up with Curt, she had spent most of the night crying and combing the newspapers, and then the Internet and the television news, for any information about the double slaying in Philadelphia.

There was nothing about Phoebe and Reno on CNN or MSNBC's news broadcasts. She gave up on the Internet, which was running sluggishly—when she did manage to check its search engines, they yielded nothing but links to Reno, Nevada, and the television show Friends, with its character named Phoebe.

However, Jordan did find the newspaper article Beau had mentioned, accompanied by a grainy photo of Phoebe and Reno. According to the caption beneath, it had been taken a year ago at a charity event.

She could see how the photo evidence had tipped off Beau that Spencer belonged to the Averills. The child was a perfect combination of his fair, pretty mother and his darkly handsome father.

Jordan had always suspected that Phoebe was drawn to Reno Averill solely for his dark good looks. There didn't seem to be much more to the man, besides his money—and Phoebe wasn't the gold-digging type.

Reno was a criminal defense attorney and the sole living heir in a well-to-do Main Line family. Both his parents had died by the time he married Phoebe, and he was an only child. That, Phoebe had explained to Jordan, was why they had opted to elope rather than have a lavish wedding. After all, Phoebe's mother had passed away years before, when they were teenagers, and her blue-collar father couldn't afford a big wedding.

Still, Jordan was stung that Phoebe hadn't told her that marriage was imminent. Jordan didn't know Phoebe was getting married until she had returned from her Caribbean honeymoon. Looking back, Jordan realized that it was the first sign that their friendship had taken a different turn.

Jordan supposed she was as much to blame as Phoebe was for letting distance come between them over these past few years. It was easier to get caught up in the details of her own life and business than to maintain on a daily—or even weekly—basis a friendship that was based on little in common at this point. Phoebe had her large home in the Philadelphia suburbs, her charity work, her child . . .

And her husband. A husband who, Jordan suspected, as had Curt, had somehow gotten entangled in some kind of underhanded business that had led to his own and Phoebe's deaths.

The newspaper articles tactfully referred to Reno as a respected, if controversial, lawyer. He had defended notoriously heinous killers, and he had gotten more than one cold-blooded murderer acquitted on legal technicalities. Jordan often wondered how he could live with himself, knowing that he had put dangerous criminals back on the street. She had wondered how Phoebe could live with him.

Now, she wondered if Reno had indeed crossed paths with somebody bent on vengeance against the lawyer and his family.

Her anger and frustration over Phoebe's death mingled with profound sorrow. She cried not just for herself and her own loss, but for Spencer's. What was going to happen to him now? When the whole mess was sorted out and Jordan was able to come forward with Spencer, some decisions would have to be made about his future.

Jordan wondered whether Reno and Phoebe had wills. Probably. After all, Reno was a lawyer. They must have arranged for legal guardianship of Spencer in the event of their deaths, and Jordan had no doubt that she wasn't named in their instructions. Reno had never given her the time of day. Surely he wouldn't have agreed to bestow custody of his only child on his wife's single childhood pal, even if she was Spencer's godmother.

Not that he knew about that. Phoebe, who was raised Catholic, had brought her infant to their hometown church to be baptized on a rare occasion when she came home, unaccompanied by Reno, to visit her father. She explained to Jordan that Reno didn't practice any religion and didn't believe in choosing one for a newborn child. He said that if Spencer grew up and decided to become a Catholic, that was fine, but he didn't want to christen him one.

Apparently, Phoebe couldn't shake the religion that had been ingrained in her by her staunchly religious mother, who died young of cancer and had clung fiercely to her faith, especially in the end. Jordan was with Phoebe at her mother's bedside when last rites were administered; she saw how comforting the ritual was for the dying woman. The image of her mother receiving the last blessed sacrament must have stayed with Phoebe through the years, so that she couldn't allow her young son to be deprived of the first blessed sacrament.

The baptism was an impromptu thing, or so it seemed to Jordan. Glad to spend some time alone with her friend and the baby, she thought they were on their way to lunch when Phoebe informed her they were meeting Father Ralph at Saint Christopher's Church. The kindly old priest, who knew Jordan and Phoebe from their catechism days, willingly baptized Spencer as Jordan cradled him protectively in her arms, touched that Phoebe had chosen her for the honor of being his godmother.

Never mind that the ceremony was conducted in secrecy or that the baby was clad in a blue seersucker romper rather than an antique lace gown. What mattered to Jordan was that Phoebe had shown her she still mattered. Reno might have come between them, but Phoebe still cared. Enough to entrust Jordan with her child's spiritual well-being—and now, with his physical well-being.

Yet Jordan knew that just as Reno would never have consented to the christening, he would never have agreed that Jordan should take custody of his son in the event something happened to him and Phoebe. They had probably chosen some suitable couple from their Main Line social circle as Spencer's guardians.

Or maybe even Curt. As she recalled, he was married with nearly grown children, was in his late forties, and was a successful business owner in Pittsburgh. Maybe he would get custody of Spencer.

Jordan's thoughts kept wandering back to Curt, alternating between regret that she had called him, and regret that she hadn't said more. He was clearly distraught over the news of his sister's and brother-in-law's deaths. He was speculating, as the authorities were, that his nephew's body was missing in the waters of the Delaware River.

I should call him back, Jordan thought. *He deserves to know Spencer is alive.*

But Phoebe had said to tell no one. And last night, Beau had said the same thing.

I can trust Curt, though. After all, here I am trusting a man I barely know. A man who never even met Phoebe.

But she'd had no choice. Beau had stumbled into the middle of this crazy scenario.

If she called Curt back now, she would again be violating not just Beau's advice, but her own promise to Phoebe—a promise she meant to keep despite her friend's death.

Jordan was sitting at the kitchen table, wiping fresh tears from her eyes and morosely stirring milk into yet another steaming cup of coffee, when she heard footsteps on the stairs.

Uh-oh.

Spencer was awake.

She had been dreading this moment all night. She had no intention of telling him yet about his parents, but she was afraid that he would take one look at her and *know*.

The little boy came into the kitchen still dressed in his pajamas with the baseball pattern, rubbing sleep from his eyes. Jordan's heart broke the moment she saw him.

"Hey, how'd you sleep?" she managed to ask, her voice sounding almost normal to her startled ears.

"Okay."

"Do you want some cereal? You've got a lot to choose from," she pointed out, remembering yesterday's shopping spree. "There's Trix, and Count Chocula, and Colonel Crunch . . ."

"It's Cap'n Crunch," he corrected around a yawn. "I'll have that."

"Coming right up." She went to the cupboard to get the cereal. She had never been allowed to eat sweetened cereal as a child. Her mother had said it would rot her teeth, and Jordan had never been big on breakfast, anyway.

Now, as she poured a bowl for Spencer, she absently munched a few pieces of Cap'n Crunch. Then, without thinking, she prepared a bowl for herself, too, and sat down on the stool beside his.

"How come you're eating that?" Spencer asked, his spoon poised over his own cereal.

"Because I'm hungry," she lied.

She wasn't hungry. Her stomach had been queasy

ever since last night. But she needed something to do. Somewhere to focus other than on the orphaned, unwitting little boy beside her.

"I thought you only ate healthy stuff," he said.

"Not always."

"But I only see you eat green stuff, and meat, and coffee."

"I ate candy at the movies with you yesterday," she reminded him.

"Oh, yeah." He was looking at her with new respect. As if maybe there was hope for her after all.

They munched in silence. Jordan forced herself to swallow around the wave of grief that was threatening to gag her again. Suddenly, she was exhausted. All she wanted to do was go upstairs, crawl into her bed, and weep for her lost friend.

Instead, she had to sit here with this little boy who missed his mommy and had no idea that he was never going to see her again.

"Is Beau taking me to the zoo today?" she heard Spencer ask. His tone wasn't very hopeful.

"Actually, he's coming over here today," Jordan said carefully. "I don't know about the zoo."

Spencer's face lit up. "He's coming over? Really? When?"

"Soon, I think."

Seeing the spark of enthusiasm that had darted into Spencer's brown eyes, Jordan could relate. She wished he would hurry up and get here. The mere promise of his presence at some point today had made the unbearable almost bearable.

She wondered how she would have gotten through last night without Beau.

Strange how somebody she had known for so short

a time could somehow be intrinsic to this most intimate, dramatic tragedy in her life.

Jordan tried telling herself that it wasn't just Beau, that anyone who happened to come along at the inopportune—or opportune—moment would have made this kind of impact. She tried to believe that Spencer would have latched on to any man who stepped in and happened to know that kids prefer grape jelly to vegetables.

No, she told herself firmly, there was nothing special about Beau himself, or her sudden and intense link to the man.

Spencer was smiling, she realized as he crunched into another mouthful of cereal. Jordan wondered how much longer she could keep the truth from him. She knew he couldn't read yet, but she had hidden the newspaper article beneath her mattress upstairs, lest he glimpse his parents' photo and start asking questions.

If the murder of a Philadelphia attorney and his wife had made the national news on a slow news day, there was no telling what the media would do with the missing-child angle. If the case heated up and attention focused on the fact that Spencer might not have been on the boat with his parents, the police—and the killer, she realized with a chill—wouldn't be the only ones on the lookout for the little boy.

"What's wrong, Jordan?"

"Hmm?" She realized that Spencer was watching her with a worried expression that must mirror her own. "Nothing's wrong, sweetie. Finish your cereal and then you can watch TV for a little while."

"Can I watch the Disney Channel? *Out of the Box* might be on."

"Sure," she said reluctantly, realizing that she should

be keeping him away from television as well as newspapers. Not that there was any chance of a news story about his parents on the Disney Channel, but what if he got hold of the remote control and changed the station in a commercial? What if he stumbled across the horrifying truth before she broke it to him?

She would just have to keep him in her sight every minute. Which was exactly what she had planned to do, anyway. If whoever had murdered Phoebe and Reno was out there looking for Spencer, they'd only get to him over Jordan's dead body.

Spencer was crying when Beau arrived at Jordan's apartment just before noon.

All the way over here, his mind had whirled with details he'd left untended at his office. The work-related worries evaporated, and his heart sank when he saw the little boy's tear-stained face peering around the doorway from the living room as Jordan opened the door wide to let Beau in.

"Hey, fella, what's wrong?" he asked, stepping into the dim air-conditioned foyer and casting a worried glance at Jordan. Had she told the child about his parents' deaths?

"She said we can't go to the zoo," Spencer sobbed.

Relief seeped into Beau as he tried to look suitably concerned. "She did? Well, there must be a good reason for that."

"There *is* a good reason," Jordan said, closing the front door again and prudently locking the dead bolt and sliding the chain into its slot.

The telltale lines and shadows around her eyes betrayed what must have been a difficult night. She looked exhausted. Her dark hair was carelessly caught up in a high, off-centered ponytail. She wore a rumpled-looking blue T-shirt and cutoffs. Her feet were bare.

She looks like a little girl, Beau thought, forcing his attention away from her, knowing that if he didn't, he might find himself reaching out to brush the strands of loose hair back from her face, the way he used to do with Jeanette.

"So what if it's too hot out?" Spencer retorted. "That's not a good reason. That's a stupid reason! And she's stupid!"

"Hey, take it easy, Spence," Beau said, seeing the wounded look on Jordan's face. "Jordan's right. It's much too hot to go to the zoo. The sun is beating down and it's so humid it's hard to breathe out there." He wiped a trickle of lingering sweat from his forehead to accentuate the point.

"Well, you said you were going to take me to the zoo. I don't want to stay in this dumb house any more. It's boring here!"

"You don't have to stay in the house," Beau heard himself say.

He could feel Jordan's dismayed, questioning gaze on him.

"We can go for a ride," he suggested, turning to look at her.

"A ride where?" Spencer asked, eyes narrowed shrewdly, as if he were weighing the possibility against another tantrum.

Beau sensed that this was out of character for him. He wasn't a bratty little kid. He was afraid, and homesick, and trapped in a strange place with strangers. The poor little guy only wanted his mommy, and he wanted to go home. Who could blame him for acting up?

"We can't go for a ride," Jordan said firmly, her hazel eyes flashing a warning look at Beau, as if to say, *how could you?*

"Why can't we?" Spencer whined.

"Because ... it's so hot out, and ... and ..." She faltered, shaking her head, silently begging Beau to bail her out.

"It *is* hot out, but my car's air-conditioned," he told her. "We don't even have to get out of it," he added meaningfully.

"We're not going to get out of the car?" Spencer protested. "But—"

"Look, we can't stay here in the apartment all day," Beau said reasonably, to both of them. "So let's take a ride around the city. I haven't had a chance to see all the sights yet, and I bet Jordan would be a good tour guide for both of us, Spence."

"I want to get out of the car," he grumbled.

"We'll see," Beau said lightly, bending over to tussle the child's hair. "Why don't you go find some shoes to wear, fella? Maybe there's a drive-through ice cream place around here someplace."

"I'll be right back!" Spencer took the stairs two at a time.

Jordan turned on Beau, green eyes flashing. "How could you? We can't go out with him! What if someone sees him?" she hissed.

"I have tinted windows," he said reasonably. "Look, the poor kid is going stir-crazy, Jordan. It's not doing anybody any good for the two of you to stay cooped up here all day. Let's get him out and make him happy, before he finds out ..."

He trailed off.

She nodded. Sadness swooped over her like an understudy who had been waiting in the shadowy wings.

Beau saw her lip begin to tremble as she wiped quickly at her eyes, averting her gaze. She was obviously distraught over her friend's sudden, violent death. She wouldn't get over that for a long time—if ever.

A wave of pain washed over Beau as he remembered his own tragic loss. Would there ever come a day when he wouldn't think of his wife and son and feel soul-searing anguish?

"Look, I know you hurt," he said softly. "And I know you're scared. It's going to be all right. Spencer's going to come out of this okay, and so are you."

"Do you really think so?" she asked, looking up at him.

He couldn't allow himself to answer her truthfully.

Instead, he found himself reaching toward the errant strands of hair that grazed her cheekbone. It wasn't a conscious gesture; it was as though his hand belonged to somebody else—as though he had no control over the movement.

As he made contact with the silky wisps, his fingers brushed her skin as well. A soft gasp escaped Jordan's lips, but she didn't flinch beneath his touch; nor did she back away.

He dared to let his hand linger there against her cheek; allowed his thumb to trace her jawline downward. When he tucked his thumb beneath her chin and lifted her face so that he could look into her eyes, he found something utterly unexpected in them.

A smoldering spark of attraction.

She was as drawn to him as he was to her.

Maybe this was the wrong time, the wrong place, but Beau couldn't tear himself away. Not now that he had seen that her need for him went beyond the emotional, that it was physical, and as real as his own sudden, fierce longing.

He closed his eyes briefly, knowing that when he opened them it would be gone, that the shared passion would prove to have been his imagination.

But when he looked down at Jordan again, there was no denying the electricity that darted between her gaze and his. He felt the warmth of desire pooling low in his belly in response, and then, before he knew what he was doing, he dipped his head and he kissed her.

Her cry of protest transformed into a moan of pleasure when his lips came down on hers.

It was a fleeting, blazing kiss, one that told him all he needed to know.

Jordan Curry was dangerous.

"Hey! How come you're kissing her?"

Startled by the voice from somewhere above them, Beau sprang back from Jordan, who instantly pressed her hand against her lips as though she'd been branded.

They both looked up to see Spencer standing at the top of the flight of stairs, a pair of black rubber sport sandals dangling from one hand.

The look of *ugh, girl germs!* disgust on his face might have struck Beau as funny if Spencer's interruption hadn't already plunked him solidly down in stark reality once more.

There was nothing the least bit amusing about reality.

Luckily, Spencer didn't wait for an answer to his question. He bounded down the flight of steps and immediately asked Beau for help putting on his shoes, turning his back completely on Jordan.

"I'll . . . I'll go change my clothes," she murmured.

Turning, she fled up the stairs. Beau heard a door slam somewhere above.

He resents her, Beau realized as he stooped to help the little boy adjust the Velcro straps around his ankles. *He resents her because she isn't his mother, and he resents her because I was paying attention to her.*

It was like one of those old movies gone awry, he thought as, sandals fastened, he helped Spencer to his feet. The kind of movie where the anguished orphan acts out his grief, tormenting his caregiver until a kindly parental figure steps in and melts the caregiver's and the orphan's hearts. Instant family.

But this wasn't a movie. There would be no instant family, Beau acknowledged grimly.

And the worst of it was that, for Spencer, still unaware that he had lost both his parents and was never going home again, the worst was yet to come.

In her room, Jordan slipped quickly out of the clothes she'd thrown on earlier, letting them fall in a heap beside the unmade bed.

It wasn't like her to let things go like this, she thought, glancing at the room's disarray. She hadn't even bothered to open the shades since Phoebe left Spencer here with her three days ago. Well, she wasn't about to do so now. Not when the world had fallen apart around her. . . .

Not when Beau Somerville had just kissed her senseless downstairs.

She glanced at her reflection in the mirror above the bureau and saw the telltale flush still coloring her cheeks. She saw, too, the rosy blotches rising on the patch of alabaster skin beneath her throat, between her bra straps.

She remembered how Kevin, her ex-fiancé, used to tease her about her tendency to flush there, almost as if she had been sunburned, whenever she was aroused.

Well, Beau sure as hell had aroused her. What was he doing kissing her? And how could she have kissed him back? This wasn't the time for romance.

There would never be a time for romance with him, as far as Jordan was concerned. If she hadn't had enough going on in her life before Spencer arrived on her doorstep and Phoebe was murdered, she was more than overwhelmed now.

And anyway, she had already sensed that Beau wasn't any more emotionally available than she was. There had been a careful distance about him every time she had seen him, and even when they talked on the phone. It didn't take a mind reader to know that he wasn't in the market for a relationship—and that Andrea MacDuff had bullied him into the date, just as she had forced him on Jordan.

And as long as that was the case, Beau had no business grabbing her and kissing her. He had some nerve, taking advantage of her at a time like this.

Jordan found herself growing indignant at his very presence downstairs until she remembered that he was here at her request.

And that if he left, she would have to deal with Spencer all alone.

She had already spent a grueling morning doing just that. Aside from her indulgence in Cap'n Crunch cereal, nothing she said or did was right as far as he was concerned. It was her fault that he had missed his favorite television program, and her fault when he'd stubbed his toe on the coffee table. He didn't want to brush his teeth, he didn't want to get dressed, and he didn't want to wear anything she had laid out for him.

On top of being generally disagreeable, Spencer had pestered her nonstop about when Beau was going to show up and whether they could go to the zoo. Finally, she'd had enough, and told him what she'd been trying to avoid: that they couldn't go to the zoo even after Beau came. *If* he came. . . .

By then, she was having her doubts that he'd show up at all, even though he'd called her twice from his office to tell her he'd be over just as soon as he could break away.

It might have been better if he'd gotten stuck at the office after all, she thought, opening a drawer and pulling out the first pair of shorts on the pile. They were black. Good. That suited her mood.

She pulled them on and checked the mirror again. She couldn't go back down there with the glow of arousal plainly visible beneath her neck. She didn't want Beau Somerville to know what that single kiss had done to her.

It had been too long, Jordan realized, since she had been touched by a man. Too long since a man had looked at her the way Beau had before he kissed her. Too long since . . .

Well, it's going to be a lot longer, especially for that, she told herself firmly, opening another drawer and pawing through it for the shirt she sought. *It's going to be forever, where Mr. Somerville's concerned.*

She refused to fall for a good-looking Southern charmer like Beau. That would just be asking for trouble.

She had vowed on her defunct wedding day that she

would never fall in love again, especially with a man like Kevin. A man who swept away her common sense with passion and promises, making her forget everything but how she felt when they were together.

Yet perhaps, somewhere in the back of her mind, she had occasionally acknowledged that she might not stay single forever. That she might someday grow weary of being alone. That somebody would come along who could make her forget the bitterness of being abandoned.

Yes, it *could* conceivably happen. Yet she also recognized that when and if a man won her jaded heart, he would be nothing like the one who had broken it.

If she really squinted into the distant future, she could see herself finally settling down someday with a safe, comfortable type—some reliable, quiet, sweet, buttoned-up gentleman like her father.

Comparing Beau Somerville to Clark Curry was like comparing a dry martini to a glass of warm milk.

Jordan sighed, pulling the sleeveless lime-green turtle-neck over her head and shaking her hair loose. It was a warm day for snug-fitting ribbed cotton and a high collar.

But right now, she could care less about the humid heat outdoors.

No, the only heat that had Jordan worried now was the fire Beau had generated deep within her with a single steamy kiss.

Dusk was falling when Beau pulled up at the curb in front of Jordan's town house. Both an old Van Morrison song on the radio and the car's air conditioner were on full blast. But when Beau cut the engine, everything fell silent.

"Is he still asleep back there?" he asked, turning to check on Spencer.

"Looks that way," Jordan replied.

They studied the little boy strapped into the backseat, eyes closed, lips slightly parted with his even breathing.

Spencer had been sleeping for the past few hours, during the whole drive back into rush hour traffic from the rural West Virginia park where the three of them had shared a picnic supper.

The day had been pleasant despite the underlying tension between Beau and Jordan, and between Jordan and Spencer. After driving through a fast-food takeout window for ice cream, they had cruised around Washington, past the White House, the Pentagon, the Smithsonian, and all the monuments—carefully avoiding the National Zoo.

Naturally, Beau had seen it all before from the windows of his SUV in his daily travels around the city, but for Spencer's benefit, he had acted newly impressed by every landmark they passed. Naturally, Spencer begged for him to park at each one so that they could get out and investigate in person. And naturally, Jordan vetoed that request every time.

He couldn't blame her. The city was crawling with people—commuters and residents, construction workers and diplomats, tourists galore: families and senior citizens' groups and kids in matching T-shirts spilling off camp buses. They couldn't take a chance that somebody who had seen the Averills' photo in the papers might take one look at Spencer's face and recognize him— or at least grow suspicious.

It was Jordan who suggested that they head to the

glorious park high above the Shenandoah River, not far from Harper's Ferry. She told Beau, in a low voice that Spencer couldn't hear above the radio, that they might be able to find a secluded spot where they could get out of the car and let Spencer run around a little. They had stopped and picked up sandwiches and beverages at a convenience store not far from the park, and they ate at a picnic table in a leafy grove. Though they saw a couple of hikers from a distance, nobody paid the least bit attention to Spencer, whose face was mostly shielded by the oversized Texas Rangers cap Beau had placed on his head just in case.

As Jordan had watched from her shaded spot on the bench, Spencer and Beau wrestled on the ground and climbed the low-hanging branches of an ancient tree. To anyone who might happen along, Jordan realized, they looked for all the world like father and son.

She wondered what kind of relationship Spencer had shared with Reno. He rarely spoke of his father, but he had repeatedly mentioned his mother today.

Each time Phoebe's son had spoken of her, Jordan felt tears springing to her eyes and was glad for the sunglasses that masked them from Spencer.

Though Spencer's slumber on the way home essentially left Jordan and Beau alone together, it had somehow been easy not to fall into a potentially awkward conversation during the long drive. With the radio playing and the air conditioner whooshing, they had traveled in near silence the entire way, aside from occasional comments about the building traffic and which routes promised less congestion.

Now Jordan wished they had taken advantage of the drive to discuss the situation.

Not the kiss, which she was trying her hardest to forget had happened.

But the situation with Spencer. Now that the initial shock of his parents' murder had worn off, Jordan was no closer to knowing what her next step should be. Logic told her to do nothing—simply to wait for something to happen.

But for what?

For the papers to report that the murder had been solved and the suspect apprehended?

For the police to come knocking at her door?

Or for a cold-blooded killer to trace Spencer somehow through her phone call to Curt and show up at her home instead?

"So you're leaving town tomorrow?" she asked Beau now, knowing they had to get out of the car and get on with their good-byes. This was her last chance to talk to him before she was left alone to grapple with her burden.

He studied her. "I don't *have* to."

"What do you mean? Don't you have a vacation planned? You probably have a flight, and reservations. . . ."

"There's no flight," he said quickly—perhaps too quickly, his eyes shadowed with an expression she didn't understand. "I'm driving out to the Outer Banks."

"That's a long drive."

He nodded. "I don't mind it. I've rented a beach house there for the week. But I don't have to—"

"No, you should go," she forced herself to say. Firmly. As though there weren't the slightest doubt in her mind.

"Are you sure?"

"What would you do here? Just more of what we did today?"

"I can," he offered.

She shook her head. "Look, you don't have to help me baby-sit him, Beau. I'll take care of him, and I'll wait and see what happens. I'll check the papers and see if they get the guy who . . . who did it," she said, conscious of Spencer in the backseat behind them. She was fairly sure he was in a deep sleep, but she couldn't chance his overhearing a reference to his parents' deaths.

Soon enough, she would bring herself to tell him what had happened. But not until the time was right.

"It could take a long time for an investigation to be carried out and for an arrest to be made," Beau pointed out. "It might never happen."

"Well, I'll figure things out," she said. "I'll wait, and when I feel like it's safe to go to the police, I will."

"But not right away."

"No," she agreed, "not right away."

"Okay."

There was a long pause.

"I'll carry him into the house for you," Beau said softly at last, opening the car door.

Jordan nodded and climbed out into the still evening air.

The heat was oppressive even now that dark was descending. Cicadas hummed a familiar rhythm, and an occasional car passed along the street behind her as she unlocked the front door and waited for Beau to carry Spencer up the steps.

She looked up and down the street, a quiet tree-and-shrub-lined stretch off a main Georgetown thoroughfare. She realized that anyone could be lurking in a window of one of the town houses that lined the block, or in the foliage-draped shadows.

The very idea that someone sinister might be looking

for Spencer made her blood run cold. She hugged herself as she stood on the stoop in the warm June dusk, stepping aside to let Beau cross the threshold with his precious burden.

Inside, she whispered, "Let's put him right up in bed."

"He's exhausted," Beau whispered back. "He'll probably sleep right through till morning."

Jordan led the way to the second-floor guest room.

She pulled back the covers and Beau deposited the sleeping child gently on his bed. Swiftly and expertly, he undressed the little boy and changed him into pajamas without waking him.

Watching his movements, Jordan was suddenly struck by the notion that Beau must have done this before. Where she was consistently awkward in her attempts to button and unbutton little-boy shirts and figure out which was the back and which was the front of his tiny pajama bottoms, Beau seemed to know instinctively.

It's because he's a guy, she told herself illogically.

But something told her that wasn't the case. It was because he had done this before. There was something too comfortable about the way he tucked Spencer's sheets and blankets up to his chin, bending to kiss the boy tenderly on the head before stepping back from the bed.

He turned to see her watching him, and was clearly startled by the expression on her face.

"What?" he asked, his voice hushed as she turned out the bedside lamp.

She shook her head, unwilling to voice her hunch, instead bending to place her own kiss on the little boy. It landed near his brow. The child sleepily swatted at the spot as though a mosquito were buzzing there.

Together, Beau and Jordan tiptoed from the room. In the hall she paused to turn the air conditioner to a lower setting. The house felt warm and close now that she was accustomed to the temperature change from outside.

She descended the stairs behind Beau. At the bottom, they faced each other.

She wanted to say good-bye. But what she heard herself say instead was, "Do you want some coffee?"

"Only if you have iced. It's too hot for anything steamy."

Too hot for steamy kisses, she found herself thinking irrationally, forcing her gaze away from his full lips. Aloud, she said, "I have iced tea."

"That would be good."

They walked into the kitchen.

She saw the light blinking on her answering machine. "I'd better check my messages first," she said. "Maybe . . ."

She trailed off, remembering.

No longer was she waiting for a call from Phoebe. That call would never come now.

Swallowing over the lump that rose in her throat, she walked to the machine and pressed the button. The tape rewound.

She had one message. It was from old Mrs. Villeroy, who lived two doors down.

The requisite pesky neighbor, Mrs. Villeroy often called Jordan to borrow something or to ask for a favor. There was no telling what she wanted this time. She said the same thing she always did, "Hello, Jordan, this is Velma Villeroy. Please call me as soon as you get back."

Jordan sighed, pressing the erase button.

With all that had happened, she wasn't in the mood to deal with Mrs. Villeroy tonight. She'd remind herself to call back tomorrow.

"Friend of yours?" Beau asked as the tape rewound. He had come up behind her, standing a few feet away.

"Neighbor."

The few moments outside in the humid night air had dampened her hair with sweat, sending trickles of it down inside the turtleneck. Jutting her lower lip to send a breath of breeze at her sticky hairline, she bent to untie her white canvas sneakers. She kicked them off, longing to shed also the confinement of the high-necked shirt and rumpled linen shorts.

She could feel Beau's eyes on her as she turned and padded past him onto the cool tile of the kitchen floor. She didn't dare look at him. She was afraid of what she might see in his expression, now that they were truly alone together.

She walked to the cupboard and took out two tall cobalt iced-tea glasses, then opened the fridge and reached for the matching pitcher. Beside it on the shelf was a wicker basket of peaches she'd bought yesterday. "Are you hungry?"

"No," he said simply.

She glanced at him as she poured, and she realized that *she* was hungry. Starved for another one of those soul-searing kisses.

Gradually, her resolve was falling away. She was growing far too weary to battle her attraction for this man. All that she had been through in the past twenty-four hours—the trauma, Spencer's adversity, the lack of sleep, the kiss—had depleted her conviction. She could no longer stand firm against the magnetic force that drew her to Beau Somerville.

He wasn't good for her. He wasn't what she wanted.

Yet right now, he was what she needed. And maybe that was enough.

Right now.

She swallowed hard, finding it hard not to let her knees buckle beneath her as she crossed the room to hand him the glass.

He took it and sipped.

She did the same, letting the cool, lemony liquid slide down her throat, though her thirst had evaporated with the realization that they were alone together again.

Errant thoughts drifted into her mind. Indecent thoughts.

She watched Beau lower the glass and lick his lips, and she knew that if she closed her eyes, she could imagine his moist mouth on the tender pulse point behind her ear, his hot tongue trailing lower . . .

Oh, Lord. How could she be thinking such things at a time like this?

Jordan tried to force her mind back to the more serious matter at hand, but her thoughts refused to budge.

How could she try to convince herself that she didn't want Beau when she wanted him as she had never wanted a man in her life?

She wanted him to carry her up the stairs as tenderly as he had carried Spencer. She wanted to be secure in his arms, her cheek cradled against his strong chest. She wanted him to lay her gently on her bed and deftly undress her.

And then . . .

And then she ached for him to make love to her, to let her prove that she was alive, that life would go on. She yearned for sweet release from the constant bonds of restraint. She couldn't stand another moment of keeping it all bottled inside—the grief, the loneliness, the pain, the desire.

Beau's green eyes collided with hers, and in that instant, she saw her own pent-up anguish mirrored there. She knew that he felt it, too. That he needed deliverance as desperately as she did.

Slowly, Beau set his sweat-beaded glass of iced tea on the counter beside them. Even more slowly, he reached out and took hers. She released it into his hand, knowing and yet not knowing what would happen next.

Jordan held her breath as she watched Beau carefully place her glass on the cool granite next to his.

Their eyes were locked once again, and Beau was looking at her in a way that left no ambiguity as to his intentions.

"Jordan, if you don't tell me to get the hell out of your house right now," he said raggedly, his face mere inches from hers, "we're both going to be sorry."

Sirens blasted in her head. He was right. Of course he was right. All she had to do was say the word, and he would go.

"You're leaving town tomorrow?" Her voice was lower, huskier than usual.

He nodded. "As long as . . . as long as you don't need me here."

She shook her head.

An unspoken agreement passed between them. They would have this one night together, and then he would go away.

After he was gone, she would be left alone with Spencer, but she could handle that more readily than she could handle having Beau here, facing the aftermath of what they were about to do.

They stared into each other's eyes for another long moment.

Jordan held her breath.

Then Beau swept her into his arms and kissed her. As his warm, wet mouth glided over hers at last, Jordan spiraled into another realm. Here, there were no conscious thoughts, no worries, no boundaries. Here, there was nothing but sensation.

Beau's tongue swirled into her mouth, igniting a passionate duel with hers that left her gasping with pleasure when he lifted his head. Then he was kissing the nape of her neck, breathing fire in the tender hollow beneath her ears where she had longed for his touch only moments before.

His arms held her fast along the length of his body. The evidence of his arousal had her squirming against him, and he groaned, lifting her so that her legs were wrapped around his waist, her arms around his neck.

"Where?" he ground out in her ear before devouring her mouth again.

"Upstairs," she replied breathlessly when they came up for air.

As though he had read her mind before, Beau carried her up the stairs, past the closed guest room door.

Crossing the threshold into her room, he kicked the door closed and deposited her on the rumpled bed. Heedless of the tangled sheets and quilt, he went to work on her clothes, pulling her shirt off and fumbling for a moment with the front clasp on her bra.

She raised herself to accommodate him, propped on her elbows as he lifted the bra away and at last her breasts spilled from the lacy silk confinement. He looked down at her almost reverently before groaning and bending to taunt one taut nipple with his hot tongue.

With a sigh, Jordan sank back against a cloud of down pillows and comforter that were heaped beneath her head and shoulders, allowing sensation to sweep her away once again. She sailed blissfully toward oblivion, borne along by the incredible sensation of Beau's wet mouth working first one sensitive nub, then the other, then sliding lower, over her stomach.

He lifted his head only briefly, to see what he was doing as he unfastened her shorts and slid them down, taking her panties with them. They were impatiently discarded over the edge of the bed before he put his hands on her thighs, pushing them gently apart. She opened her mouth to protest just as his made slippery contact with her most intimate flesh, and a purr of pure pleasure escaped her instead.

Lost to the promising ripples he sent cascading through her, Jordan wove her fingers into Beau's thick hair, clutching him to her as if she feared he might pull away. But he made no move to lift his head or cease his tongue's swirling caresses, and too soon, she felt the unmistakable quivers of impending eruption. She began to writhe in an attempt to lessen the exquisite contact, to prolong the agonizing wait. But his strong hands held her hips fast and his expert suckling went on . . . and on . . . until she exploded beneath him and around him, gasping his name.

As if the sound of his name on her lips beckoned him to her, he lifted his head at last, propping himself, fully clothed, above the length of her naked body.

"Please," she whimpered, as the waves of her climax left even greater need in their wake. She tugged at his shirt, then slid her fingertips beneath the sweat-dampened cotton fabric, stroking warm skin and firm muscle, holding his shoulders and lifting her hips to make contact with his arousal.

He groaned as she rubbed against him, his eyes drifting closed momentarily. Then he opened them and looked at her, as though he had to force himself to stay focused. She began kissing his neck, his skin salty and sweet. Their hips rocked together in an intimate rhythm until she squirmed, needing to be closer than that, needing to remove the barrier of his clothes that lay between them. She tugged at the waistband of his shorts, but he put a hand on hers to stop her.

Startled, she looked at him.

"Oh, hell, Jordan . . . I don't have . . . anything," he said raggedly, his panting breaths stirring her hair.

Protection. He didn't have protection. Her heart sank.

"Do you . . . ?" He trailed off, seeing the look on her face. "I didn't think so," he said flatly.

He rolled off her and lay, breathing hard, on his back. She lay beside him, staring at the lazily circulating paddle fan above the bed and slowly sinking back down to earth.

She landed with a thud and the realization that if Beau hadn't thought about protection, it wouldn't have occurred to her.

She had so blindly wanted him that she hadn't stopped to worry about pregnancy, or STDs. Even now, she was half tempted to throw caution to the wind. . . .

And she might have, if he hadn't sat up when he did, swinging his legs over the edge of the bed, away from her, effectively shattering what was left of the mood.

"I should go," he said, not looking at her.

She instinctively pulled the sheet up to cover her nudity, suddenly self-conscious. So they were back to this awkward sidestepping around each other, she thought darkly. She had told herself she would just allow this brief interlude, this one night with him. . . .

But her escape hadn't even lasted that long.

"Will you be okay if I go?" he asked, ever the Southern gentleman, bending to put on the shoes he had kicked off at some point.

"I'll be fine," she lied.

"Not just about this," he said, straightening and turning to look at her. "I mean, with Spencer."

"I'll be fine," she said again.

"What will you do?"

She noticed his use of the word you. Until now, she had felt almost as though they were a team. He had allowed her to feel that way, she realized. And no matter what she had told herself, or said to him . . .

She didn't want him to leave tomorrow. She didn't want him to be miles away, leaving her to grapple with her loss, and Spencer's loss, and the veiled threat Phoebe had seemed to imply.

He searched her face. "If you need me—"

"I don't," she said, and it came out sharply. "You can go. Really. I'll figure out what to do."

"Are you sure?"

She nodded.

He stood. "I'll call when I get home. I'll only be gone a week."

She nodded again, unable to speak.

"Okay, then. I'll talk to you soon." He was watching her as he headed for the door.

She made no move to follow him.

"Aren't you coming down with me?" he asked.

She shook her head.

"But you should lock the door after I go, Jordan. Just in case . . ."

"I will," she said, fighting back the bitterness—and fear—that rose in her throat. She was going to be alone again. Alone—and perhaps in danger. Yet she couldn't bring herself to ask him to stay, and he wasn't going to offer again.

He stood by the door, waiting.

She managed to speak again. "Just go, Beau. I'll come down and lock up after you leave."

"Okay."

With a slight wave, he was gone.

She lay listening to his footsteps retreating down the stairs, then heard him open the door and close it firmly behind him.

He didn't slam it, she noted dully, but he might as well have.

Chapter Seven

Tuesday morning, Beau woke to the bleat of the alarm he had set the night before.

Groaning, he came instantly to consciousness, welcoming it as he rolled over to turn off the alarm.

He saw that it wasn't quite five o'clock. He'd better get up and take another shower—this time a hot one, unlike the one he'd taken before bed last night.

Returning home from Jordan's, his body aching with frustration and unsated need, he had stepped directly into an icy stream of water, hoping to ease the tension enough to sleep.

But it was hours before he managed to drift off, and when he did, his dreams carried him back to the place his restless waking thoughts had visited. At first, he saw only Jordan and Spencer, and they were in trouble, and he was leaving them behind.

Yet as the nightmarish sequence his mind had con-

jured wore on, it took an unexpected turn. Jordan and
Spencer became Jeanette and Tyler. He knew they were
in trouble, knew he had to save them, yet he was powerless to get to them.

It was a familiar dream—one that had haunted him
over the years. But the parallel between his lost wife and
son, and Jordan and Spencer left Beau feeling uneasy.

He toweled off after his shower, and put his shaving
cream, razor, and deodorant into the small leather bag
he used for toiletries when he traveled. It already contained several items he kept in it: spare razor blades,
ibuprofin, extra shoelaces . . . and a small package of
condoms.

Seeing them, he shook his head. If he'd had them
with him last night, things would be different right now.

But he wasn't the type to carry condoms around in
his wallet, just in case. He had really only had two serious
relationships in his life: Jeanette and Lisa. In fact, it was
because of Lisa that the condoms were here in the first
place.

She had gone off the pill a year ago, saying that it
was making her nauseated. But that was right around
the time she began talking nonstop of marrying Beau
and having a child with him. He suspected that she
had stopped her oral contraception in preparation for
pregnancy. In reality, that was the beginning of the end
for them. He knew that he couldn't go down that road
ever again, and that it was unfair of him to stay with
Lisa, who deserved marriage and a family—blessings
he'd already had and lost.

In the kitchen, as Beau went through the motions of
preparing a bowl of cereal and a glass of fresh-squeezed
juice, he pondered the day ahead.

Last night, he had convinced himself that after heading over to the office this morning to tie up all the loose ends he had left yesterday, he would make the long drive to the beach house as planned.

Jordan hadn't said anything to change his mind.

If only they hadn't recklessly tumbled into bed together . . .

Oh, hell, no. The only *if only* he could logically entertain in retrospect was . . .

If only he had been prepared to tumble into bed with her.

He had no doubt that if their entanglement had followed through to its natural conclusion, he wouldn't be going anywhere today. He would still be lying in her bed, in her arms.

His caution had effectively shattered their fragile bond—the emotional one, not just the sexual one. The moment he rolled away from her, he had brought down a massive stone wall between them.

Well, what should he have done? Proceeded to finish what they had begun, and to hell with protection?

No.

He had been there once before. With Jeanette.

He had met her in Europe, while he was traveling there after finishing his graduate work at Rice School of Architecture. It was such a cliché. He was the privileged American guy, taking a year off and piddling away a chunk of his newly inherited trust fund. Jeanette was a beautiful, footloose California girl in Paris on an art scholarship. She captivated him the moment they saw each other at the café, where she was sketching passersby and he was nursing a wine hangover with a cup of strong French coffee.

They were in his bed at the Ritz before the sun went down that night, and neither of them had stopped to worry about protection. Inseparable thereafter, they were so caught up in each other that Jeanette didn't even realize when she had missed her period a few weeks later.

Not until she found herself vomiting their usual breakfast of croissants and café au lait did it occur to either of them that their first night of passion might have created more than a carefree romance.

Or that their romance wouldn't always be carefree.

But it worked out. He had proposed. She had accepted. They moved back to the States, into the sprawling Somerville plantation house, and along came Tyler.

Everyone said their marriage wouldn't last.

After all, they were opposites: Beau the scion of filthy-rich Southern WASPs; Jeanette the product of alcoholic, blue-collar West Coast parents who divorced within months of her birth.

People assumed that once the blush of falling in love with each other and with their son wore off, they would drift apart.

He and Jeanette used to laugh about it—about how Beau's father was braced for a bitter battle over alimony and a share in the family fortune, and his mother was worried about the future of her mother's sapphire earrings, which Beau had inherited and presented to his bride on their wedding day.

Well, his mother had the earrings now, Beau thought bitterly, his stomach roiling as he poured his uneaten cereal down the garbage disposal. The sapphires were safely back in Mother's jewelry box after having been dredged from the depths of the bayou. . . .

Along with the bodies of Beau's wife and son.

* * *

Somebody was screaming.

At the shrill burst of sound, Jordan sat straight up in bed, ripped abruptly from a deep sleep.

Realizing that it was Spencer—and that she was naked beneath the sheet—Jordan fumbled blindly for the robe that was draped over the bedpost. She pulled it on, noting that the screams had subsided as she raced down the hall and grabbed for the knob. For a split second, she froze, all sorts of terrible scenarios invading her mind. Then she pushed Spencer's door open, telling herself that it had to be another nightmare.

It had to be. . . .

But what if it wasn't? What if Curt's phone really had been tapped and somebody had found her and Spencer, and simply walked through the front door and . . .

Oh, God. Oh, God. Oh, God.

Spencer's bed was empty.

Frantic, she shrieked his name and hurled herself back into the hall.

That was when she heard it.

Sobbing.

It was coming from downstairs.

Jordan saw him from the top of the steps. He was sitting on the floor in the foyer, crying, rubbing his eyes. Relief coursed through her.

"What's wrong, sweetie?" She rushed down the steps to him, taking him into her arms.

He was trembling violently. "The pirate," he said, and began to cry. "He got me."

"Oh, Spencer, there are no pirates here," she said soothingly.

"Yes, there are. He was here. He took me out of my

bed and he brought me downstairs and he was going
to carry me away."

"Sweetie, it was just a dream. You must have been
sleepwalking."

"I'm scared, Jordan." He snuggled against her.
"Please don't let him come back and get me."

"I won't," she promised, because it was easier than
protesting again. "You're safe here with me, sweetie. I
won't let anything happen to you."

For now, for once, she actually believed those words.
Of course he was safe here. Nobody knew where he was,
and anyway, why would Phoebe and Reno's killer bother
tracking down a young child?

But . . .

For that matter, why would anyone with a vendetta
against Reno have bothered killing Phoebe? Well,
maybe she had been in the wrong place at the wrong
time, alongside her husband, Jordan thought uneasily.
The fact that they were dead didn't mean Spencer's life
was still in danger.

"Is it the middle of the night?" Spencer asked.

She looked at the clock on a shelf across the dimly
lit room. "It's almost dawn," she said reassuringly.

"Do I have to go back to sleep? Please don't make
me. I'm scared he'll come again."

"It's okay," Jordan said, yawning. "We can get up."

She stood, stretched, and reached for his hand.

"Jordan?" he asked, allowing her to squeeze his fingers.

"Hmm?"

"Do you think my mommy will come back for me
today?"

She froze. A terrible, sick feeling washed over her.

"No, Spencer," she said quietly. "I don't think she will."

She braced herself for the inevitable, but he seemed satisfied, if disappointed, with that answer.

At least, for now.

But sooner or later, she would have to tell him the truth.

As they headed for the kitchen, she glanced over her shoulder to make sure the front door was locked.

It wasn't.

All three locks were undone.

She stopped walking.

"What's wrong?" Spencer asked beside her.

"Nothing," she murmured, searching her memory.

She was almost positive that she had come back downstairs last night to lock the door after Beau left. She remembered lying in bed before that, growing drowsy, and realizing she was going to fall asleep and leave it open. She was pretty certain she had climbed out of bed and padded to the stairs. . . .

But everything was fuzzy.

She had been so exhausted.

Maybe she only thought she had locked the doors. Maybe she had dreamed it, just as Spencer had dreamed about the pirate kidnapping him from his bed.

That had to be it, she reassured herself, giving Spencer's small hand another squeeze.

It was almost eleven o'clock when Beau finally tossed the last duffel bag into the back of his SUV and climbed into the driver's seat. It had been a long morning at the office, followed by a quick dash back to his apartment to pack and get ready for his departure.

He still wasn't comfortable leaving Jordan and Spencer behind, but what choice did he have?

You could stay, he told himself as he drove out of the parking garage beneath his building.

At least, he could call to make sure she was all right. That thought had crossed his mind countless times this morning, but he had been so busy at the office that there was never an opportunity.

Well, it was too late now, he thought ... until he remembered that he still had his cell phone in his pocket. He hadn't even planned to take it with him on vacation, balking at Ed's insistence that he carry it to North Carolina and leave it on during the trip.

They were in the midst of designing a house to replace the historic Arlington home of a powerful—and notoriously prickly—corporate CEO after the original had been destroyed by fire.

Albert Landry wanted—no, he expected—it to be rebuilt immediately: completely redesigned, with care to preserve the antique features and update it with modern amenities. Though both Beau and Ed were involved in the design, Landry had taken a liking to Beau. The partners had decided Landry didn't need to know Beau was leaving town.

Realistically, it would be at least another few weeks before the plans were ready anyway, and Beau wasn't about to postpone his long-awaited vacation to be at a CEO's beck and call.

Beau had fully intended to leave the damn cell phone in the apartment, figuring that if something came up at the office involving the Landry project, it could wait till he reached his destination and called Ed to check in.

It was Jordan he was worried about. He had planned

to call her as well when he got to the beach, and give her the number of the phone in the house. Just in case she needed him.

He decided now that he wouldn't wait that long to contact her. Since he had the cell phone with him, he might as well call her now. Once he knew she and Spencer were okay this morning, he would be able to relax and enjoy the drive.

He pulled up to a stop sign, saw that there was no one behind him, and dialed her number.

She answered on the first ring, sounding breathless. "Hello?"

"Hi. It's Beau. Is everything okay?"

He noted a slight hesitation in her voice before she said, "Sure."

"No, it isn't. What's wrong?"

"Nothing. It's just . . ." She lowered her voice. "He had another nightmare. And he asked about Phoebe again. I just don't know how long I can go on keeping all of this from him."

"What's he doing now?"

"Watching a cartoon."

There was a honk behind him. He looked in the rearview mirror and saw that a car had pulled up to the stop sign. The driver was angrily gesturing for him to proceed through the empty intersection.

He did, telling Phoebe, "I should hang up now. I'm on the road."

"How's your trip going?" she asked.

"Great." He didn't bother to tell her that he was only two blocks from his apartment. Let her think he was merrily on his way.

"Have a good time, Beau," she said, and her voice

sounded so hollow that he almost did a U-turn and headed back toward Georgetown.

But he forced himself to keep driving. "I will. And you be careful. I'll call you when I get down there and give you the number for the house, just in case you want to get in touch."

"That's okay. Forget about all this and just enjoy yourself. I'll be fine."

"Sure, you will."

No, she won't, he thought as he hung up and turned off the power on his cell phone, tossing it over his shoulder into the backseat.

Damn it. Jordan had just lost her best friend. She had secret custody of a child whose life may or may not be in danger. And he was driving off on vacation, leaving her alone to cope.

Well, what else could he do?

He was supposed to be using this time off to escape the weight that had burdened him for far too long. It would be foolish to get further entangled with this troubled woman and child.

If anything happens to either of them, you'll never forgive yourself for leaving, Beau.

No.

But if he stayed, and let himself care for them, and tried to protect them . . .

If he did all that, and still something happened, bringing them harm . . .

He knew in his gut that it would be the end of him. He could never survive it.

Never.

If he were wise, he would keep driving and get the hell out of town as fast as he could.

* * *

Only when she hung up the phone did Jordan remember Mrs. Villeroy's call from yesterday. She realized she had better call the old woman back. If she didn't, her neighbor might decide to toddle over here.

Not that the old lady ever ventured far from her own doorstep. She suffered from arthritis that left her all but paralyzed most days. She was widowed and had no children to come by and check in on her. That was why Jordan usually didn't mind the old lady's frequent requests.

It was no trouble really for her to stop at the pharmacy on her way home to pick up Mrs. Villeroy's prescriptions every now and then, or run over there with sugar or flour or whatever the woman had run out of.

In fact, Jordan thought now with a twinge of guilt as she dialed Mrs. Villeroy's phone number, she should probably be more neighborly. It wouldn't hurt her to stop over there with a container of vichyssoise the next time she made it, or to cut a bouquet of zinnias when they reached full bloom in her container garden.

"Hello?" the old lady rasped into the receiver after the third ring.

"Mrs. Villeroy? It's Jordan Curry calling back. I'm sorry I didn't return your call last night, but . . ."

But I was swept away by passion for a man I barely know.

Jordan paced over to the doorway of the living room and peeked in to see Spencer sprawled on the couch, engrossed in his television program.

"That's all right, dear," Mrs. Villeroy said. "I thought you must be busy. After I called, I thought I probably shouldn't even have bothered you with this, but that man just left me feeling so unsettled. . . ."

Midway back to the kitchen, Jordan stopped short. "*What* man?"

Had Mrs. Villeroy peered out the window and seen her with Beau? Oh, Lord, had she somehow looked through Jordan's window and glimpsed the two of them in a clinch?

"The man who was here yesterday," Mrs. Villeroy was saying. "I was outside trying to pick up the mail that I had dropped when I opened my mailbox, and he came right over to help me. I thought that was kind of him, but then he started asking questions about you."

"Somebody was asking questions about me?" Jordan asked slowly, her heart pounding. "What kind of questions?"

"He just wanted to know whether you lived here, and whether I knew you. He seemed to think you might have a nephew staying with you, but I told him I didn't know anything about that."

Jordan sank into a nearby chair, running a distracted hand through her hair. Could it have been a police officer? Had the authorities somehow traced Spencer to her?

"Was this man a detective or something, Mrs. Villeroy?" she asked, struggling to keep her voice level.

"A detective? Oh, my, I don't think so. That is, he didn't say he was a detective, and he didn't *look* like a detective."

"What *did* he look like, Mrs. Villeroy?"

"That's the thing. I know it isn't right to judge someone based just on his looks, but I didn't trust him the moment I saw him, Jordan."

"Why not? What did he look like?"

"He was tall, with straggly dark hair, and he had a black eye patch, just like a pirate."

* * *

Beau got as far as the Maryland state line before he turned back.

He might be a fool, he thought, as he reached George-town's familiar bustling streets, but men had been fools for far lesser causes than his.

He wasn't going back because he had fallen for Jor-dan, or because of what had happened—and almost happened—between them last night. None of that fit into the big picture for him. He had no intention of pursuing a relationship with her, and as far as he was concerned, their brief romantic interlude was over.

No, he was going back because he had glimpsed the frightened look on her face when he reminded her to lock the door last night. She was alone, and afraid for Spencer, whether or not there was a real threat against the little boy's life. Beau could be there for her, to help her sort things out. He could be there to distract Spencer, and to listen if either of them needed to talk.

The streets of her neighborhood were crowded at this hour on a sunny weekday morning. As he parked on her quiet side street and stepped out of the car, Beau noticed that the weather was hot and humid again. He firmly pushed from his mind the notion of the spar-kling blue water and cooling seaside breezes that waited in the Outer Banks. He, veteran of a lifetime of Louisi-ana summers, could certainly handle this urban steam-bath.

As he marched toward the front steps of her brick town house, he wondered what he was going to say to her now that he was here. She wouldn't be happy to see him. Not after the way they had parted last night.

What if she thought he had made a trip to the drugstore and come back to pick up where they'd left off? He had to make it clear that their mutual attraction had nothing to do with why he was here.

It wasn't that he didn't feel tempted by her—especially now that he'd had a taste of the forbidden. And an utterly chaste lifestyle certainly wasn't what he had pictured for himself when he'd left Lisa and moved to D.C. He was a red-blooded man, and he knew women would come along who would make him forget, temporarily, his vow to steer clear of relationships.

But Jordan wasn't the kind of woman he could bed and then leave. There was something about her that set off warning signals in him, telling him to get away from her before he got too involved.

But you're involving yourself now, aren't you? he thought grimly as he mounted the steps.

One thing was certain: this time, he wasn't going to wait for her to tell him she needed him and ask for his help.

He reached out to ring the bell, but the door was thrown open before he could touch it.

Jordan stood there. In her eyes was the last expression he'd ever expected to see there. Sheer, wild relief.

"I heard your car pull up outside," she said, her voice hushed but urgent. "I can't believe you're here. Come in. Hurry . . ."

She reached out and pulled him over the threshold, her eyes frantically scanning the street behind him.

"What's going on, Jordan?" he asked as she closed and triple-locked the door.

"It's—my God, I can't believe you're here," she said again. "An hour ago, when you called, you were on your way to North Carolina, and now—it just seems impossible."

"I wasn't out of town yet when I called," he admitted. "I was just leaving. And I left, but—"

"But you turned around? And came here? For no reason? It's like you somehow read my mind. What are you doing back here?"

He opened his mouth to answer, but she rushed on, darting a look over her shoulder as if to make sure Spencer hadn't materialized to eavesdrop. "I didn't know who else I could call or what to do. I've been trying to reach you on your cell phone—"

"I didn't have it turned on. I hardly ever do. Why? What's wrong? Where's Spencer? Did something—"

"He's upstairs. Beau, we need you." She was clutching his arm. He could feel the tension in her grasp, and realized she was trembling from head to toe.

Worry coursed through him. What the hell was going on? "Jordan—"

"Beau, I wouldn't ask you to do this if I had any option at all, but—"

"Ask me to do what?"

"You've got to get us out of here. Out of town. Now."

Chapter Eight

They headed straight east out of Washington, following the route Beau had mapped for his solo journey. Rather than heading south on Interstate 95 through the more populous cities of the Eastern Seaboard, he had chosen a scenic route that led across the upper Chesapeake Bay near Annapolis and down the eastern shore to Virginia.

By late afternoon, they were headed along the flat, fertile, ever-narrowing peninsula on the eastern shore's only major north-south thoroughfare, Route 13. It was little more than a local highway bordered on both sides by farms, shallow bays, produce stands, a few antebellum houses, and the occasional small town or strip mall.

Beau and Jordan didn't talk much. They couldn't, conscious, as they had been yesterday, of Spencer in the backseat. The little boy was too excited to sleep. Jordan had told him only that they were going on a surprise vacation to the beach with Beau. They were on the road, their hastily packed bags joining Beau's luggage in the back of the SUV, within five minutes of Beau's unexpected arrival on her doorstep.

Jordan didn't relax until they were well out of town and she was convinced that nobody was following them. Even now she felt jittery, and couldn't help glancing regularly into the side-view mirror outside the passenger's window just to see what was behind them.

She was still rattled by the thought that an intruder might have been in the process of abducting Spencer this morning when his screams woke her. Mrs. Villeroy's mention of the shadowy stranger coincided too closely for comfort with the little boy's "pirate." And while Jordan was convinced that the mysterious "bad guy" with the eye patch had truly been a figment of Spencer's nightmares the first few times he awakened screaming, she suspected that this morning's threat had been all too real.

Beau seemed shaken by her theory that the man had somehow found out where Spencer was and had broken into the town house, meaning to spirit the groggy child out of his bed and away. Jordan figured that Spencer must have woken up, realized what was happening, and started shrieking. The intruder must have dropped the child and run off into the night when he heard her footsteps upstairs.

"Or it could have just been a nightmare, like it was the other times," Beau had pointed out, obviously trying to reassure her.

"Even if it was just a nightmare"—and she didn't believe that—"we can't ignore that Spencer has an unhealthy dread of pirates, and that a stranger in an eye patch has been snooping around. There's a connection, Beau. There has to be."

He seemed inclined to agree, though he couldn't imagine how anyone could have found Spencer at Jordan's house. But he didn't know her guilty secret—the wee-hours phone call to Phoebe's brother—and somehow, she couldn't bring herself to confess.

She was convinced now that the clicking she had heard on Curt's line meant that it was tapped, and that whoever was listening in had been led right to her doorstep, and to Spencer. She felt sick knowing that her actions might have put him in jeopardy.

Thanks to Beau, they had escaped. Spencer was safe—at least, for now.

"How much farther do we have to go?" she asked Beau as they passed yet another sign for the Chesapeake Bay Bridge Tunnel, which lay only a few miles ahead now.

"Till we get there? A few hours, at least," he said, carefully pulling into the left lane to pass a slow-moving pickup truck loaded with hay bales. "Do you want to stop for the night on the other side of the bridge?"

"No!" she said quickly.

"Are you sure? It might be better if—"

"No, let's just keep driving," she cut in.

There were countless reasons why she didn't want to stop for the night before they reached their destination.

For one thing, the area where Beau had rented his house on the Outer Banks was indisputably remote. He had told her that it was located just above the tiny northernmost town of Corolla, at the edge of the unpopulated nether regions of the narrow coastal island, where, to Spencer's delight, Beau had told them wild mustangs ran free on the beach.

Once they got to the house—which he had promised was a sprawling three-story, five-bedroom oceanfront spread with plenty of room for all three of them—they would be safe at last.

"Are you okay to keep driving?" Jordan asked him anxiously. "Because I can take over if you're tired."

"No, I can make it," he said. "I was just worried about Spencer. I thought maybe it would be easier on him if we stopped and got a room and continued in the morning."

"I'm sure he'll be fine," she said—perhaps selfishly, but she couldn't help it.

She knew *she* wouldn't be fine if they stopped.

She would feel too vulnerable alone overnight with Spencer in a mainland motel room.

She would feel even more vulnerable if the two of them shared a room with Beau.

Granted, Spencer's presence would ensure that there would be no replay of what had happened last night. But Jordan intended to shy away from any situation that had anything to do with Beau and bed—chaperoned or not.

It would be hard enough at the house, sharing a roof with him for God only knew how long.

She knew they couldn't hide forever. In fact, she had been on the verge of calling the police when Beau showed up earlier.

When she couldn't reach Beau on his cell phone, she had concluded that if Spencer's life was in danger, the authorities would be able to protect him better than she could on her own.

Then along came Beau, and the prospect of instant salvation. Getting Spencer out of town, and away from "the pirate" was her first priority. Once they reached their destination, she and Beau could decide how to proceed next.

"Do you want to hear a different CD?" Beau asked, as the Rolling Stones one they'd been listening to came to an end.

"No, that's okay."

"Are you sure? We've heard that one twice."

"Have we?" She hadn't even noticed. "How about the radio instead?"

"Nah. Long road trips are for CD listening," Beau said, as cheerfully as if they were on a regular vacation. He leaned over, pressed "Eject," and handed her the silver disk that popped out of the dashboard. "Choose something else, Jordan."

She wasn't in the mood for music. She was in the mood to brood in silence. But she glanced halfheartedly through the built-in disk holder between the seats.

She couldn't help noticing that Beau's taste in music was eclectic. Lynrd Skynrd was next to Patsy Cline, and next to that was a compilation of greatest hits from the 80s.

"Hey, look, fella," Beau said over his shoulder to Spencer as Jordan put an Elton John CD into the player. "There's the bridge I've been telling you about!"

Jordan looked up. Yes, there it was, its girders gleaming in the evening's rapidly fading light.

This was another important milestone on their journey, placing a roughly twenty-mile-long obstacle between Spencer and Georgetown, and the pirate.

That's not true—it isn't really an obstacle, Jordan reminded herself as Elton John sang the opening lines to "Your Song" on the car's speakers.

Anyone could cross the bridge.

But its meaning for her was symbolic. With every mile

that they covered and every bridge that they crossed, she could breathe a little easier.

"Bet you've never driven over the ocean before," Beau drawled, steering up the sloping incline.

"Nope," Spencer said.

He sounded subdued. Jordan turned to look at him. He was staring out the window at the pink-streaked sky and the rosy, sparkling sea.

Spencer must have felt her eyes on him, because he said softly, without turning his head, "My mom would like this bridge. She likes going places. But my dad never wants to."

A silent sob caught in Jordan's throat.

"How is my mom going to find us so far from your house, Jordan?" he asked. Now he turned to look at her. She wished he wouldn't. She didn't want to see the blatant homesick longing in his face, and she didn't want him to glimpse the grief that was growing more difficult to mask.

She forced a smile and said, "Look out there! I think I see a dolphin splashing in the surf."

Spencer squinted out the window.

After a moment he said, "Where? I don't see it."

"Maybe it was just a trick of the light," she said.

Sure. Blame it on the sunset.

She swallowed hard and glanced at Beau. He was staring straight ahead, focusing on the road now as he steered down the slope onto the flat causeway that stretched ahead as far as they could see. There was no shoulder on the two-lane road; directly beneath the low guardrails was the drop-off to the water.

She wondered what he was thinking.

After last night, she had never really expected to see him again—and certainly not so soon. The tension of what had happened in her bed paled beside what they were going through to keep Spencer safe, but sooner or later it was bound to come up again.

And sooner or later, if they spent time alone together, lust was sure to make another appearance as well. This time, Jordan thought, she would be better prepared to resist him. Last night she had been caught off guard. That wouldn't happen again. She would steel herself against temptation every second of this journey.

"What the hell . . . ?" Beau muttered, frowning into the rearview mirror.

Glancing into the mirror out her window, Jordan saw a car fast approaching their bumper. It was a sleek, black sports car, and it seemed to have come out of nowhere.

Her heart began to pound as it crept closer. She turned her head to look over the seat.

The sun glinted on the black car's windshield, obscuring the driver's face.

"Beau . . . ?" she said questioningly, and looked to see him watching the rearview mirror intently.

"It's okay," he said. He sped up a bit, but there was a minivan in front of them. A tractor trailer blocked the passing lane to the left. To the right was only the rail, and the choppy waters of the bay.

The black car was now glued to their rear bumper, dangerously close. Jordan tried to fight back panic, but her mind was racing with terrified thoughts.

If Beau had to brake suddenly, the car would slam into them from behind. Or maybe that was the driver's intent. Maybe he was going to force them off the road.

There was nowhere to go but over the side of the bridge.

Beau cursed under his breath as a sign popped up, alerting them that the first of the bridge's two tunnels was just ahead and traffic was being diverted into a single lane.

The truck in the left lane promptly began to pick up speed.

Jordan continued to face the rear of the SUV, keeping her eyes on the car behind, fearful of who was driving it. Was it the pirate? Had he found them somehow?

"Are you okay, Jordan?" Spencer asked, seeing the look on her face.

She attempted a reassuring smile. "I'm fine, sweetie."

"Then what are you looking at?"

"The bridge behind us." Her voice cracked. She managed to add, "I'm just checking to see how far we've driven."

Spencer tried to swivel his neck to see, but he couldn't see over the high back of the seat from his position. He made a move to unbuckle his seat belt.

"No!" Jordan said. "Stay strapped in, sweetie."

"Why? I just want to—"

"No!" she repeated. "It's not safe."

"Keep your seat belt on, Spencer," Beau barked, his eyes on the road, hands fiercely clenching the steering wheel.

The mouth of the tunnel was just ahead. Jordan saw that the left lane beside them was vanishing fast as the truck sped past them, maneuvering abruptly between their SUV and the minivan ahead, cutting them off. Beau braked, cursing again.

In the next instant, as the causeway sloped toward the depths of the tunnel beneath the bay, the sleek black car that had been tailgating them darted out to the nearly evaporated left lane.

There was oncoming traffic. An approaching car blared its horn and screeched its brakes.

Jordan cried out. Beau cursed colorfully, and loudly.

"You said a bad word!" Spencer bellowed from the backseat.

As the black car swept past Beau's window, Jordan, heart pounding, saw the blurred image of the occupants.

A couple of teenaged girls. Just joyriding, reckless kids.

The blond driver flashed her middle finger at Beau as they passed, just before she swerved back into their lane and cut him off, tucking the sports car into the impossibly small length of road between the SUV's front fender and the rear of the truck that had just done the same thing.

"Suddenly, I can understand road rage," Beau muttered, hitting the brake, backing off. "I think I just experienced it. If you two weren't in the car . . ." He shook his head. "That was a close call."

A close call.

Jordan nodded, leaning her head back against the seat and closing her eyes, too limp to speak.

The house was more beautiful than it had appeared in the realtor's catalogue, and much too big for the three of them. Beau had selected it because, of course, money was no object—and because Lisa had insisted that she wanted something with lots of space, a private pool and hot tub, and majestic views of the sea.

This place had all that, and more.

It was situated on a stretch of beach just beyond where the paved road tapered off to sand, accessible only by four-wheel drive. The house was private, the most isolated of a cluster of sprawling seaside homes.

Beau figured that there was enough distance between this place and the neighbors so that they would have the privacy they sought.

He left Jordan out in the car with the sleeping Spencer while he unlocked the door and checked out the layout.

The first floor contained a game room with a pool table and wet bar, a bedroom with twin beds, and a private bath.

On the second floor were three more bedrooms, all of them suites with private baths and access to outer decks and screened porches.

The top floor had a master suite, a sprawling living room, a dining room, a kitchen with a breakfast bar, two more balconies, and another screened porch.

The house was carpeted, tiled, and painted in shades of cream and white. The upholstered furniture was covered in bright-colored fabrics with splashy prints that complemented the framed artwork on the walls.

Jordan will like this place, Beau thought, looking around. Everything was bright and airy, and perfectly coordinated. Spencer would like it, too, when he woke up tomorrow and saw the blue sparkling water from almost every window.

Beau stepped out onto a third-floor porch facing the dunes. There were no stars in the night sky, and he couldn't see the water, but he could smell the salt in the air and hear the thundering surf just yards away.

He breathed deeply, relieved that he was here at last, that he had made it—and that Jordan and Spencer were with him. Somehow, this felt right.

He walked back through the house, peering into bedrooms, turning on lights, and adjusting the air conditioning. In the second floor hallway, he found the large cotton bags the rental place had left containing bed linens and towels. He quickly made up a queen-sized bed in one of the second floor rooms for Spencer and left it turned down so that he could carry the little boy up and put him in without waking him.

As he headed back downstairs and outside, Beau wondered which room Jordan would want. He assumed she would take one of the second floor rooms to be close to Spencer. That would leave him with the king-sized bed in the master bedroom all to himself. But it wasn't an appealing thought. He would almost rather be down on the second floor with the two of them.

Or was that too intimate? Would Jordan want him on the other side of her bedroom wall?

He knew where he wanted her: in his bed.

Memories of last night's curtailed lovemaking sailed into his head, refusing to budge even as he stepped back outside and saw her standing beside the car. She was leaning on the open door on her side, watching Spencer sleeping in the backseat. She looked like a mother bear standing guard over her cub.

Hearing him behind her, she turned toward him. The light he'd turned on inside the house spilled out into the night, catching her in its glow. She looked exhausted, yet—at least for the moment—serene.

"How's the house?" she asked quietly.

"Beautiful. I made up a bed for him. That's what took me so long. I'll get him and carry him up."

She nodded.

As he opened the back door and scooped the sleeping child into his arms, Beau was reminded of last night—and of countless other nights like it. But then it had been a different car, a different child, a different woman hovering at his side. A different life.

"Got him?" Jordan whispered softly, closing the car door.

Beau nodded, walking toward the unfamiliar house, remembering.

He and Jeanette used to spend weekends traveling—flying off in his private plane or sailing on one of his boats. They always prolonged Sunday nights and the leap back to the real world, stopping for a late dinner and then driving home under the stars, with Tyler sleeping in the backseat.

Beau would carry his son into the house and deposit him gently into his bed. Then he and Jeanette would tiptoe to their room across the hall, close the door, make love, and go to sleep in each other's arms.

How content he was on those Sunday nights, weary yet relaxed after their weekend adventures. Jeanette always fell asleep first, and he would lie there, holding her, listening to her gentle breathing. All was right with the world.

Beau had known he was a lucky man. He knew there were people who didn't recognize what they had until it was gone, but he wasn't one of them. No, he had always appreciated what he had while he had it. He treasured his wife and son—even wondered, from time to time, what he would do without them. But he never really thought he would have to find out.

Well, now he knew.

Without them, he would go on living. But only because he had to. There was no alternative.

But it was a life without joy. A life without promise. A life without love.

That, he knew, was the only way he could continue.

Once, he'd had everything, and lost it. Now he had nothing . . .

And nothing to lose.

Jordan woke the next morning to sun streaming through the window—and the sound of a telephone ringing.

For a moment, she thought she was back home in her town house.

Then it all came back to her.

Spencer.

Beau.

The pirate.

The drive.

The beach house.

The smile that had been about to drift onto her lips evaporated abruptly as Jordan sat up, rubbing the sleep from her eyes. She looked around the bedroom, taking in the whitewashed wooden furniture, the bright teal comforter and draperies, the oversized windows covered in blinds that were only half-closed, the slats far enough apart to let the sun shine in.

Her hastily packed suitcase lay on the floor beside the bureau, still filled with clothes. She had been too exhausted last night to put them away. Too exhausted to do anything more than find her pajamas and toothbrush and collapse into bed.

Now she stood and stretched, wondering what time it was. There was no bedside alarm clock. Well, that wasn't surprising. This was a vacation house. Most people came here to get away from everything, including clocks.

And some people came here to get away from things that were far more sinister.

As the weight of yesterday's worries descended again, Jordan made her way across the room.

There were three closed doors in the alcove opposite the bed. She began opening them and found that one led to the closet, another to the bathroom, and a third into the hallway.

When she opened that one and peeked out, she could see that Spencer's door, across from hers, was still closed.

She could also hear the rumble of Beau's voice upstairs.

Who could he possibly be talking to?

Oh. She remembered the ringing telephone. Clearly, Beau had been up long enough to have given somebody the number.

Jordan frowned as she headed into the bathroom. Surely Beau wouldn't have taken it upon himself to call the police about Spencer. They had agreed that they would figure out when and how to contact the authorities only after they reached this safe haven. But Jordan wasn't yet ready to deal with that. She needed time to collect her thoughts, to brace herself—and Spencer— for whatever lay ahead.

She showered quickly, threw on a pair of white cutoff shorts and a navy T-shirt, and hurriedly tossed the contents of her bag into the empty bureau drawers. She hadn't brought much. She hadn't had time to think about it, and she'd had Spencer's bag to pack, too.

Well, at least she had enough T-shirts, shorts, and undergarments to get through a few days out here— and a bathing suit, too. Beau had reminded her to pack one. Frolicking in the surf was the furthest thing from her mind, but she knew Spencer would want to go to the beach as soon as he realized it was right outside the door.

She stepped out into the hallway.

Now all was silent, and Spencer's door was still closed. Jordan pushed it open a crack, just enough to satisfy herself that the child was still safely sound asleep in the big bed.

At least there were no pirate nightmares last night, she thought as she padded barefoot up to the top floor, sniffing fresh-brewed coffee.

She found Beau sitting at the breakfast bar with a steaming mug and a pile of paperwork. He wore a pair of blue shorts and a faded gray T-shirt. As she came up beside him, she could smell his clean, citrusy soap-and-shaving-gel scent.

"Coffee?" she asked, peering into his cup. "Where'd you get it?"

"I went down to Food Lion in Corolla to get groceries first thing," he said, motioning at the plugged-in percolator on the counter.

"Isn't this first thing?" she asked wryly, trying to catch a glimpse of the watch on his arm. She couldn't see the hands, but she recognized the maker, and knew the watch cost a small fortune. Until now, she had almost forgotten Andrea MacDuff's mention that Beau was from a wealthy Southern family. Now she wondered just how well-off he was—and why a millionaire bachelor like him hadn't long since been snagged by a suitable debutante, or an enterprising gold digger, even.

"I've been up since five-thirty," he said. "I had to call my partner at the office last night and leave the number for this place on the voice mail. He called me back as soon as he got the message this morning."

"I heard the phone ring."

Beau nodded. "There's a little crisis at the office. One of our clients is getting a little testy. He's used to accomplishing things on demand."

"I know the type," she said, finding a mug and pouring herself a cup of coffee. "Ever since Spencer was dropped into my life, it's as though I've managed to forget about my business. I trust my partner to handle things for me, but I'm sure he's been putting out fires since I left."

"So you don't miss it?"

She considered the question. "Actually, I do. But I needed some time away. I've been working nonstop ever since we got the business off the ground. My partner calls me a workaholic."

"Mine, too. But I happen to love what I do."

Something in his expression told Jordan there might be more to it than that. Maybe, she speculated, work was as much an escape for him as it was for her.

That thought took her by surprise. She had never before considered her catering business an escape. But now, having to face head-on the loss of Phoebe and the responsibility of Spencer, she found herself longing for some insulated haven . . . just as she had when Kevin left her at the altar.

Then, she had thrown herself into plans for her future. She had planned her move to Washington, put her business plan into motion with Jeremy, and pulled out all stops to launch J&J Catering. It was easy to let her work consume her in the years since. That way, there was little time for her to spend at home, contemplating her life—or lack of one.

But now that life had thrown her another curve, there

was no buffer zone. There was no escape—except, she suddenly comprehended, into Beau's arms.

Beau began stacking the paperwork. "If Ed can't keep this client off my back, I might have to go back up there for a meeting," he said grimly.

"Back to D.C.?" Jordan was alarmed. He was going to leave her and Spencer here alone?

"Believe me, it's the last thing I want to do, Jordan. But I can't risk alienating Landry. Making him happy is key to the firm's future." He tucked the papers into a briefcase and looked at her. "Don't worry. I wouldn't leave you here if I didn't think you'd be safe. And I wouldn't be gone much more than twenty-four hours."

"Could you fly there and back in the same day?"

Again she saw the shadowed expression cross his eyes. "No," he said tersely.

"But—"

"I don't fly, Jordan." He rose and strode toward the master bedroom suite. "I'm going to change into my bathing suit and go out for a swim."

She opened her mouth to say something. She wasn't sure what; she only knew that the mood had changed in an instant. But he had already disappeared inside his room, closing the door firmly behind him.

On the other side of the door, Beau leaned against it, exhaling shakily, eyes closed.

Coward, he berated himself.

He was a damned coward.

Afraid to fly.

Afraid to confess the reason to the woman who was counting on him to be her hero.

Well, he thought bitterly, Jordan was a fool if she

thought he could save her and Spencer. He couldn't save anyone.

Hadn't he learned that in the most heart-wrenching way imaginable?

So, then what are you doing here? What are they *doing here? Why did you bring Jordan and Spencer to this remote spot? So that they could run away, just as you've been doing all these years?*

What choice did he have? She had begged him to get her and Spencer out of Georgetown, away from her town house and the stranger who was lurking, asking too many questions. He had done what he thought was right. What he *knew* was right.

There was no telling what the pirate wanted or who he was.

Now that they had Spencer in seclusion, they would have time to figure out their next move.

That made sense. It did. He couldn't beat himself up for a decision that still seemed the wisest course.

With a heavy sigh, Beau moved swiftly to the dresser and pulled out a bathing suit. As he undressed and slipped into the faded navy swim trunks, he told himself that everything would be fine. He just needed to take a swim and clear his head. He needed to burn off the tension that had been building within him all morning, ever since he'd spoken to Ed and realized that he might have to go back to Washington.

Landry was demanding a meeting. He wasn't satisfied with their progress so far. The CEO was flying home tonight from a business meeting in Zurich and expected to meet Beau and Ed at his convenience tomorrow.

According to Ed, they were perilously close to alienating the man and losing not just this project, but the promise of a contract to design Landry's new corporate headquarters in the near future. The future of the firm was riding on this man's satisfaction.

Beau should explain that to Jordan. He should explain a lot of things to Jordan, he realized. She deserved to understand where he was coming from.

He took a deep breath. He should tell her. He should go back out there and tell her what had happened. It was the only way he could expect her to grant him the emotional leeway he needed.

He grabbed a towel and stepped back out into the living area, steeling himself for the necessary confrontation.

But the stool where Jordan had been sitting was empty.

So was the third floor.

He walked slowly down the stairs, stopping at the second floor landing. From here, he could see that her bedroom door was closed. He could hear the faint sound of water running in her bathroom.

Okay.

He would leave her alone for now, he decided, continuing on down to the first floor. He could tell her about it later. There would be plenty of time for talking.

Stepping outside into the bright North Carolina sunshine, he encountered a blast of humid heat. He walked quickly toward the weathered gray boardwalk that led to the water.

The sun-heated wooden planks warmed Beau's bare feet. On either side of the boardwalk, dunes of white, powdery sand were tufted with long, pale green grasses and clumps of blooming wildflowers. At the end of the boardwalk the dunes fell away and a wide beach came into view. A gull swooped low overhead against a periwinkle sky; beyond the impossibly clean width of sand, the cornflower-blue waters of the ocean beckoned.

Beau sighed.

How he had missed the sea. He had grown up not far from the Gulf Coast, where the beach provided lifelong therapy for whatever ailed him. When things went wrong, he found solace along the shore and let the warm, rhythmic salt waves wash away his worries.

Then disaster struck, and he was cast adrift on a sea of despair. It had been years since he'd allowed himself the pleasure of a day at the beach. He had only agreed to this getaway because Lisa had insisted, but in the months since their breakup, he had found himself looking forward to the solo vacation.

It might no longer be solo—or a vacation—but Beau felt a sense of healing begin to seep into him nonetheless.

Tossing his towel wherever it dropped, he strode across the hot, shell-strewn sand to the cool, wet sand at the water's edge. The first wave washed over his feet. He looked down at the foamy water as it trailed back out to sea, leaving the sand around his feet momentarily dotted with thousands of tiny black spots.

Leaning closer, Beau saw that they were miniature mollusks. As he watched, they burrowed back into the sand, hurrying to bury themselves before the next wave washed over them. The moment they vanished without a trace, another wave swooped in and left them vulnerable again.

Beau straightened, filling his lungs with the damp ocean breeze as he looked around.

This stretch of beach was private, meant only for the use of residents and renters of the adjacent cluster of houses. A little way down, a mother sat at the water's

To start your membership, simply complete and return the Free Book Certificate. You'll receive your Introductory Shipment of FREE Zebra Contemporary Romances. Then, each month as long as your account is in good standing, you will receive the 3 newest Zebra Contemporary Romances. Each shipment will be yours to examine for 10 days. If you decide to keep the books, you'll pay the preferred book club member price of $15.95 – a savings of up to 20% off the cover price! (plus $1.99 to offset the cost of shipping and handling.) If you want us to stop sending books, just say the word… it's that simple.

If the Free Book Certificate is missing, call 1-800-770-1963 to place your order.
Be sure to visit our website at www.kensingtonbooks.com.

BOOK CERTIFICATE

Yes! Please send me FREE Zebra Contemporary romance novels. I only pay for shipping and handling. I understand I am under no obligation to purchase any books, as explained on this card.

Name _____

Address _____ Apt. _____

City _____ State _____ Zip _____

Telephone (____) _____

Signature _____

(If under 18, parent or guardian must sign)

Offer limited to one per household and not valid to current subscribers.
All orders subject to approval. Terms, offer, and price subject to change. Offer valid only in the U.S.

CN072A

Thank You!

THE BENEFITS OF BOOK CLUB MEMBERSHIP

- You'll get your books hot off the press, usually before they appear in bookstores.
- You'll ALWAYS save up to 20% off the cover price.
- You'll get our FREE monthly newsletter filled with author interviews, book previews, special offers, and MORE!
- There's no obligation — you can cancel at any time and you have no minimum number of books to buy.
- And — if you decide you don't like the books you receive, you can return them. (You always have ten days to decide.)

‖‖‖

llı.ıdııılllı.ıuılllıll.lılı.ı.b.ı.l.ı.lllı.l.l.ıuıll.lıll.ııl

Zebra Contemporary Romance Book Club
Zebra Home Subscription Service, Inc.
P.O. Box 5214
Clifton , NJ 07015-5214

edge watching over a toddler who was filling a bucket with water. A man lay snoozing in a sand chair beneath an umbrella. Two cyclists pedaled along a distant stretch of packed sand beside the water.

Other than that, there wasn't another human in sight.

Beau waded into the surf, curling his toes into the wet sand. The water was cool, especially compared to the Gulf waters he had once known. But as he waded deeper, his body grew accustomed to the temperature and it actually began to feel warm.

When he was shoulder deep, beyond the line of breaking waves, he dove in.

He skimmed the chilly, murky bottom and found himself immersed in grim, graphic memories. He held his breath as long as he could, forcing himself to stay submerged, allowing the barrage of images to torment him.

Finally, when his lungs were bursting and his head felt as though it were about to explode, it was as if his body's instinct for self-preservation overtook his need for self-punishment.

He surfaced.

After sputtering a bit and gulping air, he began swimming toward the horizon. His arms clawed the water with powerful strokes as his feet kicked and his head dipped back and forth, back and forth with the rhythmic breathing he'd learned as a little boy.

He swam with a purpose.

He swam as though he were being chased.

As though, were he to lift his head to look behind him, he would see a couple of demons doggedly following him.

Demons . . .

Or ghosts.

He kept swimming, slowing his pace only when he was nearly spent. Treading the deep water, seeing how far he'd come from shore, it occurred to him that he could keep going. He could keep swimming toward the horizon until he wore himself out and let the waves wash over him, carrying him down into oblivion.

Then, would he feel what they had felt?

No.

No, because he wouldn't be fighting for his life.

For him, the cold oblivion would be welcome.

Beau tipped his face toward the warm sun, floating on his back as he contemplated his options.

He could keep swimming toward the horizon and a certain fate.

Or he could swim toward shore and uncertainty.

Shore, where Jordan and Spencer waited.

He floated a few moments longer.

Then, his mind made up, he lifted his head, plunged his face back into the water, and began stroking toward the distant sand.

Chapter Nine

"What do you want to do for dinner?" Beau asked as Jordan came up the stairs after her shower.

"What do you want to do?" she countered, conscious of Spencer's presence. The little boy was sprawled on the floor beside the couch, where Beau was leafing through a coffee table book about Outer Banks shipwrecks.

"I want a Happy Meal," Spencer announced, looking up from a couple of miniature metal cars Beau had brought back from his earlier trip to the supermarket. Spencer had built a ramp for them using Beau's beat-up loafers and a local telephone book.

"A Happy Meal?" Jordan echoed, wondering what the heck that was.

"I don't think there's a McDonald's out here, fella," Beau said, leaning over to ruffle Spencer's hair.

Okay, so a Happy Meal was clearly some kind of fast-food kiddie fare that Spencer would have to do without.

Spencer gave the glass coffee table a disappointed kick.

"Careful!" Jordan said, reaching out to steady a sculpture of a seagull that sat in the middle of it.

"Don't worry about him hurting that thing," Beau said. "It's solid and it weighs a ton. It's not going anywhere."

"When can we go back to the beach?" Spencer wanted to know.

"Tomorrow, if the weather's nice," Jordan promised.

"Can I play on my rock?"

She smiled. "Sure."

Spencer's "rock" was a jutting boulder just in front of the dunes. It seemed out of place there amid the mountains of soft sand. He had spotted it not long after they arrived on the beach today and seemed fascinated by it. He scaled it fairly easily and sat up there, looking out at the sea, wearing a pensive expression. Jordan had found herself wondering whether he was thinking about his mother. It was Beau who had broken the spell, coaxing Spencer down from the rock and into a spirited game of Frisbee.

Jordan handed Beau the bottle of aloe lotion he'd loaned her. "Here you go," she said. "Thanks. It helped."

"Did you get all the burned spots?" he asked, looking concerned.

"I think so."

"What about your back? It looked pretty bad when we left the beach."

"I couldn't reach it," she said. The moment she saw

the look that crossed his face, she wanted to take the words back.

"I'll do it for you. Come here."

"It's okay. It isn't—"

"Come here," he repeated, moving over and patting the couch cushion beside him.

She plunked herself down, her back to him. Her skin did feel tender and sore from the sand and the blistering sun. She'd worn sunscreen, but had foolishly applied a lower SPF to her skin than she had to Spencer's.

Now she would pay the price. The little boy's cheeks were barely rosy, while every inch of Jordan that had been exposed to the hot Southern rays had been singed a light, painful pink.

"Lift up your T-shirt in back," he said, almost gruffly, all-business.

She wanted to protest, but she didn't, again conscious of Spencer's presence. The little boy had gone back to his cars, grumbling about wanting a Happy Meal and clearly oblivious to the taut undercurrent between Jordan and Beau, just as he had seemed to be all day at the beach.

Not that the day had been entirely fraught with tension. There had been moments of fun, when the three of them frolicked in the water or joined forces to build a sand castle.

It was Spencer who came up with the idea of burying Beau in the sand, an enormously satisfying occupation for a preschooler. But he insisted on Jordan helping, and that was where she got into trouble.

It was impossible to ignore Beau's finely sculpted physique when she was crouched over it, letting warm sand trickle over his firm, tanned muscles. It was too easy to recall what it had felt like to lie against his naked skin, and to imagine what would have happened between them if the time and circumstances had been right.

This was another of those moments, Jordan realized, as Beau's hand made contact with her naked shoulder as she bent forward, the hem of her T-shirt gathered near her shoulder blades.

She gasped, nearly leaping off the couch at his touch.

"I'm sorry. I thought I warmed the lotion in my hands. Is it cold?"

"Not too bad," she managed.

In truth, the lotion was warm . . . and her thoughts had darted into steamy territory.

"I'll try to be gentle," Beau said.

"Mmm-hmm."

His fingertips swirled the moist lotion into her hot, thirsty skin, bringing instant relief from one problem and exposure to a far greater one.

How could she be thinking about making love to him at a time like this?

The truth was, it was far too easy for sensual thoughts to take over.

Time and distance had brought her to a false sense of security. She could simply forget why they were here, could forget all about Spencer, and poor Phoebe, and the pirate.

She could almost convince herself that this was nothing but a decadent beach vacation, and that later, when the sun went down and Spencer was asleep, they could pick up where they'd left off.

He had fallen silent, she realized. And his movements had slowed, less clinical and efficient than before. She wanted to protest when he lifted his hand away, then heard him squeeze the bottle to drizzle lotion over his fingertips again. Thankful the massage wasn't over, she closed her eyes and bent farther forward to give him access to the untouched region above her bra clasp.

He obliged, resting one hand on her shoulder to hold her steady as the pads of his fingers on the other worked the rich, fragrant moisture into her parched flesh. He used circular movements, a heavenly swirling pattern reminiscent of her far more intimate encounter with his tongue.

Fighting back a moan of pleasure, Jordan managed a half-strangled-sounding, "Thank you. That's great. Thanks."

"Are you sure? Did I get every spot?"

No. Not every spot.

Jordan tried to ignore the part of her that tingled with electric reminiscence and wistful anticipation. She tried to turn her thoughts—and the conversation—to a safer brand of hunger.

"I'm starved," she said, struggling to attain lightness as she pulled down her T-shirt and rose from the couch. "How about you guys?"

"I want a Happy Meal," Spencer announced, as though sharing a late-breaking bulletin. He looked ominously capable of a tantrum.

"Fine," Jordan said, heading him off. "I'll make you one."

There was a moment of silence.

"You'll make me one?" Spencer echoed, looking at Beau, who looked at Jordan.

"Yeah," he said, setting the bottle of lotion on the coffee table. "You'll *make* him one?"

"If the mountain can't go to MacDonald's, MacDonald will come to the mountain. I mean, the beach. *Whatever,*" Jordan said, brushing off their blank looks as though they were the ones who didn't have a clue.

She went on briskly, "I checked out the contents of the fridge and cupboards earlier. Beau did a great job stocking up on the basics. I think I can whip up a decent Happy Meal for all three of us."

Beau and Spencer exchanged a dubious glance.

"Let's see what she can do, fella," Beau said with a shrug. "Give her a chance."

"Okay," Spencer said reluctantly.

Jordan started toward the kitchen, displaying a confidence she didn't feel. Halfway there, she turned and called, "Beau? Can you come here for a second?"

He did, ambling toward her wearing a good-natured *now what?* expression.

When he was close enough, she leaned toward him and whispered, "What the heck is in a Happy Meal?"

"Okay, Spencer, you can open your eyes!" Beau said, his hands on the little boy's shoulders after having propelled him to the dining area.

Spencer opened his eyes and gasped. "Wow! What's that?"

"It's a Happy Meal," Beau said, as the little boy picked up the white paper bakery bag. Beau had recycled it from the rolls he'd bought this morning and had decorated it using markers he'd found in a kitchen drawer. It looked almost like a bag that might hold a fast-food kid's meal.

"Thanks, Beau!" the little boy said, opening the bag and peering inside.

"Thank Jordan," he said, turning toward her. She stood a few steps away from them, looking hesitant to take the credit that was due her.

"Thanks, Jordan," Spencer mumbled, not looking at her.

Beau saw the disappointment in her eyes before she turned away. His heart ached for her. She was doing everything within her power to win Spencer over, but the child still maintained a cautious distance from her—and a stubborn resentment. Yet with Beau, Spencer was affectionate and playful. That had to be painful for Jordan.

As Jordan carried food for her and Beau over to the table, Spencer plopped into his seat and began removing the items she had packed into his bag.

Along with a juice box, napkins, and real McDonald's ketchup packets from the glove compartment of Beau's car, there was a hamburger wrapped in waxed paper Beau had decorated to resemble an authentic fast-food wrapper, and homemade french fries in a small waxed-paper pocket he had made.

"This looks great," Beau said, lifting his own hamburger from the plate Jordan had set in front of him. "Thanks so much."

"You're the one who bought the burgers and buns and potatoes," she said. "All I did was cook them."

"You spent an hour cutting the potatoes into those thin strips before you fried them," he said, mainly for Spencer's benefit. "That was an incredible amount of work."

The little boy was oblivious, having just discovered the cellophane-wrapped "prize" Beau had tucked into the bottom of his bag. It was a miniature box kite he'd bought in the supermarket with Spencer in mind. He'd picked up quite a few small toys and trinkets for the child, thinking Spencer might grow bored here without a television.

"Wow, thanks, Beau," Spencer said, putting the kite aside and reaching for a ketchup packet. "Can we fly it later on the beach?"

"Maybe tomorrow," Beau said. "It's already dark out there."

He watched Jordan take a halfhearted bite of her own burger. Their eyes met as she chewed. He could see the worry etched in her gaze once again, and he knew what she was thinking.

While she was cooking, the telephone had rung. It was Beau's partner, Ed. He was trying to keep Landry at bay, but it looked as though Beau might have to head back to Washington tomorrow morning. Ed was going to call back in a little while to let Beau know for sure.

"You know," Beau said quietly, "it's only a six-hour drive."

His meaning registered on her face. He saw her glance at Spencer, who was busily squirting more ketchup onto his fries from yet another red-and-white packet.

"It took us longer than six hours yesterday," Jordan said.

"There was traffic, and we didn't take the interstate. I would. I'd leave at dawn, take Ninety-five up away from the coast, get to D.C. by noon, have my meeting, and drive back. I'd be here before dark—okay, maybe later at night. Or in the middle of the night. The point is, I'd be back."

"That's too much driving for one day."

"Not for me."

"It could be dangerous. You'd be exhausted."

"I'll drink coffee," he said simply. "Look, I might not even have to—"

As though summoned by fate, the phone rang.

Avoiding Jordan's gaze, Beau put down his burger, walked over, and picked up the receiver.

It was Ed, of course. Nobody else had this number.

"I'm sorry, Beau," his partner said. "I tried to get him to reschedule, but he wouldn't. He demanded to see both of us, tomorrow afternoon."

Beau wanted to tell Ed to forget it. That he should tell Albert Landry to forget it. The billionaire CEO could find another architect, another firm . . .

Torn, he looked toward the table. Jordan's eyes collided with his. He was surprised at what he saw there.

Go, she mouthed.

And she really meant it. He could see it in her expression.

"Hang on a second," Beau said into the receiver before lowering it and pressing the mouthpiece against his shoulder.

"We'll be fine," Jordan told him in a low voice. "Really."

"Are you—"

"I'm sure. Go."

He shot her a grateful look, but renewed worry ignited within him. Yes, she and Spencer were isolated here. Nobody knew where they were. They would be safe until he got back. But . . .

No. He couldn't let paranoia get the best of him. They were safe here, and Ed needed him. If he didn't meet with Landry, they could kiss the future of the firm good-bye.

Beau lifted the receiver again and spoke into it, saying simply, "Okay, I'll be there."

* * *

When Spencer was tucked safely into bed, Julia took another shower. She had taken one after the beach, but the cool, gentle spray felt good on her sunburned skin. Afterward, she realized that she'd better apply more lotion to her back and shoulders if she wanted to avoid peeling. She should have brought some of her own— or at least, should have kept the bottle Beau had loaned her earlier.

Maybe he had left it on the coffee table, she thought, as she quickly combed her damp hair and pulled it back into a ponytail.

All was quiet upstairs. He'd probably gone to bed early, in anticipation of tomorrow's long drive.

Instead of the short cotton nightgown she'd laid out on the bed, Jordan slipped on her terry-cloth robe, tying it quickly at her waist. It would conceal more of her just in case Beau was up and about, which she doubted.

As she left her room in search of the aloe lotion, she wondered what it would be like here tomorrow, alone with Spencer.

She knew this place was safe. She was certain nobody had followed them here. Theirs had been the lone pair of headlights crossing the long causeway onto the Outer Banks late last night.

There was no reason for Beau to miss his important meeting. She and Spencer would be fine without him. Yet the thought of being here alone was unnerving.

Today, playing with Spencer on the beach, had felt almost like a vacation.

Yes, there was tension between Jordan and Beau; there was underlying fear and grief, too.

But they couldn't discuss the situation or their next move in front of Spencer.

Nor could they take their eyes off him for even a minute to get away by themselves and figure out what they were going to do.

So there were times when she could almost forget why they were here. Times when she could almost pretend that things were normal.

Then reality would intrude and she would realize that she and Beau and Spencer didn't belong together.

This man and this child were strangers to her, to each other. Fate might have made them a temporary threesome, but it would soon send them on their separate ways.

But what about Spencer? she found herself wondering. What would happen to him when she and Beau brought him forward to the authorities?

Would he go to live with some family friends Jordan had never even heard of?

Or, she wondered with a pang, with an uncle he had barely seen?

Yet she supposed either of those scenarios made more sense than his staying with her.

Even if she were capable of caring for an orphaned four-year-old boy, she knew that Phoebe and Reno must have left wills. She also knew that they couldn't possibly have named her—a single, self-employed full-time businesswoman who lived in another city—as Spencer's guardian.

Even if she wanted to fight for custody, she knew she wouldn't have a legal leg to stand on. No judge would award the child to her under the circumstances. And if given a choice, Spencer certainly wouldn't choose to be with Jordan.

Who would he choose?

Beau. He would choose Beau.

What a ridiculous thought! Beau was more a stranger to Spencer than Jordan was. Yes, he had bonded with the child more than she had, but that didn't mean he had any stake in Spencer's future. When this was over, he would walk away.

How will Spencer feel when that happens?

Jordan couldn't let herself think about that any more than she could let herself think about Spencer's reaction when he found out about his parents' death. She had to tell him—or leave it to the authorities to do. There must be social workers who were brought into situations like this—people who were experienced with children and loss.

But they'll be strangers, too, Jordan thought grimly.

Spencer was surrounded by strangers.

Funny, aside from repeatedly asking for his mother and the few passing references he'd made to his father, Spencer hadn't even mentioned anybody else from his old life. She found herself wondering about the people who must surely have populated it.

Then Jordan remembered that Phoebe had chosen to reach out to *her* when she realized danger was imminent. Not to someone who might be nearer, or closer. Phoebe had turned to someone she had barely seen in years. She had gone to the trouble of traveling all the way to Washington through stormy weather to deliver Spencer into Jordan's hands.

Had there been nobody else in her life that she could trust?

Was there nobody else who would care enough about Spencer to keep him safe?

Filled with renewed determination to honor the last

promise she had made to her cherished friend, Jordan approached Spencer's closed bedroom door. She opened it softly, tiptoed into the room, and leaned over the sleeping child. He looked innocent and vulnerable lying there in the night light's glow.

Jordan leaned over and kissed him on the cheek.

She half-expected him to swat at her sleepily as he had before.

But he didn't.

As she turned to walk away, she heard a soft sigh escape him.

The hushed sound tugged at her heart.

This child needed her desperately. For all she knew, she was all he had. And she wasn't going to let him down.

On the deck that opened off the living room, Beau sat on a teak lounge in the darkness overlooking the sea, listening to the waves pounding the shore. Tonight the sky was a murky canopy above him, with not a star in sight. The air was humid and warm, bordering on oppressive. It would probably rain tomorrow. Good. That meant Jordan and Spencer would stay inside while he was gone.

It wasn't that he thought there was any chance anyone would recognize the child on the beach. It was private, which meant that it was sparsely populated. Nobody on it today had come within a hundred yards of them, and even if they had, they couldn't have got a good look at Spencer. Beau had bought him one of those floppy sun hats while he was out shopping this morning. The low brim shielded most of his face.

Still, Beau again contemplated telling Ed he just

couldn't come back to Washington right now, Landry be damned. But Ed would demand an explanation. He thought Beau was out here by himself. He wouldn't understand how Beau could possibly put the firm's future in jeopardy simply because of a vacation. He was already having a hard time understanding why Beau wouldn't just catch a flight in from Norfolk to make the trip easier. He had even offered to charter a plane for him.

"You know I don't fly anymore, Ed," Beau had said quietly.

"I know, but Beau, you're making things harder on yourself than they have to be. If you would just—"

Beau had cut him off there with a curse and an order to stay out of his personal life. He'd regretted his harsh words right after he spoke them, but he couldn't take them back.

Ed had a wife and children. He had never been in Beau's shoes. Nobody should ever be in Beau's shoes.

He clenched his jaw and rubbed his tired eyes, craving bourbon.

If there were a bottle in the house, he would be filling a glass right now. He longed for the reprieve it would bring.

Restless, too warm, he stripped off his T-shirt and draped it over the rail. That was better. It eased his discomfort from the heat, but not the hunger for something to numb the bitter taste of sorrow.

There was a time when, struck by the craving for liquor, he would have gotten into the car, driven to the first liquor store he found, and indulged.

But that was when the wound was still raw, the grief still all-encompassing. It had dulled over the years until it was mostly just a vague, throbbing ache tinged more with regret than agony.

But the guilt was still there, tormenting him, begrudging him every breath he took. And tonight it was stronger than ever.

Because there was another woman.

Another child.

They needed him, and he couldn't be here to—

Suddenly, a pool of light spilled over him.

Startled, he turned toward the living room. He had closed the French doors because of the air conditioning, but through them he could see that Jordan had come into the room.

Her hair was damp. He knew it smelled of her fragrant shampoo. He inhaled, and it was almost as if her scent mingled with the dank salt air.

She wore a white terry cloth robe that covered her to her knees, but as she leaned over the coffee table, it fell open at the waist. Startled, he realized that she was naked beneath it. He glimpsed the span of pink skin on her neck and shoulders; the snowy slopes of her breasts.

All at once, his craving for bourbon was replaced with a need whose urgency drove him to his feet.

He found himself striding toward the French doors, stopping short before he got there only because he realized he needed to put himself in check.

He couldn't barge in there, take her into his arms, and ravish her.

He had to think this through. Think of the consequences.

All right, what will the consequences be?

Right now, his thoughts clouded with desire, his eyes

feasting on the woman before him, he couldn't think of any.

Only of pleasure.

He opened the door.

Jordan cried out.

Their eyes met.

"It's only me," he said, stepping into the sterile chill of the house.

"You scared me. I thought you were in bed."

He saw that she was holding the lotion bottle in her hands.

"Why don't you come out here with me?" he invited, trying to keep his eyes focused on her face and not the V-shaped crevice between the folds of the robe.

She looked past him, at the empty deck where two wooden lounge chairs seemed to beckon.

"It's a beautiful night," he lied.

It wasn't beautiful. There were no stars, and the temperature was uncomfortably humid.

What the hell was he doing?

Quite simply, he was luring her out there. There, under cover of darkness, with the sound of the crashing surf, she wouldn't be able to see the blatant hunger in his eyes. His words wouldn't sound so hollow.

"All right," she said, glancing down and pulling her robe firmly closed. "I'll come out for a few minutes. We need to talk about Spencer."

"We do. We do need to talk about him," Beau agreed, holding the door open for her. As she passed him, the herbal scent he had imagined became tantalizingly real, wafting in the air so that he found himself longing to bury his face in her hair.

"I'll be right back," he said.

"Where are you . . . ?"

He was already on his way to the master suite. In his bathroom, he swiftly reached for the leather bag that held his toiletries. As he slid a foil-wrapped packet into the pocket of his shorts, he caught a glimpse of himself in the mirror.

What are you doing? What are you thinking?

He *wasn't* thinking.

The truth was, he was tired of thinking. All he ever did was think. For once, he wanted just to feel.

He turned away from his own accusatory gaze and made a hasty retreat back to the deck, where he settled again in his lounge chair.

They were side by side, facing the shadowy dunes, legs outstretched.

"It looks like it's going to rain," Jordan said, surveying the sky as she adjusted her chair's back to a more comfortable slant.

"Maybe."

"Did you hear a weather report on the radio or get a newspaper when you went shopping this morning?"

"I didn't bother. If it rains, it rains," he said with a shrug.

"I guess." She paused. "We should be checking the papers. Just in case there's been any news. . . ."

About Phoebe and Reno. He knew that. Why hadn't he thought to buy the paper this morning? Was it because he didn't think it likely that the local news would carry the story? Or was he subconsciously trying to prolong their time here together? Was he fearful that, if they discovered that the murders had been solved and the culprits were in custody, there would be no reason for her to stay?

If that were the case, he could bring her and Spencer back to Washington with him tomorrow. He could go to his meeting and Jordan could go to the authorities, and that would be that. When he returned here, he would return alone, just as he had intended.

But now the thought of a solitary week in the Outer Banks seemed terribly depressing.

"What are we going to do?" she asked.

And for a moment, he was so struck by the *we* that he didn't really comprehend the question. He was part of a *we*. They were in this together. He was no longer alone. Incredible what a simple pronoun could do to—

"Beau . . . ?"

He turned to her. "When I go back, I can try to see what I can find out," he said. "If there's been any progress in the case, we'll have a better idea whether it would be safe to go to the police."

She sighed, looking out over the railing, toying with the cap on the lotion bottle in her lap. "I'm starting to think that's what I should have done all along."

I. It was back to *I.* She had separated them once again.

"No," he said, trying to stay focused on Spencer. "You shouldn't have gone to the police. Phoebe didn't. There was a reason for that. She went to you. She trusted only you. You couldn't be sure you could trust anyone, even the police."

"I trusted you," Jordan said, looking at him.

He turned to meet her gaze. "Why did you trust me?"

"For one thing, it wasn't as if I had a choice. You kept showing up. You figured it out. But even then . . . there's something about you, Beau. The way you bonded with Spencer . . . and how you knew what to do. You always knew what to do, with him, and . . ."

She trailed off.

He waited.

"How did you know what he needed, Beau?" she

asked softly. "Was it because you were a little boy once? Or because . . ."

He didn't want to say it.

But somehow, the words spilled from him.

"Because I had a little boy once, Jordan."

He could see by her expression that those were not the words she expected to hear.

"You *had* a little boy?" she echoed.

He nodded mutely, a massive lump choking further words from his throat. And in that instant, her face changed. She knew. He could see that she knew the terrible truth that he couldn't utter.

"Oh, Beau." She reached toward him.

He thought she would take his hand, or squeeze his arm.

She didn't. She laid the backs of her fingertips against his cheek, like a concerned mother checking for fever. A flood of emotion surged forth as he realized the gesture was made not out of pity or obligation, but because she cared for him. She felt his pain, and she wanted to ease it.

"They both died, Jordan."

There. He had confessed the tragic truth. The words were wrenched from him on a shuddering sob. He struggled to maintain control, but the dam had broken and the words cascaded from his tortured soul.

"Tyler and Jeanette . . . they were my whole world. And they died. I couldn't save them. Oh, Lord, I tried to save them."

"Oh, Beau." Jordan was out of her chair now, sitting on the edge of his, alongside his outstretched legs. She cradled his head against her, stroking his hair. "Oh, my god, Beau. What happened?"

"I was flying us home from the Keys after a weekend trip."

It all came back to him now. How they had lingered in the warm aquamarine water behind the hotel until late in the day, then meandered into Key West for conch fritters and key lime pie as the sun set. They didn't set out for home until well after dark that Sunday night. He was too carefree—no, too reckless—to worry about the remnants of a tropical storm that was hovering along the Louisiana Gulf Coast.

"You were flying?" Jordan's gentle question brought him back.

He nodded. "I got my pilot's license right after Jeanette and I were married. We wanted the freedom of being able to take off at a moment's notice and go wherever we felt like going. We loved the sensation of being up there in the clouds, alone together—just the two of us, and Tyler . . ."

Another sob broke loose. He clasped a hand over his mouth.

"It's okay," Jordan said softly. "You can let it out. Don't bottle it up, Beau."

"Tyler was only . . ." He gasped, sobbed again. "He was only three. He and Jeanette were strapped in back. I was about to land. It was wind shear."

Wind shear.

He remembered the awful moment when he lost control. . . .

The plane plunging toward the water . . .

Waking up, what felt like hours later—he later learned it had only been a minute, maybe less. . . .

Struggling to free himself from the submerged wreckage, surfacing to find himself alone in the eerie dark-

ness, alone in the strangely still, snake-and-gator-
infested bayou . . .

The moment he realized that they were still in there,
trapped in the crumpled remains of the plane, was the
worst moment of his life. It was a moment he was des-
tined to relive countless times in waking nightmares and
in the real thing.

"The plane crashed and you tried to save them." It
wasn't a question. It was a statement. He could tell by
her expression that Jordan seemed to see, somehow,
the horrific vision in his mind.

"I didn't try hard enough. I was disoriented. I went
down a few times, but . . . I couldn't even find the
plane." His voice had become a wail. "Later, I saw
pictures—the wreckage wasn't even entirely under
water, Jordan. All I had to do was look, and I would
have seen . . ."

"You were disoriented. It was dark. You were probably
injured yourself, Beau."

He was. A concussion. Lacerations. Fractured ribs.
Nothing compared to what happened to them.

"They drowned, Jordan," he sobbed. "They were
alive when we hit, and they were alive under there,
struggling, waiting for me . . . and I didn't come. While
I splashed around helplessly, they were drowning a few
feet away."

"Don't torture yourself, Beau." Jordan's hands were
on his shoulders, her face inches from his, her eyes like
magnets drawing his gaze. "Nobody could have saved
them."

"I could have."

"If you could have, you would have."

Yes.

If you could have, you would have. . . .

Somehow, her words pierced the armor of his profound contrition, his self-inflicted punishment.

If he could have saved them, he would have.

In hindsight, he had done nothing. He had failed.

But then, and there . . .

Had he done all that he was capable of doing in that terrible time and place?

A last shuddering sob escaped him, and with it the first shard fell away from the impenetrable fortress he had built.

Jordan's simple words had brought him a glimmer of peace. Not the temporary numbness the bourbon allowed, nor the illusion of normalcy forged by his work.

This, he somehow recognized, was real. There was hope for him. Hope for healing. Hope for the future.

Jordan gently dried his tears with the sleeve of her robe, her movements wafting more of her scent around him.

As he breathed deeply, the storm subsiding, something other than calm settled over him. He recognized it, of course.

It was the same need that had taunted him earlier, driving him to bring her out here.

His next movement surprised him—clearly, it surprised both of them.

He pulled her down into his lap.

It just happened, the way their first kiss in her town house had just happened.

Jordan didn't resist. As he pulled her against him, her face tilted up expectantly. The wonder of it nearly took his breath away. She knew he was going to kiss her; she wanted him to; she was waiting.

His lips met hers tentatively at first. But in no time caution gave way to passion. Groaning, he slid his tongue past the moist barrier and entered an erotic duel with her tongue and her lips, probing, stroking until they were both moaning and their hands began to roam.

He was caught off guard by her feather-light touch when it sent shivers of anticipation through him as she explored his bare chest. He kissed her more deeply and was gratified by the sensation of Jordan's hands splayed on his naked shoulders, as though she were pulling him closer still.

Tonight she seemed to meet his unbridled desire with a fierce need of her own, welcoming him, teasing him, making him crazy with need.

He untangled his hands from her damp hair and reached swiftly for her robe. He slipped it effortlessly off her shoulders. When he began to kiss her neck, she gasped. For a moment, he thought it was pleasure, but then she pulled back slightly. Looking at her nude body, at the stark contrast between her breasts and her arms and shoulders, he remembered: the sunburn.

"I'm sorry," he whispered, trying to slow his panting breath. "I forgot. You're in pain. We don't have to—"

"Yes, we do," she said, and pressed his head to her breast. "It doesn't hurt here."

He kissed one rigid nipple, lapping it gently with his tongue.

"Or here," she said, and he moved to the other as she arched her head back. The purring sound that escaped her throat drove him into an inner frenzy, but he fought to maintain the languid pace, to keep his movements gentle as he nuzzled the silky mounds she offered.

She squirmed in his lap, grazing his arousal beneath the barrier of his shorts. For a moment he didn't realize her movement was deliberate. When she did it again, and he understood, it was all he could do not to take her into his arms, lower her onto the wooden deck, and ravish her right there.

He held his breath as she wriggled against him, then began to stroke him. The fabric did little to desensitize her exquisite touch, and he was almost dismayed when she stopped to tug at his waistband. But he lifted his hips and allowed her to pull his shorts down so that they were both naked and in each other's arms at long last.

She straddled his knees and bent over to kiss his chest. She did to him what he had done to her, suckling his nipples and sparking an erotic tension that only increased when she moved away . . . moved lower. She trailed kisses down his abs, and he could feel his muscles clenching in anticipation when she didn't linger there.

She moved lower still. He groaned when he realized what was going to happen, and he groaned when it happened. He allowed her mouth only a few moments to lavish his rigid flesh before gently tugging her away.

"I can't hold out," he said, his breath ragged. "Not like that. And I want to be inside of you when it happens."

"But . . ."

"It's okay," he said, fumbling for his shorts on the deck beside his chair. He retrieved the square packet from his pocket and held it up.

She stared.

For a moment, he thought he had made a huge mistake. She knew now that he had come out here prepared. She knew this wasn't entirely spontaneous. Not for him.

He waited for the icy veil to descend in her eyes, waited for her to scold him, to walk away.

Instead, a smile teased her lips. "You were pretty sure of yourself when you asked me to come out here, huh?"

He felt a lazy grin spreading across his own face. "Nope. Not at all. I was hoping . . ."

"So was I," she confessed.

That did it. He needed her. Now.

He ripped into the packet and sheathed himself swiftly, ready, willing and . . .

"I don't want to hurt you," he remembered, seeing her sunburn again. "Your skin . . ."

"It won't hurt this way," she whispered, reaching for the chair beneath him. She released the lever that held the back in an upward slant, lowering it—and him—into a flat position.

Then she inched her way up, from straddling his knees to stradling his hips, her hands on his shoulders. As she lowered herself over him, her groan mingled with his and he was blinded by sheer ecstasy.

He was careful not to touch her sensitive shoulders or back as she began to move rhythmically above him, allowing his hands to roam over her breasts, her flat belly, her firm backside.

Her breath was coming in soft little pants as she began to gyrate her hips in a movement that sent him over the edge. His body bucked beneath hers as they exploded in tandem, ripples of pleasure giving way to a deluge.

As the waves subsided, he pulled her head down against his chest and stroked her hair as they listened to the pounding surf.

"I wish I didn't have to go," he said softly.

"So do I."

"Maybe you and Spencer should come with me."

"No," she said, pulling back so that he could see her

face. "I can't take him back to D.C. Not until I know it's safe. We're better off here."

He knew that. He had told her that himself. But now that he had her in his arms, he never wanted to let her go.

So much could happen in twenty-four hours.

So much could happen in an instant.

Nobody was ever truly safe.

But fate had given him a second chance. A chance to deliver this woman and child from peril. This time, he was going to succeed. Even if it meant making himself vulnerable once more to the very loss that had shattered his life.

He had come into this of his own accord, telling himself he could maintain the necessary detachment. He had been a fool to believe that . . . and he was most certainly a fool right now.

But it was too late for detachment.

He had learned the hard way that you could never turn back the clock.

You could only go forward blindly, and live with the choices you made.

Chapter Ten

Jordan woke to the sound of rain against the roof. As she rolled over and pulled the covers up to her chin, she remembered where she was.

In North Carolina.

In Beau's bed.

Her eyes jerked open. The room was still dark, but not so dark that she couldn't see the empty pillow beside her.

She sat up, running a hand through hair that was oddly matted. She wondered why, then remembered the details of last night in a rush.

When it began sprinkling outside, he had led her into the house and into his room, where they made love again. The second time was less frenzied, more languid. Afterward, they fell asleep in each other's arms.

Now he was gone.

Had he left already on the long drive back to Washington? Would he really leave without waking her to say good-bye?

She swung her legs over the edge of the mattress, then realized she had nothing on. Her robe from last night was probably still out on the deck, sopping wet by now.

She spotted a T-shirt of Beau's draped over a doorknob and put it on. It came down to her mid-thighs, making her decent enough to run into Spencer—not that he was likely to be up at this hour.

Whatever hour it was.

She opened the door and found the living area quiet, seemingly deserted.

"Go back to bed."

Beau's hushed voice startled her.

She turned to see him in the corner by a low desk, gathering a stack of manila folders and putting them into a brown leather satchel.

"Are you getting ready to leave?" she asked, suddenly feeling awkward. Last night's natural aura of intimacy seemed to have evaporated the instant she spoke.

He nodded, not looking at her, focusing instead on closing the bag's zippered compartment with exaggerated care.

"I'd better get on the road," he said. "It's pouring out. It'll take me a little longer until I drive out of it."

Classic morning-after strain, she thought, wishing it away. Not even the broad light of day yet, and still they were facing each other like two people who had made an embarrassing mistake.

Was it a mistake?

How could it have been, when it felt so right?

She watched Beau pull on a hooded forest green

pullover and fought back the image of him naked beneath her.

"What time is it?" she asked.

"Almost four-thirty." He slung his satchel over his shoulder. "You should go back to bed."

"I will." She yawned and followed him across the room. "Please be careful, Beau. The roads will be slippery."

"I'll be careful. Do you want me to stop at your place and get anything for you?"

"No!" How could he even think such a thing? "You have to stay away from there, Beau. He might still be prowling around my place, looking for Spencer, waiting for us. . . ." The very thought made her shiver. "Don't take any chances."

"Don't you, either. You have my cell phone number if you need me. I'll keep it on. And I'll be back as soon as I can. The meeting should be over by five at the latest. I'll get right on the road. Maybe I can be back here before midnight."

"Don't rush. We'll be fine."

"I know you will."

They were facing each other now, a few feet apart, lingering at the head of the stairs.

"I looked in on Spencer before," Beau said. "He's sound asleep."

"Good. I'll go back down to my room so that he'll find me if he needs me."

He nodded, jangled his key chain. "Well . . . I've got to go."

"Okay."

He leaned toward her. She braced for a quick peck, but his kiss belied the strain of just moments before.

Perhaps she'd been wrong about that. Perhaps the tension had been only in her imagination.

It lasted longer than a standard good-bye kiss; long enough to set her heart pounding and spark a quiver of need in the depths of her stomach.

His hand lingered on her cheek as he pulled back. "Good-bye, Jordan. When I get back, we'll talk."

She nodded, knowing that he was referring to more than just the dilemma involving Spencer.

Then he was gone. She heard his footsteps descending two flights of stairs; heard the first floor door close and lock; heard the engine of his SUV roar to life.

It was then that she was seized by sheer, unexpected panic.

She wanted to run after him, to tell him to stop—to take her and Spencer with him.

She forced herself to stand her ground, to listen as his car rolled away toward the road, toward the one route to the mainland.

She was alone here with Spencer.

What if the pirate tracked them down here while Beau was gone?

That would be impossible, she told herself. *If nobody followed us out here—and I'm sure of that—then there is no way he could know where we are.*

She hadn't told a soul she was leaving town. It had happened so fast. And even if the pirate managed to track down Jeremy or one of her clients, nobody would ever connect her with Beau.

Nobody except Andrea MacDuff, she thought uneasily.

But the woman had only set them up on a blind date. She had no idea what had happened between them since.

Still . . .

What if the pirate got to Andrea, and Andrea inno-
cently mentioned Beau?

The thought was ludicrous. Half the time, Jordan
herself couldn't even reach the often elusive Andrea.

She was just paranoid, searching for reasons to be
afraid.

Still . . .

The pirate had been snooping around her town
house, asking questions of the neighbors. He might
even have gotten inside, tried to abduct Spencer from
his bed. The man was brazen and clever.

What if he had been spying on her and Beau on the
few occasions they had come and gone together?

The man could have seen Beau's car parked in front
of her house. He could have followed him back to his
place. Found out who he was. Asked some questions,
and figured out that when Beau left town, he had
brought Jordan and Spencer with him.

Why didn't we think of that before? Jordan wondered,
trying to keep the frantic fear at bay.

Because she hadn't been thinking clearly while Beau
was around. Obviously, neither of them had been.

She had told herself that the only way anybody could
find her here would have been to follow her. She hadn't
stopped to realize that all it would take would be a
glimpse of Beau at her place—or even of his car parked
out front—to launch sufficient detective work to trace
Jordan to this house.

What if the pirate was here already?

What if he was out there somewhere in the dunes or
even in a neighboring house, watching Jordan right now
with a pair of binoculars?

She was suddenly aware of the well-lit room in which
she stood.

Of the several pairs of French doors leading onto various decks, unobscured by draperies or blinds.

Anyone could see right inside.

You're letting your imagination get the best of you, Jordan scolded herself, pressing a trembling hand against her wildly pounding heart.

She strode over to the nearest double doors and stared out into the sodden, inky predawn light. She could see nothing but the reflection of the room behind her superimposed over a shadow of the deck beyond, and sheets of rain.

She reached out and flipped the light switch beside her, plunging the room into darkness.

Now she could see a bit more outside.

The looming, distant roofline of a neighboring house.

The silhouette of the dunes.

Nothing more.

The place was desolate, she realized.

It wasn't a haven at all.

With Beau gone, she and Spencer were more vulnerable here than they had been in Georgetown.

At least at her town house, there were neighbors to hear her if she screamed for help. Here, the other houses were so few and far between that her screams would be swept away on the wind, obscured by pattering rain and the incessant roaring of the sea.

She didn't even have a car so that she could escape if she had to.

How could Beau have left her here without a car?

How could Beau have left her here at all?

You told him to go.

You told him you and Spencer would be fine.

She had believed it then.

Not anymore.

* * *

Thanks to the crummy weather, there wasn't as much traffic on the I-95 corridor as Beau had anticipated. By late morning he was passing the exits for Fredericksburg, about an hour south of Washington.

He had exhausted his supply of CDS, listening to the Rolling Stones a couple of times before getting as sick of it as he was of the steadily bobbing windshield wipers.

He was growing restless, his thoughts on Jordan and Spencer. He wanted only to get the drive and the meeting over with so that he could head back to them.

He had stopped only once, to get gas, a jumbo-sized coffee, and a stale service station blueberry muffin. Now, thanks to all that coffee, he had to stop again.

He pulled off the highway at an exit that had a Seven-Eleven. They usually had clean restrooms, and their coffee was more palatable than the bitter brew he'd ingested earlier.

He parked the car and put up his hood before venturing out into the rain. Here it was more drizzly than it had been earlier. It must be a coastal storm. It would be nice if it let up before he made the return trip, he thought as he stepped into the small, brightly lit mini-mart.

He made his way toward the back of the store to the rest room.

Standing before the mirror above the sink as he washed his hands, he saw his reflection. The lack of sleep was visible on his face. He'd been up so early that razor stubble had already sprouted on his chin. His hair was matted from the hood. He looked like hell. He couldn't show up for a meeting with Landry looking like this.

He was planning to stop back at his apartment to change into a suit anyway. Checking his watch, he realized that he had made such good time, he should have time to shower and shave while he was at it. And if the return trip went as quickly as this one had, he should be back on the Outer Banks long before midnight.

Back out in the store, Beau hurriedly fixed himself a large cup of coffee at the self-service counter. He was dumping a third packet of sugar in when he overheard two truckers talking on the other side of the counter.

"Nah, I'm headed down to Norfolk," one was saying. "Should get there right before the storm makes landfall. Figure I'll stay the night, at least."

"Yeah, but you'll be sleeping in the rig. You won't get a room anywhere within a hundred miles of there if they start evacuating the Outer Banks like they said."

"Evacuating the Outer Banks?" Beau cut in, a sick feeling washing over him. "Excuse me, I couldn't help hearing—what's going on? How bad is this rainstorm?"

"Rainstorm? This ain't no rainstorm, buddy. It's Tropical Storm Agatha. Where you been?"

Tropical Storm Agatha . . .

Beau was struck by a sudden memory of something he'd read about that in the paper on Sunday. Something about forecasters keeping an eye on that storm in the Caribbean, and about its being unusual for a potent storm to pop up so early in the hurricane season, which had only begun June 1.

He hadn't paid much attention to the article, and he hadn't heard or read the news since. He'd been trying so hard to isolate Spencer from any bulletins about his parents that he hadn't even risked turning on the radio.

Oh, hell. How bad was this storm?

"No, Gus, it's not Tropical Storm Agatha anymore—

they just upgraded it to Hurricane Agatha," the second trucker contradicted the first.

"Yeah?"

"Yup. I heard they evacuated Hilton Head. Mandatory evacuation. Storm's moving up the coast and they're talkin' about evacuating everyone in its path. She's gonna make landfall around Nag's Head."

Beau fumbled with the lid on his coffee cup, sloshing the scalding liquid over his hand. He cursed.

"Careful, there, buddy. Stuff'll burn ya." One of the truckers offered him a napkin, but Beau was already striding toward the register, barely noticing the stinging pain where his skin was already blistering.

He grabbed a copy of *USA Today* from a nearby display, threw several dollar bills at the clerk, and headed for the door.

"Wait! Mister, I didn't even ring it up yet."

"I'm in a hurry," he tossed over his shoulder.

"But your change—"

"Keep it," he said, and dashed through the rain to the SUV. Inside the cab, he scanned the headlines. Agatha was right there on the front page. That was an ominous sign.

Beau skimmed only half the article before reaching for his cell phone and the—

Damn!

Damn, he had forgotten to bring the small pad on which he'd scribbled the telephone number for the beach house.

His heart pounding, he dialed Ed at the office.

"Beau! Where are you? Did you know there's a hurricane—"

"I know. Why the hell didn't you tell me last night?"

"I just found out. Hell, Beau, I've been holed up

working on this plan for two days straight. I only know about it now because I happened to hear the weather forecast while I was in—"

"Ed, I need a favor."

"Please don't tell me you can't get here. The weather can't be all that bad yet, and Landry's flight landed on time. He'll be here in less than two hours, Beau."

"I'm on my way. I'm in Fredericksburg. But I need the phone number for the house I'm renting. Do you still have it?"

"Yeah, I still have it. In fact, yesterday I—"

"Ed, this is an emergency. I need that number. Give it to me."

"Hang on."

Beau waited, thrumming the steering wheel impatiently with a pen, worried about Jordan.

She would have no way of knowing a storm was headed for the Outer Banks. She would have no way of evacuating.

She'd have to call somebody for help, he thought, if the weather got as bad as the National Weather Service was predicting. He should be able to make it back there on time, but if he didn't, and there was an evacuation, the local police would have to get her and Spencer out of there.

Jordan would balk at calling the police, for any reason. But this was serious. It, too, could be life or death. And if somebody somehow figured out who Spencer was, well . . . they'd worry about it then.

Ed came back on the line. "Here's the number, Beau."

He scribbled it on a margin of the newspaper.

"But Beau, listen, I just want to—"

"I have to go, Ed. I'll see you when I get there."

He hung up on his friend, certain he knew what Ed had been about to ask him.

Beau, why on earth do you need the phone number for that house if you were staying there alone?

He dialed the cell phone so quickly that he punched a number in wrong.

Twice.

"Calm down," he muttered to himself. "Just calm down."

The third time, he entered the number correctly. He pressed Send, then waited through several seconds of static before the phone began to ring on the other end of the line.

It rang once . . .

Twice . . .

Three times . . .

Four . . .

Five . . .

Where are you, Jordan?

He let it keep ringing. She had to be there. She had to answer sooner or later.

Unless . . .

Had something happened?

Had the pirate found her and Spencer?

Beau slammed the steering wheel with the fist that had already been burned. Pain exploded, searing all the way up his arm. He didn't care. He wanted to hurt. He deserved to hurt.

He was going back to her. Now. He had to. He had to . . .

He jammed the key into the ignition and the engine roared to life. He peeled out of the parking lot with a screech, his eyes searching for the entrance to the interstate's southbound ramp ... not noticing an oncoming minivan in his path.

The driver leaned on her horn and swerved.

As he passed the vehicle, Beau could see a shaken mother at the wheel, and four small children strapped in back.

Hell.

He could have wiped out a family in that one reckless instant. Somebody's wife and babies ...

Hell.

He had to get hold of himself. He had to calm down.

You can't turn around and drive right back down there. Not in this condition. You need to think logically.

Maybe Jordan just hadn't heard the phone. Maybe she was in the shower.

And maybe the storm wasn't as bad as those truckers—and the newspaper—made it seem. And even if it was ...

Jordan and Spencer would be fine. He would get back down there to them before it got bad. He would be back there tonight. He just had to do one thing at a time.

He cautiously steered toward the on-ramp for I-95.

Northbound.

He would go to D.C. He would fulfill his obligation to Ed, and the firm, and Landry. He would find out what he could about the storm. And he would be well on his way back to North Carolina before nightfall.

Everything is going to be fine.

Everything is going to be fine.

It became his mantra as he drove along, heading for home.

Everything is going to be fine.

If only he believed it.

* * *

"Jordan! Check out that one! It's bigger than every one we've seen so far!" Spencer bellowed above the wind and rain.

She nodded, watching the enormous, foaming white wave cresting a few yards from shore before spilling onto the beach.

"This is awesome," Spencer shouted. He was standing right next to her, but the water, wind, and rain were deafening, especially when they both had their hoods up.

They were standing on Spencer's rock. The surface was surprisingly flat and level, once Jordan had managed to climb up there with him. It was slippery, but they were being careful. And from this vantage point, they had a prime view of the glorious storm.

"It is pretty awesome," she called back to Spencer, watching another towering wave building at sea.

"Thanks for coming out."

His words caught her off guard. She looked at him, touched. He looked away.

"You're welcome, Spencer."

He shrugged, watching the water.

She hadn't wanted to stay inside another minute any more than Spencer did. She was feeling uneasy in the house—wary and claustrophobic. Out here on the deserted beach, she somehow felt safer.

From the windows upstairs, they could see the choppy sea and frothing whitecaps out beyond the dunes.

Down here on the beach, they could feel the mist and salt spray mingling with the rain that hadn't let up for a moment. It was wild and beautiful, and she wasn't afraid here. Not of the storm.

A storm was the last thing to fear right now.

"Can we stay out here a while longer?" Spencer shouted.

Jordan nodded.

She never wanted to go back to the house. Not until Beau came back.

As though he were reading her thoughts, Spencer asked, "What time will Beau be home?"

Home.

That he referred to this unfamiliar place as "home" made a lump rise in Jordan's throat. This wasn't home. Not for him—not for any of them.

Her town house in Georgetown wasn't home for Spencer, either.

The little boy's only home was a Philadelphia mansion that now lay empty and deserted forever by its owners.

Spencer had asked about his mother a few times this morning.

But he had asked about Beau first.

His face fell when she reminded him that Beau had gone back to Washington for a meeting. And Spencer certainly didn't perk up when she once again evaded his follow-up question about when he was going to see his mother again.

How long could she avoid telling him about his parents' deaths?

Guilt seeped into her when she thought about last night—about the pleasure she'd found in that fleeting interlude with Beau.

How could they have been thinking of anything but Spencer's plight? How could they have allowed themselves to give in to temptation, to think of their own needs when this little boy would never again have the one thing he needed most?

If Beau hadn't told her about his own loss, it never would have happened.

But she had found herself caught up in his tragic tale, wanting to ease his pain.

No, Jordan. Your motives weren't as noble as that.

Maybe at first. But when she looked into his eyes, and knew he was going to kiss her, pure desire had overtaken her.

She couldn't let that happen again. She needed to keep her head clear and her mind on Spencer's welfare.

"Whoa! Whoa, Jordan, look!"

She jerked her gaze back toward the horizon, where Spencer was pointing.

Against the backdrop of an ominously black sky, the green-gray sea seemed to be growing more frenzied by the moment. As the wind whipped strands of damp hair against her cheek, Jordan stared at the furious lather of monstrous waves.

Moments ago, she had told herself that she wasn't afraid of this storm.

Now she wasn't so sure.

Now she was having trouble finding anything that *didn't* frighten her.

Hurry back, Beau, she begged silently, fervently, hugging herself against the clammy wind.

Beau reached his apartment in record time. Soaked to the bone from the rain, chilled despite the warm, humid weather, he was in and out of the shower in a matter of minutes. In the bedroom, he saw that he had time to spare before he had to be at the office for his meeting.

Again, he tried dialing the beach house. He had called

every five minutes for the past hour, to no avail. This time was no different. The phone rang incessantly before he finally hung up.

He tossed the receiver aside and reached for the television remote control. There was a commercial on The Weather Channel, so he quickly tuned to MSNBC News, figuring they would have an update on Hurricane Agatha.

Sure enough, a reporter was shown in a blustery live shot with a caption that indicated she was in Myrtle Beach, South Carolina.

Beau toweled himself dry and dressed slowly, riveted to the television screen.

The hurricane was tracking up the coast, now expected to make landfall in Nag's Head, North Carolina around daybreak. The severity of the storm depended on several factors, but most areas along the South Carolina coast were being evacuated.

Beau had apparently missed the live report from the Outer Banks, but he managed to piece together that the evacuation there was still voluntary at this point. The network would broadcast regular updates throughout the day.

When the anchor turned his attention to other news, Beau muted the television and again tried dialing the beach house.

This time, to his shock, Jordan answered on the third ring.

"Where have you been?" he demanded, relief coursing through him.

"Out on the beach," she said breathlessly, as though she had dashed for the phone. "We just came back in. You should see the waves, Beau. Spencer wanted to—"

"Jordan, there's a hurricane headed up the coast,"

he cut in, his eye on the television set, where there was a graphic regarding the Fed's latest interest rate. "You should be safe until I get back tonight, but then we're going to have to get out of there."

There was a pause.

"A hurricane?" she echoed softly. "Oh, God. I had no idea. No wonder . . ."

"Jordan, there's a voluntary evacuation of the Outer Banks now. They're talking about the possibility of a mandatory one. If that happens, we'll have to leave. Or maybe we should leave anyway."

"But . . . where would we go?"

"Back here?" he said, frustrated. "Hell, I don't know. We can't keep running. Can we? Is that what you want? Is that what's best for Spencer?"

"All I know is that I made a promise to a friend," she said, so softly that he realized Spencer must be right there with her. "I'm planning to keep it, Beau, at any cost."

"I know you are." He gazed idly at the television, where a report from Sunny California was apparently showing the latest Hollywood star getting his footprints on the sidewalk outside Mann's.

Jordan was silent.

"Look," he said, checking his watch, "I'm on my way to my meeting now. I'll be out of there in an hour or two, even if I have to cut it short. I'll be back to you and Spencer as soon as possible, Jordan. And then we'll figure out what to do. Don't worry. No matter what, we'll keep that little boy safe."

"Thanks, Beau."

"Hang in there. And for God's sake, stay inside. It's getting rough out there, and this is only the edge of the storm."

"We'll be fine. Don't worry. Get back safely."

"I will."

He heard a click as she hung up.

He walked toward the television, pointing the remote at the screen to turn it off.

Then the graphic over the anchor's shoulder captured his attention.

There was a streamer of yellow police tape and a chalk outline of a male and female silhouette, captioned "Murder in Philadelphia."

Beau hurriedly jammed the mute button to restore the sound as the scene switched to a reporter standing outside an elaborate brick Georgian-style home on a leafy street.

". . . police have not been forthcoming about possible suspects. But a source here now says that there may be a link between Reno Averill's death and a high-profile client he recently agreed to represent."

Beau stood frozen in front of the television screen, his heart pounding.

"Convicted, paroled pedophile James Shelton now stands accused of the strangulation deaths of several teenaged girls in the metropolitan Philadelphia–New Jersey area—including the murder of Lisa Gisonni, daughter of reputed mob soldier Joseph "the Moose" Gisonni, a member of the notorious Beramino crime family. Shelton, who selected his victims at random, has reportedly confessed to abducting, raping, and strangling the girl on Christmas Eve of 2000. He faced certain conviction when the case went to trial—until Averill, notorious for winning acquittals in cases like this, replaced defense lawyer Howard Goff."

Beau sank to the edge of the bed, riveted to the courthouse footage of a no-nonsense-looking lawyer escorting his client, a pock-marked loser that even a fresh haircut and an obviously newly purchased suit and tie couldn't transform.

"Now Shelton may be facing acquittal on a technicality. But NBC News has just learned that Shelton's sixteen-year-old daughter, who lives in New York City with her mother, Shelton's estranged wife, has been missing for several days."

There was a school photograph of a lank-haired young girl wearing a vacant expression.

"While the girl has a history of drug and alcohol abuse, and has been known to vanish for a day or two at a time, there is speculation among those who know her that this time she met with foul play—and that Joseph Gisonni may be behind her disappearance as well as the double murder of Reno Averill and his wife, Phoebe."

Beau felt sick at the sight of two tarp-covered bodies being loaded into an ambulance in a waterfront scene.

Those were Spencer's parents' bodies.

Tears sprang to Beau's eyes. He swiped them with the back of his sleeve, not caring that he was wearing a two-thousand-dollar suit coat.

"Though Gisonni has an airtight alibi for the night they were slain, a source confirms that his ties to organized crime suggest he might have ordered the killing of the Averills. Gisonni was heard threatening the defense attorney and his family after he joined the Shelton defense."

Beau gasped as a familiar face filled the television screen. The snapshot couldn't have been taken more than a month or two ago. It showed Spencer exactly as he looked now. He was smiling into the sun, holding a fishing pole on the deck of a boat.

"As for young Spencer Averill, Reno and Phoebe Averill's four-year-old son, police originally assumed he was on board his father's yacht, was killed with his parents, and that his body simply had yet to surface. Now that several days have passed and police divers have turned up nothing, there is speculation that the child may have been abducted from the scene by the killer. Police are asking anyone who has seen Spencer Averill to contact them at one-eight-hundred, five-five-five, three-oh-four-nine."

The words *Confidential Police Hotline* and the 800 telephone number replaced the photograph of Spencer's face.

"Meanwhile, the official search for a motive and suspect in the Averill slaying goes on. Now back to you, Brian."

The scene shifted back to the anchor and a story about a shark attack on a surfer in Oregon.

Beau rose, strode across the room, and turned off the television set.

His mind was reeling as he picked up his keys and his cell phone. He headed blindly for the door.

As he closed it behind him and turned the key in the lock, it occurred to him that maybe he should have brought an umbrella.

But he didn't go back.

Two-thousand-dollar suit and Ed Landry's expectations be damned, there wasn't a moment to waste.

For a moment, as he dashed down the quiet carpeted hallway toward the elevator bank, he again considered skipping the meeting and heading straight back to North Carolina.

But he was already here in Washington.

Ed was counting on him.

He owed Ed. His friend had given him more than a job. He had presented a chance for a fresh start when Beau most desperately needed one.

He could go to the meeting and cut it short as he had planned.

He would still have plenty of time to beat the storm.

Thank God he had happened to catch that story on the news. Now, at least, he knew what they were dealing with—or might be dealing with.

The newscaster had been careful to attribute the speculation to an unnamed source. The police weren't officially linking the Averill murders to the mob, but the implication was crystal clear.

Beau had heard of the Beramino crime family. He knew that they were powerful and lethal.

What the hell had Reno Averill been thinking, getting tangled up with them?

Okay, Beau conceded as he got on the elevator, the defense lawyer wasn't directly connected to them. But he was representing the serial killer responsible for a mob soldier's daughter's death.

If Gisonni intended to get even with Shelton and his attorney, he would probably do so in exactly that manner: by hurting Shelton's daughter, since he couldn't get to Shelton himself, who was in prison. And by going after not just Reno, but his family, too.

So who was the mysterious pirate?

A hit man hired by Gisonni and the Beramino family?

Jordan and Spencer are safe where they are, Beau reminded himself as he got off the elevator and crossed the parking garage toward the SUV.

With Spencer's photograph being flashed on the national news, they couldn't afford to be seen anywhere the child might be recognized.

So Hurricane Agatha was, it now seemed, a blessing in disguise. In bearing down on the Carolina coast, the storm had further isolated the beach house and sent people fleeing the Outer Banks.

He had to call Jordan and let her know what was going on.

In the car, Beau steered his way out into the busy weekday traffic before turning down the volume on the radio and reaching for his cell phone.

As soon as he tried to dial, he realized he'd made a mistake.

A huge mistake.

The display screen was flashing an orange "Low Battery" image.

He cursed under his breath. He wasn't used to carrying the damn thing, and he sure as hell never left it on all day as he had today.

He'd left the charger kit in the Outer Banks, along with his other possessions.

He clenched his jaw, focusing on the traffic through the rain-spattered windshield.

Calling Jordan with the latest would only alarm her, he told himself. The news could wait until he got to her.

The trouble was, without the cell phone, Jordan had no way of getting in touch with him if she needed him.

And anyway, from here, he was all but helpless.

A familiar feeling of guilt washed over him—along with renewed determination to get back to the beach house as soon as possible.

He wasn't far from his office now, stopped at a red light at Massachusetts Avenue. He turned up the radio volume again and tuned it to the all-news station he sometimes listened to.

When the light changed, he would only have to drive straight ahead another block and turn into the entrance ramp for the parking garage beneath his office.

Frowning, Beau willed the light to change.

The radio newscaster announced that the latest on Hurricane Agatha would be right ahead, after this message.

Hurricane Agatha.

A mob hit.

Beau closed his eyes and leaned his forehead against the steering wheel as Spencer's and Jordan's faces mingled with Tyler's and Jeanette's.

You have to save them.

This time, you have to.

Behind him, a horn blared.

He lifted his head and saw that the light was green.

Without giving it another moment's thought, he stepped on the gas and whipped around the corner, heading away from the office—and right toward the entrance ramp for I-395 and the quickest route out of town.

Why hadn't Beau called?

Frustrated, Jordan paced from the French doors leading to the deck overlooking the sea to the French doors leading to the deck overlooking the driveway.

Neither view offered anything but dismal, gray, mist-shrouded rain. It was like being on an airplane and looking out the window in the midst of a bank of clouds . . .

Except as the plane gains altitude, you rise above the clouds and there's sunshine and an incredibly blue sky, Jordan thought morosely. She had the feeling there wouldn't be any sunshine or blue skies today.

But seeing Beau's car emerge through the storm would be better than sunshine.

Even a phone call would be a glimpse of blue sky.

She glanced at Spencer, who lay on his back on the living room floor, driving his miniature metal car up and down the coffee table leg. He made a low-pitched "brrmm brrmm" sound in his throat, then softly mimicked the squealing of tires.

He hadn't been playing so softly a few minutes ago. Not until Jordan, encouraged by the temporary rapport they'd established out on the beach, made the mistake of crouching beside him, asking, "Can I play, too?"

He had scowled at her. "No."

She'd foolishly made another try. "But it sounds like fun, Spencer. And I can be the police car. I can make a great siren sound. Listen."

Her self-conscious, halfhearted siren attempt went over like a lead balloon.

What the heck was she going to do with this kid for the rest of the day until Beau came back?

Damn it, why didn't Beau call? Was he okay?

She had tried his cell phone a little while ago, but got a recorded operator's voice saying the cellular customer she was trying to reach was unavailable. She figured he must have driven out of range.

But surely he would have cell phone service at some points along the road.

She decided to try again.

"What are you doing?" Spencer asked as she lifted the telephone receiver.

"Just checking to see if I can reach Beau now."

"Can I talk if you do?"

"Sure . . ."

She frowned, her finger poised above the dial.

The receiver was silent against her ear.

There was no dial tone.

She cursed softly, conscious of Spencer sitting up, watching her expectantly.

"What's wrong?" he asked.

She pasted on a bright fake smile. "Nothing," she said. "Nothing at all."

Everything.

Everything was wrong.

Chapter Eleven

"Want to play another game?" Jordan asked Spencer hopefully.

"Nah." He tossed his depleted hand of cards in the center of the table and looked toward the window, moping.

"Are you sure? Because—"

"I don't want to play," he said, his eyes flashing angrily at her. "I'm sick of cards! It's all we've done all day."

He was right.

But thank God for the deck of cards Jordan had found in a kitchen drawer. Without it, she would have been hard-pressed to keep the child entertained. The miniature cars Beau had bought him had long since inspired boredom.

Outside, a gust of wind slammed into the house, shaking it violently.

Spencer gasped and looked anxiously toward the window again. Darkness was falling rapidly, though it shouldn't be time for dusk yet.

"It's okay, it's just the storm," Jordan said, forcing her voice to remain calm.

"I know that." He sounded irritated with her.

"Do you want another sandwich?" she asked. She had made him two peanut-butter-and-jelly sandwiches already. Remembering Beau's wizardry, she had cut one sandwich into an awkward seahorse shape, and another into a shark with a jagged fin.

"No."

"Are you sure? This time I could make it look like an octopus, if you want. Or you can choose another—"

"No," he said again, glowering.

She busied herself collecting the cards from the table, stacking the deck neatly in her palm so that the edge of each card aligned precisely with the edge of the one beneath it.

Cards. She hadn't played in ages. Not since she was a little girl.

But she and Spencer had just played every card game she could recall from her childhood with Phoebe. She remembered games she hadn't thought of in years, making up the rules where they were fuzzy in her mind.

As they played, she'd repeatedly pushed back the memories that threatened to surge forth, along with tears of grief for her lost friend. She had to keep her composure now more than ever, for Spencer's sake.

Yet it was impossible not to think of Phoebe now especially, as Jordan sat across from a child who not only looked like her, but who played games as Phoebe had played them. He had been dead serious, focused on his cards, even chewing on his lower lip while pondering a move, just as Phoebe used to do.

"Want me to show you how to build a house out of cards?" Jordan asked, desperate for a distraction.

"Nope."

"Come on, I bet we can build a great house of cards." Spencer shook his head.

The rain pattered loudly on the roof overhead. It wouldn't be as loud downstairs. Maybe they should go down to one of the bedrooms, or to the game room on the first floor, Jordan thought.

She looked at Spencer and tried again to engage him. "Beau's an architect, you know. That means he designs houses for a living. Bet we can really impress him if we design a card house that won't fall down."

"Card houses are stupid. They always fall down," Spencer said flatly.

"How do you know?"

"My mom and I build them."

"I thought you said your mom never taught you how to play cards," Jordan said, surprised.

"Not this kind of cards. We play 'go fish' and 'I spy.' And then sometimes, we use the cards to build houses."

"Oh." Jordan took a deep breath. Outside, the wind gusted. The lights flickered. "Well, why don't we build—"

"No!" Spencer shouted. He pushed his chair back from the table and glared at her. "I want my mom. How come I'm stuck here with you and you won't let me call her?"

"Spencer . . ."

She half-expected him to interrupt her again. But he didn't. He just stared at her, waiting. Waiting for her to explain.

"Spencer . . ."

"What? Where's my mom?"

Jordan took a deep breath.

Then the wind howled and slammed into the house again, this time plunging it into darkness.

This was insane.

Beau had been driving for hours, and he had still only made it as far as Richmond. He was miles from the coastline, but the rain and wind had picked up in intensity. The traffic headed toward him—away from the coast—was far heavier than it was here. But it was slow going because of the weather. And twice accidents in the northbound lanes caused rubbernecking delays on Beau's southbound side.

According to the radio, the storm had been upgraded to a Category 3 hurricane, with wind speeds in excess of a hundred miles per hour.

The storm's precarious path was crucial. If it stayed over water, it would only intensify. If it veered toward land, some of its power would be diffused.

Timing was also crucial. If the storm hit the Outer Banks during high tide, the entire peninsula could be swept underwater in the storm surge. The governor had issued a mandatory evacuation order for the region.

Beau was losing precious time.

As traffic slowed to a near stop alongside an exit for Richmond's airport, Beau stared at the green-and-white exit sign, allowing the idea that had been building in the back of his mind to take hold with a vengeance.

He looked at his watch, then at the pouring rain and the line of traffic that snaked in front of him.

It was the only way.

The only way.

He jerked the steering wheel to the right and pulled onto the shoulder, driving toward the exit.

Toward the airport.

"I don't like candles," Spencer said, warily looking at the small votive candle Jordan had lit and placed in the center of the coffee table.

"Why not? I think candles are cozy," Jordan said, making a tremendous effort to keep the anxiety from her voice.

"Because I don't like fire." Spencer's voice grew smaller and he seemed to burrow into the couch cushions.

Jordan put the book of matches and an unlit candle on the table and sat next to him. She longed to put her arms around him and pull him close, but she sensed that he would only pull away. He was still embarrassed at the way he'd reacted when the lights went out.

Actually, he had done exactly what she wanted to do: burst into tears and wailed for his mother, and then for Beau.

But Jordan couldn't afford to do that—or even to admit to the child that she wanted to. She had to appear strong and in control. She had to make him feel safe.

That was getting harder by the minute. The storm had intensified.

When she was looking for a flashlight, she had found a small battery-operated radio in a cabinet downstairs, but there was too much static to hear much of anything. She did hear the words "hurricane" and "evacuation," but it was impossible to decipher the context.

Besides, the radio broadcast seemed to make Spencer even more agitated, so she turned it off.

She hadn't found a flashlight, either. There were several books of matches in the kitchen drawer, and at least half-dozen small, scented votive candles scattered around the house. She had collected them all and lined them up on the counter.

"Where's Beau?" Spencer asked again. "I don't like this storm. He's supposed to be back by now, isn't he?"

"Not yet," Jordan said, looking at her watch. Even if Beau had left Washington when he said he would—and in decent weather—he still wouldn't be due out here for another hour or two at least.

"Is something bad going to happen to us?" Spencer asked, watching her face carefully.

She hoped the flickering light would conceal the truth as she feigned shock that he would even consider such a thing, saying, "No! Of course not! Why would you even say a thing like that?"

"Because . . ."

The little boy hesitated.

"You don't have anything to worry about, Spencer," Jordan lied. "This big old storm can't get us."

He seemed to consider that.

Then he caught her completely off guard, asking, "If the water is rough like it was when we were out on the beach, it means a pirate can't sail his pirate ship on it, right?"

"Oh, Spencer . . ."

She fumbled for words. What could she say?

That there was no such thing as pirates? That wouldn't cut it anymore. Not now that she knew that his eye-patch-wearing nemesis might be made of flesh and blood.

"Tell me about the pirate, Spencer. Where did you first see him?"

The little boy was silent, looking down at the pillow on his lap. For a moment she thought he was going to evade her question.

Then he began to speak, his voice low and quivering, his eyes glued to the pillow. "I saw him when my mom and I were getting out of the car at home one day."

"How long ago?"

"I dunno."

No, he wouldn't know. Spencer was too young to have any sense of time. He had told her earlier today that his mother had been gone for months. It probably seemed like that to him. It even felt that way to Jordan.

"What did the pirate do?"

"He just came up to us and started talking to my mom. He was waiting for us or something. He didn't have a ship. But I still knew he was a pirate."

"Because he looked like one, right? He had a black eye patch like a pirate, didn't he, Spencer?"

The little boy nodded. "He said something bad to my mom. He made her cry."

"Did you hear what he said?"

"Some of it. He said my mom had to tell my dad something about his job. To stop doing something." Spencer's voice trembled. "And he said that if my dad didn't stop doing it, the pirate was going to hurt me and my mom."

A tide of nausea coursed through Jordan. She tried to imagine what Phoebe must have felt, coming face to face with some kind of thug—and a threat against her own life, and her child's.

"What happened then?" she asked Spencer, as though he were giving her a blow-by-blow of a play date. She didn't want him to know how crucial this information was, and she certainly didn't want him to perceive any kind of peril, or that the pirate still lurked somewhere.

"Then he told my mom she'd better not tell anyone what he said. And he left." Spencer was looking at Jordan now, his guard down, his expression earnest. "And we went inside, and my mom told me to go into my room. And I went, but I still heard her on the phone with my dad. She told him to come home from work right away."

"Did he?"

"Uh-uh. My dad gets really busy at work. Sometimes he can't come home at all."

Jordan nodded, hating Reno Averill with all her heart. Clearly, his profession had placed his family in jeopardy.

"My mom and dad had a big fight when my dad did come home, though," Spencer volunteered. "I woke up and heard them. My mom was crying."

Oh, Phoebe . . .

"What were they saying?" Jordan managed to ask.

"I couldn't really hear. All I know is that the next day, my mom brought me to your house. When is she coming back, Jordan? You don't think the pirate did something bad to her, do you?"

Now was the time.

Now was the time to tell him the truth.

Jordan had been prepared to do it before, but then the lights went out.

Now she stared at the child's worried, frightened face, and she knew she couldn't do it. Not here. Not now. Not with a storm raging outside and Beau still gone.

"Jordan . . . ?" Spencer prodded. "Did the pirate get my mom?"

"Spencer, you said yourself that the pirate can't sail his ship on rough seas, remember?"

"Yeah, but maybe the seas aren't rough in Philadelphia."

Jordan cleared her throat unsuccessfully. It was still clogged with emotion when she said, "Right now, I think seas are pretty rough everywhere, sweetie."

Beau's body was trembling from head to toe as he sat behind the controls of the small twin-engine plane.

A plane.

Hell.

He hadn't set foot on a plane since the accident.

Hadn't even been near a plane, for Christ's sake. What was he doing here?

His stomach was roiling. He had eaten nothing all day since that stale muffin, which had long since dissolved in all the acrid coffee he'd poured down his throat in an effort to cope with the day's demands.

Could he actually fly this thing?

Of course he could. He could fly any plane. He'd been an expert at this, once.

All he had to do was start up the engines, radio the tower, and wait for the go-ahead.

Beau shook his head in amazement at what had transpired back there in the terminal. Most people couldn't walk into an airport off the street and find themselves in a charter plane within the space of an hour. Even after a lifetime of opening doors with his wallet and the Somerville name, Beau was sometimes stunned at the extent of what money and connections could buy.

All it had taken was an astronomical sum of money—

a sum he could easily afford—a few well-placed phone calls, and here he was.

Rain pattered against the windows.

Wind buffeted the wings.

Yet miraculously, they had given him the okay to fly this plane out of here.

Beau started the engines. As the plane rumbled to life around him, he closed his eyes, struggling to calm himself.

It was going to be okay.

He could do this.

He could.

Even the charter people thought he could.

But they didn't know where he was really headed.

He had filed a northwest flight plan, away from the storm—not dead into the center of it.

Once he was up, he'd head for the coast. He'd get as close as he could to Jordan and Spencer—preferably all the way to Dare County Regional Airport.

That was the plan.

But if he had to land on the mainland and find some other way to the Outer Banks, he was prepared to do that.

After all, it wouldn't be helping Jordan and Spencer if he got himself killed.

He took a deep breath.

Then another.

He looked out the window at the storm, remembering what the weather had been like that long-ago day.

Something like this weather.

You're a fool to try this, Beau Somerville.

But that flight was different.

His wife and his son had put their lives in his hands. This time, the only life in his hands was his own.

No, that wasn't true.

Jordan and Spencer were counting on him. They were alone in the beach house with no means of escape, a hurricane closing in, and God knew what else.

A mob hit man?

He pushed the thought from his mind.

One thing at a time.

First, he just had to get back to them.

Or die trying.

With a violently trembling hand, Beau pressed the intercom. He radioed the tower and uttered the four words he never thought he'd say again.

"Ready for takeoff."

A distant thumping sound roused Jordan from a light sleep.

She found herself still on the couch, with Spencer's head on top of a pillow on her lap. Her neck was stiff from having fallen asleep in an upright position, and she winced as she turned her head, listening.

It must have been the wind, she decided. It was still blowing like crazy, hurling sheets of rain against the windows.

She tilted her head back and forth several times, rubbing her neck to get the kinks out. She should really carry Spencer down to his bedroom so that he could sleep comfortably in his own bed.

As for her, she had no intention of going to bed. Not with Beau out there somewhere in the storm. Shouldn't he be here by now?

What if something had happened to him?

Maybe he'd been in an accident . . .

Or maybe the pirate had gotten to him . . .

No! Stop thinking that way! Jordan scolded herself. Of course Beau was fine. There was an indestructible aura about him.

Or maybe she just wanted to think that of him because she couldn't bear to consider the alternative.

Her world had become an infinitely more interesting and less lonely place with Beau in it. Granted, they had shared more drama in the past few days than some people lived through in a lifetime.

Jordan couldn't help wondering what would have happened if they had simply met for the blind date Andrea MacDuff had arranged.

Would they have shared a polite dinner and then gone their separate ways?

Probably. Neither of them had been willing to take a romantic risk. Now she knew why he was emotionally distant. He had no idea about her past, or Kevin. . . .

But being a jilted bride paled in comparison to what Beau had been through. Her curtailed wedding and losing Kevin paled in comparison to the trauma of these past few days.

How had she managed to hang onto that pain for so long? If Kevin came to her tomorrow, single, available, and contrite, she wouldn't want him back. He belonged in another lifetime, to another woman—the woman she had once been.

Yes, what he had done to her had hurt. But it hadn't come as close to destroying her as she had once thought.

What Beau had been through, that could destroy a person.

But it hadn't. He had somehow survived.

Just as Jordan had survived.

Just as Spencer would survive whatever lay ahead.

Jordan stroked the little boy's silky hair, looking down

at him lying asleep in her lap. She would miss him when he was gone, she thought tenderly. Maybe she could visit him, wherever he wound up living.

She could tell him stories about Phoebe. Stories only she knew. She could make sure that he grew up knowing what his mother had really been like—knowing her as only a best friend could.

Tears were trickling down Jordan's cheeks.

She thought about how it had been Phoebe who cradled her, very much like this, as the sun set on her wedding day. Jordan couldn't seem to drag herself out of bed for at least twenty-four hours after leaving the church, and Phoebe had stayed right there with her. Jordan had allowed her to do what she wouldn't let her mother do: hug her while she cried, and assure her that everything was going to be all right.

Jordan hadn't believed her, of course.

But everything really was all right. She just hadn't realized it until right now. She had picked up the pieces of her old life and she had built a better life. And if she hadn't been so damned frightened of being hurt again, it might not have had to be such a lonely life, either.

Well, that was going to change.

When she got back to Georgetown, she was going to start living again. She was going to start taking time for herself, to do the things she used to enjoy. To bake, and garden, and maybe even travel.

What about dating? she asked herself. *What about Beau?*

Being with him, lying in his arms, had awakened needs Jordan had buried for years. Needs she had tried to forget even existed.

Thinking about those stolen moments together sparked renewed hunger inside her even now.

Was she anxious for Beau to get back only because she

was worried about him, and because she was frightened here alone with Spencer?

Or was it partly because she craved close contact with him: the kind of intimacy they had shared last night?

A little of both, she admitted to herself . . .

And then she heard it again.

A thump.

It had come from somewhere outside.

Perhaps just the wind. Or maybe a tree branch hitting the house, Jordan thought, as her heart began pounding.

But she didn't remember seeing any trees nearby.

Maybe it was just deck furniture, then. Maybe it blew off somebody's deck—or even one of ours—and was swept against the side of the house by the wind. . . .

As she tried to quell the wayward fear that had suddenly surged inside her, Jordan heard another sharp, sudden sound.

Breaking glass.

Spencer stirred in her lap as she jerked her head toward the sound—and the nearest set of French doors leading to a deck. . . .

Just in time to see a black-gloved hand reaching through the shattered glass panel to turn the knob from the inside.

Beau clenched the controls as the little plane bounced violently. He reminded himself that storm chasers flew into hurricanes all the time.

But they were experts.

And maybe they had a death wish.

He didn't.

Not anymore.

If he survived this, he would never again entertain thoughts of suicide. Not even for a moment. He had never wanted to live as badly as he did right now.

His chances of doing so had never been slimmer.

He was close to the Carolina coast, but he wasn't going to make it past. He wasn't going to make it to the airport on the Outer Banks. He wasn't going to make it to any airport. He had lost communication with the tower that had been trying to guide him in at Elizabeth City.

He had to put the plane down now—literally on a wing and a prayer.

All he could hope for, at best, was a long, deserted stretch of highway below. What were the chances of finding one? At night, in a storm?

He descended another thousand feet.

He was flying by instruments alone. He could see nothing. It was pitch black outside the windows.

Panic swelled within him.

He pushed it back.

Panic now would be deadly. If he managed to keep his wits about him, he might be able to survive a crash landing.

He cursed, wrestling with the wind for control of the plane.

He should be able to see lights below as he descended.

He went down another thousand feet.

Again, he nearly lost control of the plane.

Memories rushed back at him. He could feel the plane spiraling earthward, could taste the metallic flavor of fear in his mouth, could hear Jeanette's screams, Tyler's frightened whimpering . . .

No.

That was then. This was now. Now, he was alone. If

he lost control and this plane went down, it would carry only him with it.

And he wasn't going down without waging one hell of a battle.

He descended again. He was flying dangerously low. Coming in for a landing, if he could just find a place to land. He glimpsed occasional lights through the rain-shrouded mist. . . . Twin pairs of white lights. And red lights.

Head and taillights, he realized. There was a road down there.

But it wasn't deserted.

He cursed.

He couldn't put the plane down on a highway full of cars.

Not full *of cars,* he told himself. The lights were few and far between. This wasn't a well-traveled road. Maybe if he just . . .

No.

He couldn't take even the slightest chance of placing innocent men, women, and children in harm's way.

He descended lower, the little plane jarring and bumping along its turbulent course as he frantically sought a place to put it down.

He could now see a vast black patch below, devoid of lights. It was either a large empty field, or water. From here, it was impossible to see which.

Water . . .

He remembered the sickening smell of jet fuel mingled with the dank scent of the bayou.

The terror of surfacing alone with nothing but black sky overhead and black water all around.

The ominous, barely-there current signaling him that

a large gator or snake was moving silently through the murky water nearby.

The sickening knowledge that an encounter with either of those predatory bayou creatures would be nothing compared to facing the chilling, heart-wrenching certainty that everything that mattered to him was lost forever in the twisted metal wreckage mired in muddy water.

The plane jerked violently. He wrestled it lower.

That was then.

This is now.

This is only about me, alone in the plane—about my survival.

He would have to come down right here, and right now.

No, it isn't just about me.

If I die, Jordan and Spencer will be on their own.

If I make it, I can get to them. I can save them.

Once again, in a cruel twist of fate, the lives of a woman and child hung in the balance with his own.

He scanned the sprawling darkness below.

If it was a large, flat patch of farmland, he might survive.

If it was water . . .

Oh, hell. *Was* it water?

There was only one way to find out.

He braced himself for the answer.

The shadowy figure blew into the room in a swirling gust of wind and rain.

Seized by terror, Jordan felt a strangling scream lodge in her throat.

Spencer was slowly sitting up on her lap, rubbing his

eyes. She squeezed him tightly against her, warily staring at the intruder as the child squirmed, trying to pull free.

The man's clothing was black, as was the eye patch that left only one frighteningly dark eye to glare at Jordan and Spencer as he crossed swiftly toward them.

Jordan's thoughts whirled.

She had to do something.

She couldn't just sit here and wait for the stranger to attack.

But there was no escape. There was no way she could lift the struggling child into her arms and run. She wouldn't get anywhere.

"Jordan . . . what are you . . . *doing?*" Spencer tried to wrench himself from her viselike grasp, then twisted his head to look up at her face.

He followed her gaze . . .

And screamed.

"Shut up!" the intruder rasped.

"The pirate! Jordan!" Spencer buried his face against her shoulder, crying.

"On second thought, go ahead and scream," the man said. He was standing over them now, a murderous gleam in his eye. "Nobody's around to hear you."

Jordan found her voice. It emerged low, trembling, stricken with fear, and she fought to keep it level. "Who are you?"

"Didn't you hear the kid? I'm the pirate." He laughed, a sinister sound that sent icy fingers of dread down Jordan's spine.

"What do you want? Why are you here?"

"Just following orders, ma'am," he said mockingly. "The man I work for, he doesn't want the kid around spreading stories. He doesn't want the kid around at all."

Jordan's stomach lurched.

She saw the man reaching into his pocket as he continued talking.

"I tried to leave you out of it, lady. My boss, he doesn't like things to get more complicated than they have to. I tried to take care of business back at your place, like he wanted. But the kid had to wake up and you had to come running."

"You really were in my town house," Jordan said, dread mingling with a new emotion that sprang forth deep inside her.

It was fury.

Fury that this man had been prowling in her home in the dead of night.

That he had taken a defenseless little boy from his bed.

That he had come here to finish the diabolical deed.

She had to buy time.

To keep him talking.

If she did, maybe Beau would get here. . . .

Though the stranger kept his hand concealed at his side, she glimpsed the familiar dark metal object he had removed from his pocket. She knew it was a gun. She knew he was going to use it to kill both her and Spencer.

And even if Beau showed up any second now and caught him in the act, he couldn't save them. He would only be shot, too.

Spencer was whimpering, his face buried against her breast, soaking her with hot tears. His entire body was quaking in fear. She stroked his hair, wanting to soothe him with words, but afraid to trigger a violent response in the intruder.

Jordan knew she had to do something. Fast.

"How did you find us here?" she asked, as though it mattered.

He laughed again, as though she were a source of great amusement. "You can't be serious."

She was silent, waiting.

He had left the doors open.

Rain was blowing in, and the wind's gusts banged the doors repeatedly against the walls, rattling the panes. He didn't seem to notice.

"It wasn't difficult to find you," he said with a shrug. "You were careless. I was watching."

"You didn't follow us here." She tried not to let her eyes drift to the gun in his hand. Forced herself to hold his gaze with her own, to keep him focused, and talking.

"No," he agreed. "I didn't follow you. I didn't have to."

"Then how . . . ?"

"Mr. Beau Somerville."

The mere mention of Beau's name sent a ripple of hope through Jordan. He had promised to come back. She hadn't even known him for a week, and she didn't know much about him, but she was certain of one thing: he was a man who didn't make promises lightly. He would be back. She just had to keep herself and Spencer alive until he got here.

"Beau Somerville told you where we were?" Jordan asked, as though that were an actual possibility.

"Do you think he would do that?"

She forced a shrug, clinging tightly to the terrified little boy in her arms. "I have no idea. Did he?"

He greeted her question with one of his own. "Do you know how easy it is to trace a license plate, Ms. Curry?"

So that was it. He had seen Beau's SUV parked at the curb in front of her town house and traced the plate.

"The plate led me to a lease in the name of an architectural firm in Washington. Your friend should be more careful who he tells about his plans. One phone call to his business partner was all it took for me to find out where Mr. Somerville had gone off to."

Jordan searched for something to say—*anything*. She had to keep the conversation going, knowing that when it died, *they* would die.

"Beau's partner just came right out and told you where he was?" she asked.

The man nodded, looking pleased with himself. "He thought I was a potential client. I said I would only speak to Mr. Somerville himself . . . and here I am. But unfortunately for both of us, he isn't here, is he?"

"No. He isn't here."

"I didn't see the car." But he looked as though he didn't quite believe her. Almost as though he half-expected Beau to leap from a hiding place any second now and wrestle him to the ground.

Oh, Lord, if only that could happen.

"He isn't here," she repeated, hearing an edge creeping into her voice, and forcing it back.

She perceived the slightest movement of this hand holding the gun. Panic welled within her. How much time did they have? Was he just going to shoot them here and now? Would Beau come in and find their bloody bodies?

She knew what that would do to him.

The man had already lost his wife and child.

She and Spencer weren't his wife and child—not anything close to that—but Beau felt responsible for them.

He was already riddled with guilt over the accident that had stolen his loved ones. If he came back here and found an innocent child murdered, he would be destroyed. He cared deeply about Spencer.

And what about you, Jordan?

Does he care deeply about you as well?

She shoved the thought from her mind. Now was not the time to ponder what she might mean to Beau.

The wind gusted and the French doors banged against the walls again, punctuating the tense silence.

"How did you get up to that deck?" she asked the intruder.

"I climbed. With a rope. You didn't know how vulnerable you were, did you?"

I did know, she thought fiercely. *I knew, and there was nothing I could do about it. We were trapped here.*

"What about the storm?" she asked, fighting against her growing panic.

"What about it?"

"How will you get back to the mainland? You're trapped here, just as we are."

"That's my problem, isn't it?" he said, sounding impatient now. His one glittering ebony eye seemed to probe into her soul, seeing the stark trepidation that was rapidly overtaking her.

She looked away.

Her gaze fell on the coffee table.

On the flickering, dying flame of the candle.

And the pile of nautically themed books beside it.

And the sculpture.

The seagull sculpture that Beau had said weighed a ton.

Jordan shifted her weight on the couch, so imperceptibly that the intruder couldn't possibly notice. She slowly slipped her right arm out from beneath Spencer's weight, holding it poised.

Just in case.

Just in case there was the slightest chance that she could act.

"Get up," the pirate ordered suddenly. "Both of you. Get over there against the wall."

He gestured with the hand that was holding the gun.

This was it.

It was now or never.

As she stood, Jordan calculated the distance between her and the pirate, and how long it would take her to cover it.

"Go!" he barked.

Spencer whimpered as she set him on his feet. "What's he going to do?"

Jordan didn't answer.

Instead, she shouted out in surprise, as though she had glimpsed something shocking behind the pirate.

He instinctively whirled around to see what it was.

In one swift movement, she swooped over the statue, knowing before her hands closed on it that this might be her fatal mistake. Beau had said that it was heavy. She had no idea how heavy, or whether she could even budge it.

Fueled by adrenalin and sheer desperation, she hoisted the sculpture off the table.

"Spencer, run! Run! Downstairs, outside! Run!" she shrieked as she swung the massive hunk of stone toward her target.

It all happened at once.

The little boy obeyed, barreling toward the stairway.

The pirate cocked his gun and fired after him.

The bullet ricocheted off the railing.

Spencer disappeared from view, his feet pounding down the stairs as Jordan's makeshift weapon made contact with the stranger's skull.

It wasn't water.

It wasn't water!

It was a farmer's field, heavily planted with a low, leafy, green crop.

It was rough, but it wasn't even a crash landing. The plane remained intact.

Beau maintained control until the wheels touched down on the marshy surface. Even then, even as the plane careened across the field, it was nothing like what he'd expected. It was almost as though an invisible hand had reached out of the sky and guided him in.

He was alive.

Alive!

He hadn't even lost consciousness.

Exhilaration swiftly gave way to pain and urgency.

Wincing, he extracted himself from the cockpit. Suddenly, he ached all over. Weariness seeped into him, but he couldn't afford to give in to it. Couldn't even acknowledge it.

He had to get to Jordan and Spencer. There was no time to waste.

He began hiking across the field toward a distant house, barely conscious of the steady wind-driven rain that soaked him. He had to bend his head against the tremendous gusts, trudging through the mud that soon caked him from head to toe.

As he slipped and went down with a splash amid the muck, he realized he was still wearing his suit and his polished dress shoes.

The thought of being dressed like this in a place like this was so ludicrous that he would have laughed aloud if there were anything remotely funny about the situation. But he was consumed by worry.

He tried to calm his fears. Tried to tell himself that Spencer and Jordan were fine. That she would have known enough to call the police to evacuate them from the house.

But what if she didn't realize the mandatory evacuation was in effect?

Or that their portion of the Outer Banks was only fifteen feet above sea level—low enough to be completely underwater with the storm surge if the hurricane made landfall at high tide.

He had to get to her.

He could only take comfort in the knowledge that if he was having this much difficulty in locating her and Spencer, Gisonni's hit man wouldn't get there easily, either.

At last he reached a house, an unremarkable clapboard structure. Behind it was a small orchard of laden fruit trees and an old pickup truck beside a leaning barn. The windows of the house were dark, but he could see the eerie beam of a flashlight moving through a room. They must have lost power in the storm.

He knocked several times on the back screen door.

The howling wind seemed to drown out the sound.

Finally, he pushed the door open—it was unlocked—and poked his head inside. "Hello? Anybody home?"

He took several steps into a small kitchen with worn linoleum, laminate countertops, and ancient appliances.

"Stop right there," a voice said.

Across the shadowy room, an old man in a white

sleeveless T-shirt aimed a shotgun squarely at him. Beside him, and old woman in a short floral housecoat and curlers trained the flashlight's beam directly on Beau, momentarily blinding him.

He lifted his arms to shield himself—whether from the light or from a potential shotgun blast, he wasn't sure.

"Wait!" he called out. "I need help."

"You one of them looters they been talkin' about on TV?" the old man asked, eying him suspiciously.

"Looters?" Confused, Beau searched his mind for meaning. "You mean, people are looting because of the storm? Listen, I'm not a looter. I promise you."

"Then who are you? What're you doin' prowlin' around here at night in weather like this?"

"I just crashed my plane in your bean field."

"I don't have a bean field. I have tobacco."

Beau clenched his jaw. "Tobacco field, then. I just crashed my plane in it. And I'm going to pay you for the damage. But I need to use your phone to call for help."

He braced himself for the inevitable news that they didn't have a phone—or for them to toss him right back out the door again.

"Phone's over there on the wall," the old man said, lowering the gun and peering at him.

"Jake!" the old lady said fearfully.

"Shut up, Emmie. He's not lyin'. Those lights we saw and that sound we heard musta' been his plane landin' over in the field. I told you it wasn't one of them UFOs."

Again, Beau thought that if the circumstances had been different, he might be moved to laugh. But all he did was cross purposefully to the phone on the wall.

"You get hurt in that crash?" Jake's wife asked him.

"No, I'm fine." He lifted the receiver, praying for a dial tone.

There was one.

"Thank you," he added breathlessly, deliriously grateful for the dial tone and for Jake's wife's concern.

"Who ya calling?" the old man asked.

He paused. The truth was, he had no idea whom to call.

"Nine-one-one," he decided, and began dialing.

Jordan stared in horrified relief at the man whose body lay crumpled at her feet.

Blood trickled from a jagged split in his forehead, oozing down over his brow and soaking the black eye patch.

The sculpture had been flung from her grasp when she hit him, and it had shattered into a zillion pieces that scattered wildly on the tile floor.

For a moment, she could only take in the scene.

Then, hearing a door banging on the first floor, she realized what had happened and burst into action.

"Spencer!" she called, rushing toward the stairway. "Spencer! Come back!"

She started down the steps, knowing that she had to stop him.

She couldn't let him go out into the stormy darkness alone. The scenario that had seemed like Spencer's only salvation moments earlier filled her with sick dread now that she had taken care of the more imminent threat.

As Jordan hit the second step, her foot caught on something—a chunk of the sculpture. She struggled to keep her balance, grasping for the railing.

Her arms flailed helplessly, windmilling at her sides before she pitched forward.

She was falling . . .

Falling . . .

She landed in a heap at the landing several steps down, her body exploding in pain as her right foot twisted at an impossible angle beneath her.

Fighting back the tears of frustration and anguish, she pulled herself to her feet, grasping the rail.

"Spencer!" she bellowed again.

She had to get downstairs.

It was pure agony to put her weight on her right foot. She hobbled slowly, clutching the railing, screaming the child's name.

It took far too long for her to reach the second floor, cross the hallway, and start down the next flight of stairs.

"Spencer!" she screamed, knowing it was futile. He couldn't possibly hear her from outside.

Hot tears streamed unchecked down her cheeks.

Oh, Lord, what had she done?

On the first floor at last, she hopped to the door and flung it open. She was greeted by buckets of rain and a wind gust so violent it nearly ripped the door from its hinges.

"Spencer!" she shrieked into the night.

"Spencer! You can come back now! It's safe! It's okay! Spencer!"

The only reply was the fierce howling of the hurricane gale.

Chapter Twelve

Wearing a bright orange life vest, Beau clung to the seat beneath him as the Coast Guard search-and-rescue cutter lurched wildly on the black, roiling waters of the Currituck Sound. The channel between the mainland and the Outer Banks was just a few miles wide at this point, and famously shallow. Somehow, that knowledge did little to dispel the sensation of being tossed on a violent, open sea.

Landing the small plane in a farmer's tobacco field was like an amusement-park ride compared to this, Beau thought, as a towering, foaming wave crested and broke inches from where he sat, spraying him with icy water.

He had literally been soaked to the bone for hours now. Yet he paid little heed to the chill and discomfort. What mattered now was getting to Jordan.

There was no phone service. He had tried calling her, to no avail.

According to the local police, most of the northern Outer Banks region was already flooded and without power or telephone service. Those who hadn't been evacuated when the governor's orders came through earlier were now being taken out on Coast Guard boats and helicopters, since the Wright Memorial Bridge, Currituck Sound's lone crossing, had long since become impassable.

Beau had fought long and hard to be allowed to accompany this boat on its run to locate Jordan and Spencer. He'd claimed that it was his family stranded out there. Just saying the words "wife and son" had been heart-wrenching enough to bring real tears to his eyes. Seeing them, the boat's captain relented.

"All right. You can come aboard," he had said. "I have a wife and son myself, and if they were stranded out there, you can bet I'd want to be the one to get them out. Besides, you know exactly where we can find them."

Now Beau watched the seasoned sailor fighting to control the small boat in the angry sea, much as he himself had wrestled with the plane earlier. When this was all over, he knew there would be hell to pay for that wreck, between the charter company whose plane he had destroyed and the farmer whose crop he had damaged. It seemed the old man would probably have been happier if Beau had been a looter he could heroically hand over to the county sheriff's department, but that was because he didn't recognize the Somerville name or the extent of the money behind it. Beau figured that when and if the crash made the local papers and the farmer figured out who he was, he'd be looking at a hastily filed lawsuit.

It had taken longer than he'd expected for the police

to pick him up after he called 911. Plane crash or not, they had more on their hands than they could handle tonight. The roads away from the coast were clogged with evacuees, there were widespread power outages and accidents galore, and businesses really were being looted in urban areas.

They wanted to bring Beau to the local hospital to be checked out, but he insisted he was fine and that it was his "family" that he was worried about. In no time, he was delivered to the water's edge, where the Coast Guard rescue operations were underway.

And here he was.

It was hard to believe that this wasn't even the brunt of the storm, but only the leading edge. He had been through many a hurricane growing up on the Gulf Coast of Louisiana, but always from the warm, dry safety of home—or a comfortable hotel on the few occasions they had been evacuated away from the coast.

Never had he faced the raw elements or witnessed nature's fury as he had tonight.

Looking up, blinking against the spray and the wind, he saw that the cutter had almost reached land—or what was left of it.

Even from here, Beau could see buildings rising from the stormy sea, seemingly floating in it.

He told himself that even if the first floor—or more— had flooded in his rental house, Jordan and Spencer would be safe. He reminded himself that his architect's eye had discerned that the place was sturdily built. Surely it must have withstood other storms of this intensity.

But the truth was, he didn't know that for certain.

As renewed fear and self-doubt filled him, he decided that for all he knew, the house was newly built and flimsy as a cardboard box.

The cutter reached the bay and headed north, hugging the partially submerged shore. He saw the captain scanning the houses for landmarks.

Beau had pointed out the location of the house on a map for the captain before leaving shore. The house faced the ocean side of the peninsula, but it was less than half a mile wide in that spot. The plan was that the boat would pull in on the Sound side and they would reach the house on foot from there.

"This is as far as we can go with the boat," one of the men shouted to him as the engines idled. "The house should be right in there. Stay here with the Captain and we'll go in for them."

"I'm coming too!" Beau shouted, standing. He nearly toppled over as the boat pitched beneath him, but managed to keep his balance.

They looked at each other, and then dubiously at the angry sea.

"I'm coming," Beau repeated, tightening the straps on his life vest and joining them at the rail.

Hang in there, Jordan. Be brave, Spencer. I'm on my way.

Huddled on the stairway above the rapidly flooding first floor, Jordan prayed as she had never prayed before.

She prayed for Spencer, out there in the storm.

She prayed for Beau, wherever he was.

She prayed that the monster upstairs wouldn't suddenly regain consciousness and come after her like Glenn Close rising from the bathtub at the end of *Fatal Attraction*. If he did, she could at least rest assured that he couldn't shoot her. She had crawled back up the stairs and taken his gun.

She had no idea whether she could actually use it,

but she had seen enough movies to have a basic understanding of how it worked. She had even practiced cocking the weapon, but was afraid to try firing it.

She would only use it if she had to. In self-defense.

"Oh, Spencer, come back," she pleaded softly, her voice hoarse from screaming his name above the wind.

If it weren't for her ankle, she would be out there despite the rising water, looking for Spencer. But she had tried—several times now—and couldn't get far hopping. Her foot was enormously swollen and so tender that she was convinced it was broken.

She had even tried dragging herself through the water on her hands and knees, succeeding only in getting soaked and filthy before retreating to the house, where despair washed over her.

She had cried so many tears that her eyes were hot and raw, and her cheeks stung from wiping at them with the soaked sleeve of her T-shirt.

She had never felt so miserable and alone in her life.

What now?

Was this how she was going to die? Would the water keep coming in, forcing her to climb higher and higher on the stairway until it swept her away?

Would she drown?

The mere thought of that sent a violent trembling through her.

She thought about Beau's wife and son. They had drowned.

He had to live with that—live with knowing what their last moments must have been like as the plane went down and the bayou closed in and they struggled for air, finding nothing but water.

No. Don't think about that. You can't. It isn't helping

anything, she warned herself, brushing away a fresh flood of hot tears.

Suddenly, she thought she heard something.

Voices.

She thought she heard voices.

Oh, Lord. She must be hallucinating. Was she that far gone?

"Jordan!"

There it was: her name, carried to her on the screaming wind.

The voice was achingly familiar.

You're only hearing it because you want to hear it, she told herself. *He's not really out there. He's not—*

"Jordan? Spencer?"

The door burst open directly below her.

Beau's face peered inside, framed by a bright orange life jacket.

At first he didn't see her.

Not until she choked his name on a sob.

His face lit up when he spotted her there on the stairs.

"My God! Jordan! Are you all right?"

He looks like hell, she thought incredulously. He was caked in mud, filthy, his clothing tattered. Yet no sight had ever been more heavenly than seeing him there.

He took the stairs two at a time as two other men, wearing Coast Guard uniforms, appeared below.

"Jordan," he said, pulling her into his arms, holding her tightly against him, "where's Spenc—"

Beau's voice faded abruptly as he saw the gun clenched in her hand.

His eyes met hers.

She opened her mouth to speak, but nothing came out.

"Where's Spencer, Jordan?" Beau asked in a low voice laced with apprehension. "Where is he?"

"Beau," she choked out, "he's lost out there somewhere."

"Lost?" He looked bewildered. Again, he glanced at the gun. "Lost, but not . . . ?"

"He found us, Beau. The pirate . . ."

"No . . ."

"Yes. He's here."

"Here?" he echoed in shock, looking around wildly. "But—"

The story spilled out of her then. All of it. She spoke in a rush, aware of the Coast Guard men listening in wary confusion, their gazes fixed on the gun she still held in her trembling hands.

"Give that to me," Beau said gently when she had finished.

She did, and he immediately turned it over to the young officers. "I'll explain what this is about in more detail," he promised them, already headed down the stairs for the door again. "But first we have to find a little boy who's wandering out there alone."

Jordan sagged against the step in relief. Beau was here. Beau would help. He would take care of everything.

"I knew you'd come back," she said softly, gratefully. "I knew you would."

Beau stopped, his foot on the bottom step. For a moment, her words had struck him motionless. Then he turned to look up at her.

"I'll find him, Jordan," he promised, determination in his eyes.

* * *

"Spencer! Spencer!"

Beau knew his voice had as much chance of being heard as a whisper in a packed stadium, yet he kept calling the little boy's name. Kept praying that he might hear an answering shout.

So far, he hadn't.

But he refused to give up hope.

The sea was a maelstrom of foaming whitecaps now, the storm surge at its height. Beau waded through waist-deep water on what had once been a road, surveying structures that had once been majestic beachfront homes.

They would be again, he supposed, if they remained standing.

But for now, rising eerily from the flooded landscape, they were like big, deserted ships bobbing on a remote stretch of ocean. It was impossible to believe that only two days ago, this place had been a serene seaside resort.

Beau kept the other Coast Guard officer, Mike, in sight. He was easy to spot in his orange life vest. They were combing the submerged houses, one by one, for the missing child.

Beau had felt sick inside when Jordan told him Spencer was out in the storm. He didn't even know if the little guy had learned to swim.

He had scoured every hopelessly soggy house within a reasonable range, and there had been no sign of Spencer. He had checked decks, ledges, cars—everything short of actually breaking into the houses.

"What do you think?" Mike called above the wind.

"We've got to keep looking," Beau called back. "He's got to be somewhere."

Yes.

Assuming that the worst hadn't happened—and Beau refused the even consider that notion—then yes, Spencer had to be somewhere.

Somewhere nearby.

Somewhere dry.

Somewhere . . .

"I think I know where he might be!" Beau suddenly shouted.

Jordan lay on the couch, her foot wrapped and elevated.

Rhett, the Coast Guard officer who had stayed behind with her, still stood guard over the pirate, whose inert body lay where it had fallen earlier. He was alive, but out cold. The officer had radioed for help, then settled in to wait with Jordan.

"Do you want more ice for your foot?" he asked.

Jordan shook her head, mute.

Every bit of energy she possessed was focused on the search. It had been a long time since Beau disappeared out into the night again. Too long.

The storm seemed to be picking up in intensity.

Spencer was out there somewhere.

So was Beau.

Jordan's foot throbbed and her head ached and she felt weak, almost dizzy from lack of food and sleep.

But none of that mattered.

Beau would find Spencer, she told herself.

After all, he had promised.

A glimmer of doubt pressed into her consciousness, despite her effort to concentrate on positive thoughts only.

Beau shouldn't go around making promises he can't keep, she thought, irrational anger welling within her.

But it wasn't Beau's fault that Spencer was out there. It was hers.

No. You were trying to save Spencer, not doom him. You only did what you thought was best, Jordan.

If only she hadn't fallen on the stairs.

If only she had been able to catch up with the fleeing little boy before he vanished into the tempestuous night.

"Are you okay?" Rhett asked her.

She nodded, afraid that if she tried to speak, her voice would break. Yet she was all cried out. She couldn't believe that there were any more tears left inside her.

So she closed her eyes and went back to praying.

Praying to Phoebe, wherever she was.

You've got to watch over him, Phoebe, she thought fervently. *You've got to keep him safe until Beau can find him and bring him back to me. And then I swear—I swear—I'll never let anything happen to him again.*

She cried out and jerked her head around at a sudden crashing sound behind her.

To her horror, she saw that the Coast Guard officer lay slumped on the floor.

Standing over him was the pirate, his face caked with dried blood, a gleam of hatred in his lone eye—and his menacing half-gaze fixed on Jordan.

Scrambling to the top of the dune, Beau said a silent prayer that this nightmare was about to end.

Spencer had to be here.

He had to be.

If he isn't, Beau thought grimly, *there's no place else. We'll have to give up.* . . .

Give up?

No, he thought fiercely, clawing his way toward the soggy sand pinnacle, struggling against the numbing exhaustion. He wouldn't give up. Not the way he had before, with Jeanette and Tyler.

This time, he wouldn't give up until he knew for certain that there was no hope.

He had reached the top.

He could see over the dune.

At first, realizing the beach was no longer there, he was disoriented. There was nothing but blue-black, rushing water wherever he looked.

Then he saw it, rising from the edge of the sea like a volcanic island.

The rock.

And he saw him.

The child.

Spencer.

Relief swept over him, even as an enormous wave swept over the rock.

"Spencer!" Beau bellowed, his heart lurching as he watched the little boy desperately grasping for a hold on his massive granite refuge.

Spencer didn't hear him. The power of the sea drowned out Beau's voice.

He stared, his heart in his mouth, praying harder than he had ever prayed before. For a moment, his view was obscured by the water.

He squeezed his eyes closed.

When he opened them again, the wave had ebbed.

Spencer was still there.

And Beau understood in that instant that this wasn't the first wave that had threatened Spencer's life—or the first time he had triumphed, holding his territory.

Pride swelled within him to meld with the sheer terror of the little boy's predicament.

Spencer had been out here too long. He was soaked, weary, rapidly reaching his limit. The next wave might be the last for him. There was no time to waste.

Beau turned to Mike, who was scrambling up the dune behind him.

"He's there!" he shouted over the hurricane's roar. "We have to get him now, before he's swept out."

He swallowed hard over a sudden lump in his throat and raised his voice to shout, "Hang on, Spencer! I'm coming! You're going to be all right, fella!"

"Where the hell is the kid?"

The pirate was moving slowly but purposefully toward Jordan.

She stared at him in mute defiance, grateful that Spencer was anywhere other than here.

"Where's the kid?" he demanded again, nearly stumbling over a low table.

He was obviously in pain, perhaps a bit disoriented.

Yet that didn't help her.

Her foot was so swollen and painful that she knew her own movements, should she try to flee, would be even more sluggish than his.

Yet she had to try. She couldn't just lie here and let him close in on her like a black bear lumbering ominously toward a wounded kitten.

Besides, he no longer had the gun—a fact he might not be aware of.

Not that she had it, either. Rhett had said he was going to put it somewhere safe, and she had no idea where. Thankfully, neither did the pirate.

Jordan forced herself to meet his violent gaze as she pulled herself to her feet. The pain was intense, but her instinct for self-preservation was even sharper. She was going to get away from this madman—or die trying.

"You're not going anywhere," he snarled, upon her more quickly than she had thought possible. He was reaching for her before she could move.

She ducked, wrenching herself from his grasp.

He grabbed her again.

She struggled. She kicked, bit, scratched, screamed, all to no avail. She found herself being dragged across the room.

Yet she realized, first with incredulity and then with panic, that he wasn't taking her toward the stairs. He was heading to the French doors that led to the nearest deck.

The one overlooking the turbulent sea, whose waters now covered the ground three stories below.

Beau held his breath as he dove into the choppy sea, the rope around his chest providing little reassurance.

The rope was anchored to a nearby post, and Mike stood by, ready to assist if he got into trouble. Mike had volunteered to be the one to swim over to the rock to get Spencer, but Beau insisted. The little boy was incredibly shaken, probably in shock. After what he had been through with the pirate, there was no telling what he might do if he saw a stranger swimming toward him.

He still hadn't seen or heard Beau.

He was facing the black horizon as he huddled on the rock, soaked and shivering, his knees pulled up to his chest. He looked as bedraggled and forlorn as Jordan had when Beau spotted her on the stairway at the house.

The sight of Spencer, and the knowledge that his intervention was sorely needed, tugged on Beau's heart now as it had before, with Jordan.

He couldn't let anything happen to either of them.

A wave washed over his head the moment he surfaced, and he emerged sputtering, with a bellyful of burning saltwater.

He battled the churning sea, determined to get to Spencer as wave after wave pounded the rock.

Exhausted, he could hear Mike's shouts of encouragement as he swam within reach. The wind seemed to have died down, if only slightly. Beau realized that Spencer would hear him now, too, if he called out.

He opened his mouth to shout the child's name just as another skyscraper of a wave bore down on the rock.

It swept over Beau as well, tossing him upside-down and dashing his skull against the unforgiving granite. Miraculously, he recovered, surfacing for air as a searing pain in his head nearly blinded him.

"Spencer!" he shouted, his voice hoarse with strain and acrid salt water. "Spencer, hang on! I'm going to get you down from there!"

There was no reply.

Beau looked up at the rock and saw that it was empty.

A deluge of rain soaked Jordan as the pirate shoved her out onto the deck. The painted wooden planks were slippery beneath her bare feet. She lost her balance and toppled toward the floor, but he reached down and yanked her upright again.

"You're done," he lashed at her, his face a twisted mask of rage. "This is it, you understand? And when I'm through with you, it's the kid's turn."

"Try and find him," she retorted, breathless with fury.

"Believe me, I will."

Not before Beau does, she thought vehemently, clenching her teeth as he slammed her body against the wooden railing.

As a new pain exploded within her and his rough hands closed over her upper arms, she realized his intent.

And there was nobody to stop him.

"Beau!" Jordan heard herself screech as the pirate bent her upper body backward over the rail, high above the torrent of charcoal-colored water. "Beau!"

Where was he?

Where was Spencer?

Now only one thing was certain: if Beau didn't appear to rescue her in the next split second, she would be flung over the railing to her death.

For a few long, desolate moments, Beau was alone in the stormy sea.

He opened his mouth and howled Spencer's name, the effort torturing his raw throat and his strained lungs.

Then, miracle of miracles, he saw something bob up only yards away.

"There he is!" Mike shouted behind him.

Stunned, elated, Beau frantically paddled toward the child.

Spencer was struggling in the water, thrashing about, his arms flailing helplessly, making it clear that he couldn't swim.

"Keep your head up, Spencer!" Beau screamed, only

to see the little boy plunge from sight beneath another fierce wave.

"No! Spencer!"

Beau dove for the spot where Spencer had disappeared. His arms were outstretched, his searching hands encountering nothing but water.

It was just like before.

Anguish ripped through him as he surfaced only long enough to gulp another breath before diving again.

He went deeper this time, swinging his arms in wide arcs from front to side, praying as fervently as he had on that other stormy night.

Then, his prayers hadn't been answered.

Tonight, they were.

Just as his breath ran out and he was rising toward the surface again, Beau's hand ran into something soft . . .

Squirming . . .

Alive.

"Beau!" Jordan shrieked. "Beau! Help!"

But he wasn't here.

He wasn't coming.

He couldn't save her.

Jordan struggled against the pirate's viselike grip, knowing that this time, she could only rely on herself. The battle was hopelessly mismatched, and the pirate had the upper hand. She couldn't possibly overpower him.

She was bent backward over the railing, his evil face looming above her.

Looking into the black depths of his gaze, she thought about how this monster had killed Phoebe. Her best friend. Phoebe, who had everything to live for, had been murdered in cold blood, along with her husband, leaving their only son an orphan.

Jordan thought about what would happen if the pirate got his hands on Spencer. How he would slaughter an innocent, terrified child to settle some score for some maniac.

There was only one way to make sure that didn't happen.

A fresh burst of fury-fueled adrenalin pumped through Jordan's depleted veins. With a grunt of exertion and a burst of superhuman strength, she pushed upward, forward, with all her might.

Caught off guard, the pirate wobbled . . .

Loosened his grip . . .

Lost his balance and sprawled on top of Jordan.

She heard a sharp crack.

For an instant, she was convinced it was gunfire.

Then she felt the railing beginning to give way beneath their combined weight.

Time seemed to slow down so that every second felt like a minute.

She got hold of her attacker and pushed down on his body, using it as leverage to push herself forward.

She felt the planks of the deck firm beneath her feet once again.

Felt the pirate's hands clawing at her.

Heard the splintering sound beneath him.

Then, just as she wrenched herself free, it was over.

The railing broke, hurtling the pirate over the edge in a three-story free fall.

And then, for Jordan, everything went black.

* * *

Clutching the water-logged child in his arms, Beau allowed Mike to haul them both to safety with the rope.

As he staggered onto the dune with Spencer cradled against his chest, Beau could hear the little boy choking and gasping for air. It was the sweetest sound he had ever known. Spencer was alive.

"You saved him, Beau!" Mike threw an arm around him. "I don't know how you did it."

"I don't either," Beau murmured, stroking Spencer's soaked hair.

Looking skyward, he muttered silent thanks as tears mingled with the salt water streaming down his face.

"Jordan?"

Dazed, she opened her eyes.

Had somebody called her name?

She was lying on the deck.

Rain was falling.

It all came back to her in a rush.

The pirate.

Beau going after Spencer.

The storm . . .

The storm?

As Jordan turned her head, wincing from the terrible throbbing above one ear where she must have hit it on the deck, she realized that something was different.

There was a strange lull in the wind.

How long had she been unconscious?

She started to sit up.

Somebody stopped her, touching her face.

"Jordan, take it easy."

She realized that it was Beau, hovering over her, caressing her cheek.

Again she tried to turn her head, needing to see him. She moaned as the pain sliced through her skull once more.

"Shh," Beau said, "it'll be all right."

"Spencer?" she managed to ask. "Is he . . . ?"

"He's fine."

Those two words flooded her with relief. Spencer was fine. Beau had promised that he would save Spencer, and he had.

Gratitude surged through Jordan. She struggled to find the words to tell him, but a deep-seated numbness had taken hold.

All she managed was, "Where . . . ?"

Beau knew what she meant. "He's inside. There's a cut on his arm that Mike's bandaging for him—not a deep cut, so don't worry—and then we have to get out of here before the back end of the storm swings through."

Out of here? She didn't want to get out of here. She didn't want to go anywhere. All she wanted was to lie here forever in the gentle rain with Beau's fingertips stroking her.

"I'll carry you," Beau said softly, and she felt him lifting her into his arms. Then she could see his face— his beautiful face—looking down at her with an expression she had never seen there before. She had never seen it on anyone.

He carried her across the deck, away from the broken railing where the pirate had fallen. Did Beau know what had happened? She tried to tell him, but he shushed her.

"It's okay," he said. "We know. His body washed up."

"What about Rhett?"

"He's okay. Everybody's going to be okay, Jordan. Including you."

"Thanks to you."

"No, thanks to you," he said. "I can't stand thinking about you out here with him. He was trying to push you over, wasn't he?"

She nodded. Again, the blinding pain in her skull. Her eyelids fluttered, wanted to close, but she forced them to stay open. She wanted to look at Beau, as long as he was looking at her and wearing that expression.

Balancing her in one arm as though she weighed no more than Spencer, he reached for one of the French doors leading back to the living room.

"We have to go," he said again, opening it. "Before the wind kicks up again."

"Maybe the worst of it is over," she said hopefully as he carried her inside.

"It isn't, Jordan," he told her grimly. "This is just the eye of the storm. The worst is yet to come."

Chapter Thirteen

"Ms. Curry?"

Jordan looked up from the lukewarm Styrofoam cup of coffee she was clutching in both hands. A balding middle-aged man in an ill-fitting suit stood in the doorway.

"I'm Detective Rodgers with the Philadelphia police. I've been working on the Averill case."

He looked like every police detective she'd ever seen on television, from his wardrobe to his no-nonsense demeanor as he strode toward her.

She set her coffee on the scarred table in front of her and rose slightly to shake the detective's hand before sinking once again to the cheap metal folding chair. It groaned beneath her weight. This police station in rural Dapple Cove, North Carolina wasn't exactly the lap of luxury—not that Jordan would expect it to be.

But this was where the Coast Guard had brought them

after the rescue. There was a hospital here. And a low-budget hotel, which happened to have a couple of empty rooms, once the storm had passed and evacuees started returning to their coastal homes.

Here it was, two days after Agatha had blown out to sea, and all Jordan wanted was to go home to Georgetown, collapse in her bed, and sleep for a week.

But that couldn't happen for at least a few more hours. Her flight out of here wasn't until later this afternoon, and before she could go back to the hotel, check out, and leave for the airport, she had to meet with this man who had flown all the way down from Philly to discuss the case with her.

"I know you've been through the wringer," the detective said, flashing her a sympathetic look.

She smiled grimly. " 'The wringer' doesn't even begin to describe it, Detective."

"I'm sorry about the loss of your friend."

Phoebe.

A lump rose in her throat. She nodded.

"I'm sorry, but I have to ask you some questions," the detective said.

"I understand. It's all right. I'll answer what I can."

And she did. They spoke for well over an hour, with Jordan recounting every detail she could possibly remember about what had happened from the moment Phoebe showed up on her doorstep last week.

Finally, Detective Rodgers leaned back in his chair and said, "I just want you to know that we've managed to get Gisonni in custody on an unrelated charge, but we're going to get him for this, Ms. Curry. One of his associates is willing to testify that Gisonni hired that hit man to go after your friends, and after you and the kid."

Jordan's head throbbed where she had hit it on the deck the other night. She knew that she still had a faint purplish-green bruise on one temple, and didn't even have any makeup to cover it up.

The Coast Guard hadn't allowed them time to gather their belongings from the beach house before they fled during the eye of the storm. All she had thought to bring was her purse containing her keys and her wallet containing her identification, cash, and credit cards. At least she had been able to buy a few articles of clothing and some toiletries at the local five-and-dime, to get her through these few days. Makeup wasn't among the necessities.

But when she got back home, she would cover the bruise. She didn't want to see it every time she looked into a mirror for the next few days. It made her think of the ugly scene on the deck.

She told herself that she should be glad the pirate was dead. That it was either him, or her and Spencer. That he deserved his violent end.

But the truth was, she couldn't seem to shake the chill that came with knowing a man had died right in front of her. And *because* of her. She had sent him over that railing to his death. Yes, it was self-defense. But she had the feeling that she wouldn't soon recover from the knowledge that she had caused somebody's demise.

Nor would she feel completely safe again, even with the hit man out of the picture.

"Why would anyone testify against Gisonni?" Jordan asked wearily, sipping her coffee, now grown cold. "Especially one of his own associates?"

"Trust me, Ms. Curry, this guy's not doing it because he's looking for a good citizenship award. He knows he's going down on a couple of other charges—racketeering, for one—unless he testifies against Gisonni."

"But what's going to stop Gisonni from hiring another hit man to go after him?" she asked dubiously. The detective was making it sound too easy.

"Witness Protection," the detective said simply. "Look, the point is, you took care of Calacci for us."

She closed her eyes briefly. Calacci, she now knew, was the name of the pirate. She didn't want to know his name, though. She didn't want to make him more human when she thought of him.

"Now," the detective said, "we're going to take care of Gisonni for you. And for the kid. Cute kid," he added, a bit gruffly. "I talked to him a little while ago."

"How is he?" Jordan asked, sitting up straight in her chair.

She hadn't seen Spencer since last night, when Phoebe's brother, Curt, had arrived at the hotel. The little boy had been sleeping when Curt carried him off down the hall to his own room.

"The kid's doing all right," Detective Rodgers said. "I guess he's been crying since his uncle told him this morning about his parents, but what do you expect? He'll get through it. We've got a social worker over there at the hotel with them to help smooth things over."

A social worker.

A stranger.

Spencer knew now about Phoebe and Reno. He was crying.

Jordan's heart twisted. She was overcome by nausea— and an urgent need to get to Spencer, to bring him comfort somehow.

But Curt is there, Jordan reminded herself. *Curt is Spencer's uncle. He's with family now, where he belongs.*

"Did Spencer tell you anything helpful about the encounter he and his mom had with Calacci?" Jordan asked.

"Everything that kid said was helpful, Ms. Curry. Like I said, cute kid. Damn shame about his parents."

Tears stung Jordan's eyes. She merely nodded.

"If it weren't for you and Beau Somerville, that kid would be dead," Detective Rodgers said bluntly.

Jordan looked up.

Beau Somerville.

"Have you spoken to Beau?" she asked, trying not to appear too eager for news of him. She hadn't seen him since they had come back to the mainland, where all three of them had been hospitalized overnight. By the time she and Spencer were reunited and released, Beau was gone.

"We haven't interviewed him yet, but we expect to at some point today. He's been up in Richmond, trying to straighten things out with the charter airline and his attorneys. They've already filed a lawsuit. So has that farmer whose field he crashed into."

"The farmer is suing Beau?" she echoed in disbelief. The airline, she could understand, since Beau had filed a bogus flight plan. But the farmer?

The detective nodded in disgust. "Apparently, it caused them mental anguish, having him show up at their house in the middle of the storm."

"That's ridiculous!"

"What do you expect? He's a Somerville. That's what happens."

A Somerville?

Jordan frowned. "What do you mean?"

The detective raised a quizzical brow. "How well do you know Somerville, Ms. Curry?"

Well enough to have fallen head over heels for him.

"Fairly well," she said, feeling her cheeks grow hot at the memory of just how well she had gotten to know Beau during that fiery, passionate interlude at the beach house.

"But you don't know who he is?"

"What do you mean?" Jordan asked again.

The detective steepled his fingers beneath his chin and looked at her. "Beau Somerville is one of the richest men in the South, Ms. Curry. His family is worth a fortune—and you must be one of the few people who doesn't know that."

"I'm not from the South," she murmured, shaking her head.

She had known Beau was wealthy. But she'd had no idea that his name alone was enough to inspire get-rich-quick schemes in farmers.

Andrea MacDuff had tried to tell her that, she realized. But it hadn't sunk in, because Jordan simply hadn't been interested in dating Beau—or anyone else. She hadn't realized what was missing from her life until after she met him.

And now he was gone.

So was Spencer.

But her life was waiting.

She swallowed hard, trying to muster enthusiasm for going home.

But suddenly, she only wanted to cry.

"Are you all right, Ms. Curry?" the detective asked in the awkward tone of a man who was unaccustomed to drying tears.

"No. But I will be," she said firmly, as much to him as to herself.

Seated at the wheel of his SUV, Beau watched Jordan come out of the small clapboard police station. She stopped to toss a white Styrofoam cup into a wire trash basket, then walked slowly, head bent, as she headed down the quiet, leafy main street of Dapple Cove.

There were few people about on this gray, muggy morning. The Outer Banks had suffered the brunt of the storm, but the Carolina coastline had been ravaged as well. Everywhere you looked, there was evidence of water damage, and downed branches still littered the streets.

Beau hesitated, watching Jordan walk away. He wondered if he should just let her go. He knew she was flying out of here this afternoon. He could always look her up when he got back to D.C. . . .

For what? To tell her it was nice knowing her and wish her well?

Somehow, that seemed ridiculous.

But what did one say after all they'd been through together? It wasn't as though he expected their relationship to continue when they got back to the city. She had her life there, and he had his. When they met last week he wasn't looking for . . .

For what?

For love?

Of course not.

And he didn't *love* her. What had happened between them had transpired because of extraordinary circumstances.

Circumstances that no longer existed.

He should remember why he was here. He should go into that police station and talk to the detective who had summoned him here.

He cast one last look at Jordan.

There was something about her. . . .

He couldn't let her go.

Not without saying good-bye, at least. And finding out how Spencer was. The little boy hadn't been far from his thoughts.

He got out of the car abruptly, quickly striding after her.

"Jordan!" he called when he was close enough.

She looked up. He watched an expression of surprise cross her features. Pleasant surprise. She was glad to see him, he realized, hurrying his pace, feeling almost giddy.

When he reached her, it seemed perfectly natural to hug her. He intended it as a friendly hug, but it was more than that from the moment he felt her in his arms and breathed her heavenly, familiar scent.

"Honeysuckle," he murmured, his heart beating faster.

"What?" She pulled back and looked up at him, puzzled.

"You smell like honeysuckle. I've noticed it before. It's your shampoo."

"I used the hotel's sample packet of shampoo," she said with a faint smile. "It's not my usual brand."

"It's not?" He pondered the fact that she must just smell that incredible naturally. He fought the urge to bury his face in her neck and inhale, reluctantly releasing her from his embrace instead.

"I thought you were in Richmond," she said.

"I was. Since yesterday morning, trying to take care

of a few issues with the charter company." He didn't want to get into the lawsuit.

Now that he was here by her side, he realized that it was enough just to be with her. He would worry about everything else later. The detective, the airplane, the farmer—everything.

"Did you get things straightened out?"

"I will."

"Good." She looked as though she wanted to say something else, but didn't.

Realizing how easily she could walk away, Beau was suddenly seized by the need to prolong his time with her.

He looked around for inspiration. "Do you want to get something to eat?" he asked, spotting a diner a few doors down the street.

She hesitated, then nodded. "I guess I just realized I'm hungry."

"Great. So am I."

They began walking toward the diner.

"How did you know where to find me, Beau?"

"Lucky guess."

She didn't look as though she bought that.

And truth be told, he hadn't come here looking for her. Finding her had merely been a pleasant surprise. He had left for Richmond without saying good-bye, and thoughts of her had pervaded his time there. Only because he was worried about her, of course. Or so he had repeatedly told himself.

"Actually, I got a message at the hotel from a Detective Rodgers," he admitted. "He said he would be speaking with you here today, and that he needs to talk to me as well. I had just pulled up in front of the police station when I saw you come out."

"That's what I figured." They had reached the diner's entrance, but she hesitated on the step. "Do you think you should go back there and talk to him now?"

He shook his head. "He can wait. I'd rather talk to you first. I know you have a plane to catch."

"How about you? When are you going back home?"

"Tomorrow." He had a meeting this evening with the farmer's lawyer. He wasn't looking forward to it any more than he had been looking forward to the ordeal in Richmond, but it had to be done. Now that they had connected him with Somerville Industries, they fully intended to bleed him dry, as did the plane charter company.

Beau's father's attorney, Anton Parr, had flown from Baton Rouge to Richmond to represent him yesterday and was due to arrive in North Carolina in time for tonight's appointment. Parr wanted to fight both cases—especially the farmer's outrageous demand for excessive damages—but Beau intended to settle.

The sooner he could put all of this behind him and get back to his life, the better.

Even if "all of this" includes Jordan? he asked himself, holding the door open for her as they stepped into the diner.

Yes, he decided firmly. He had no choice but to go back to the real world, and his real world didn't include either of them.

The diner was exactly what he expected—a rural Southern greasy spoon. A long counter ran along one side of the room, a row of booths lined the other, and a haze of cigarette smoke hung over all of it. Beau felt right at home here: squeaky screen door, buzzing flies, country music on the radio, and all. It was a true taste of his deep Southern roots, carrying him back to a simpler time.

He smiled, remembering how he and Grammy had loved to eat at the local diner back in DeLisle, much to his parents' frustration. According to his mother, the place was germ-laden; according to his father, Somervilles could afford to frequent finer establishments. All true, but nobody could beat a blue plate heaped with hush puppies and chicken-fried steak.

Beau and Jordan settled into a booth adjacent to one that was occupied by a family of three: mother, father, and toddler boy. He saw the child painting the table with mashed potatoes, watched the mother dunk her paper napkin into a glass of ice water to clean the mess while the father looked around for the waitress and the check.

It was a scene he had lived.

Jeanette, who'd had a lumberjack's appetite despite her petite build, had loved to eat in places like this. So had Tyler.

Oddly, today, watching the little family in the next booth didn't spark the usual gut-wrenching pain inside Beau. Today his memory didn't chill him—it wrapped him in a warm, nostalgic glow merely tinged, but not infused, with the familiar sorrow.

The waitress came over to them. She was a faded blonde with deep wrinkles around her eyes and mouth that betrayed years of sun and smoking. Setting down water and menus, she asked, "You two need a few minutes before you order?"

Beau looked at Jordan.

"I do," she said.

He knew what he wanted without opening the menu,

but he needed a few minutes, too. Anything to prolong this time with her.

He waited to ask Jordan about Spencer until the waitress had gone back to the kitchen. The moment he spoke the child's name, her eyes clouded over.

"He's with his uncle," she said simply.

"Phoebe's brother? The one he barely knows?" For some reason, that notion disturbed him.

"He barely knows us either, Beau," she pointed out. "I called Curt from the hospital. He got the first plane that was able to get down here when the weather cleared. He wasn't even angry that I hadn't told him Spencer was with me when I called him from Georgetown. He was only grateful his nephew is alive."

Beau stared at her, his mind swerving back to those tense days before North Carolina. "You called him from Georgetown?"

She gasped and clasped a hand to her mouth. "I forgot . . . you didn't know. I knew it was a mistake as soon as I made the call, Beau."

He contemplated that. "Why was it a mistake? If you didn't tell him you had Spencer, what did you say?"

"That I was sorry about Phoebe," she said miserably. "But as soon as I heard Curt's voice on the other end, I knew I shouldn't have called. Phoebe had told me not to tell anyone where Spencer was. She must have known that Gisonni would be watching her brother closely, tapping Curt's phone, even."

"How do you know that he was?"

"I heard clicking on the line. I was sick about it. If I hadn't called, they never would have found Spencer with me."

Beau could see the blatant guilt and regret etched on her face. He knew what she was going through, how she was tormenting herself over one irrevocable misstep—one that might have led to disaster.

But it hadn't.

Spencer was alive. They were all alive.

Her mistake hadn't been deadly.

Perhaps the phone call hadn't even been the trigger that set Gisonni's hit man on their trail.

"Jordan, did you ever stop to think that maybe the phone call wasn't how they found us?" he asked gently, understanding and needing to ease her pain.

"What else could it have been?"

He shrugged. "We'll probably never know. Maybe somebody followed Phoebe to your house that night. Maybe they ransacked the Averills' house and found your name and number in her address book. Maybe they found out you were Spencer's godmother. None of it really matters now, does it?"

"I don't know," she said softly. "I keep telling myself that I should have been more careful. Calacci saw your car parked in front of my town house. He traced the plates. He talked to your partner. . . ."

"I know."

When they spoke yesterday, Ed had told Beau about the phone call from a potential "client."

I tried to tell you someone had called looking for you when I talked to you that last day, Beau, but you hung up too fast.

Of course he had. Because he thought Ed suspected he wasn't at the beach house alone, and that that was what he was going to say.

In trying to protect Jordan and Spencer's whereabouts, he had unwittingly helped the cunning killer set the trap. If he had allowed Ed to tell him about the stranger's inquiry, he would have realized far sooner that Jordan and Spencer were in peril.

"Look, Jordan, we both made mistakes," he said slowly. "But we both did what we thought was right at the time. Neither of us meant to put Spencer in danger. How could we have known any better? How could we have behaved any differently?"

She looked down at the tabletop. "I just keep thinking that I should have—"

"No," he said, reaching out to touch her hand. "No should-haves. Should-haves will torture you. Don't torture yourself, Jordan."

It was what she had said to him on the deck that night.

Don't torture yourself, Beau.

By uttering those words, he now realized, she had given him permission to heal after so many years of blaming himself for something he couldn't have changed.

She looked up at him. He saw in her eyes that she knew what he was thinking. That she had recognized the words he had repeated back to her.

"You'll never know how much you helped me that night, Jordan," he said softy. "I haven't talked with anybody about the . . . accident."

Accident.

That was what it had been. An accident. Nobody's fault.

"You couldn't carry that burden of guilt around forever, Beau," Jordan said.

"And you can't, either," he said simply.

There was silence for a long moment.

Then Beau asked her the question whose answer he was dreading. "Did Curt tell Spencer about his parents?"

She nodded, her eyes somber. "A social worker was

with them to help—" Her voice broke. She reached for
a napkin from the metal holder on the table and wiped
her teary eyes. "I'm sorry."

He placed his hand over hers. "It's okay. I know. This
is hard."

"I want to be with him. I keep wondering if he's
afraid. And if he's even asked about me."

"Of course he has, Jordan," he said with conviction
he didn't feel. He knew as well as she did that Spencer
had kept his emotional distance from her from the
moment Phoebe left him in Jordan's care.

"No. You were the one he bonded with," she said.
"But there were a few times, on the last day, when I felt
like he might be willing to let me in. Then everything
exploded, and now I'll never know what it would have
been like to feel as though he didn't hate me."

"He doesn't hate you," Beau said. "He was scared
and confused, and he took it out on you."

"But he didn't take it out on *you*. You knew how to
reach him. You knew exactly what to say and do. Of
course, you would have. I mean, you were a . . ." She
trailed off and looked down at the scarred Formica
tabletop.

"I was a what?" he asked, wondering if he even wanted
to know what she was going to say.

"A dad," she said softly, looking up at him. "You
were a dad."

He waited for the usual current of grief to sweep him
off to that bleak, lonely place. But this time, for some
reason, it didn't come.

"I'm sorry," she said.

"For what?"

"For reminding you."

"I think about Tyler every second of every day," Beau

told her. "I don't have to be reminded. And you know what? I need to think about him."

And maybe even talk about him, he realized. So many years of happy memories had been shut away in the dimmest recesses of his mind, shadowed by the omniscient recollection of those last dark moments in the midnight waters of the bayou.

Maybe it was time to push that one away. . . .

To bring the other memories out into the light at last.

"There were so many things we used to do together," he murmured, his thoughts drifting back, back, back . . .

"Like what?" she asked gently

Memories began flooding him. Happy, long-obscured memories.

"I carved him a little boat once," he said, smiling. "Out of an old chunk of wood. My grandfather had taught me how to whittle and I hadn't done it since I was a kid, but I made Tyler that boat for the bathtub— he used to love to take his bath, you know? Not like some kids. He never complained . . . and it actually floated. The little boat I made."

Jordan squeezed his hand.

"Jeanette made a little sail for it out of an old handkerchief of my mother's," he went on, "only Tyler didn't like the sail because it had lace on it. Only a little shred of lace, but he said it made his boat into a girly boat. And I agreed."

He laughed at the recollection of Jeanette's feigned indignation, of her dismay and Tyler's thrill when Beau cut up a perfectly good pair of jeans and made a denim sail for the boat instead.

"You folks ready to order?" the waitress asked, materializing beside their table once again, pad in hand.

"I need another second," Jordan said, reaching for the menu.

"How about you, hon?" The waitress looked at Beau.

"I'll have fried chicken, mashed potatoes with cream gravy, corn, biscuits, lemonade, and a slice of pecan pie for dessert," Beau rattled off without hesitation.

Jordan looked up in amazement. "You didn't even look at the menu."

"I didn't have to," he drawled with a grin, suddenly feeling lighthearted. "This is a good old-fashioned Southern diner, and I'm a good old-fashioned Southern boy, remember?"

"You know what? That all sounds great. I'll have the same." Jordan closed her menu with a snap.

They grinned at each other as the waitress left.

And for a fleeting moment, Beau wondered what it would be like if he could sit across from her at every meal. Forever.

Just as quickly as it had come, the thought vanished, leaving in its wake a familiar trail of regret. He only thought he wanted her because . . .

Because why?

There were a zillion reasons.

Because she was a beautiful woman.

Because she knew how to make greens the way his grammy had.

Because he had bonded with her in a way that he hadn't bonded with a woman since Jeanette.

Because being with her and Spencer had almost been like being with Jeanette and Tyler again.

That was it.

The reason he couldn't *let* himself want her. He knew that what he'd felt out there in that storm when he was trying to reach her wasn't about her.

It was about him.

About his twisted sense of guilt and responsibility.

About his irrational longing to replace what he had lost.

"What's wrong?" Jordan was asking, watching him intently.

"What do you mean?"

"You were looking so happy, and then all of a sudden it's like this dark cloud came over you."

"Oh . . . I just . . . I just remembered something."

"What did you remember?" Her eyes searched his for meaning.

Why I can't let myself get involved with you. Why this has to be over.

"Nothing," he said, and looked away.

Chapter Fourteen

Jordan walked into the hotel lobby less than an hour later, the lunch with Beau having left a sour taste in her mouth.

Lord knew it wasn't the food. Beau's order had been right on target. All of it—the chicken, the gravy, the pie—had been delicious.

But it didn't go down very easily when you were sitting across from a person who suddenly seemed like a stranger.

They had eaten quickly, and when the meal was finished, went their separate ways—he to the police station to meet with Detective Rodgers, and she to walk the few blocks back to the hotel.

When they parted on the street in front of the diner, Beau had simply said, "Maybe I'll catch up with you back at the hotel before you check out. What room are you in?"

She told him, but added, "I won't be there much longer than it will take me to pack my bags and check out."

"I thought your flight wasn't until later."

"It's not. But I'd rather hang around the airport than in that room." There was something depressing about the starkly decorated low-budget room with a view of the courtyard pool, its water littered with storm debris and having taken on a greenish algal cast.

Beau didn't hug or kiss her, but only gave her a detached little wave before striding off down the street.

She didn't know why that should have caught her by surprise. After all, what did she expect? A long embrace? A passionate promise to see her again?

Beau was essentially a stranger. Or if not technically a stranger at this point, then a mere acquaintance at the very most.

Shared turmoil and responsibility for Spencer—and, okay, a few passionate interludes—had created a false sense of intimacy between them.

So why couldn't she accept that for what it was? Why did she feel as though there should be more between them? Why, now that the rest of it was over, couldn't she accept that they were over, too?

He's everything I don't want in a man, she reminded herself.

He didn't come close to matching the image she had created about her imaginary future husband. Beau was incredibly handsome, a billionaire playboy, a busy, successful professional—the kind of man who couldn't possibly be content with a wife who canned her own jam, sewed her own curtains, and planted her own flower garden—or at least would do all of those things if she could. That would be heaven for her.

Beau, on the other hand, was used to a far different lifestyle. . . .

But so are you, Jordan reminded herself. She was totally absorbed in her career these days. She didn't have time for any of those things, let alone a husband. Or babies.

A husband?

Babies?

Beau had already had a wife. He'd had a child.

To assume that she could fill the void in his life—or that he even wanted to fill it again, especially with her— would make her a fool.

So would thinking that she was cut out for a man like him.

She sighed as she crossed the air-conditioned lobby toward the elevator bank. She passed the small sitting area with its meager furnishings—a couple of uncomfortable-looking vinyl-upholstered chairs and a low, fingerprint-dotted glass-topped table covered with outdated magazines. Water had seeped in when the flood waters rose during the storm, and the pale green carpeting gave off a dank, mildewed odor.

She would check out of this place, thank goodness, and she would go back to her life, and she would be content.

She promised herself that after a few days . . .

Or maybe a few weeks . . .

She wouldn't even miss Beau.

Or Spencer.

But her heart wasn't listening to the hollow reassurances of her inner voice.

Her heart knew better.

"Jordan!"

She looked up, hearing a male voice calling her name.

Her first thought was that it must be Beau, coming after her, wanting . . .

Wanting what?

It didn't matter.

Because it wasn't Beau. It was Curt, Phoebe's brother, stepping off the elevator. He was carrying a suitcase with one hand, and holding Spencer's small clenched fist in his other.

Jordan noticed that the little boy looked even more diminutive than usual next to his tall, broad-shouldered uncle.

"Hi!" she said, waving, pasting a happy smile on her face.

There was a desolate expression in Spencer's eyes as he gazed up at her.

Jordan bent down to hug him. His little body seemed to stiffen in response.

"My mommy and daddy are dead," he said dully.

A sob choked her reply. "I know, sweetheart. I'm so sorry."

She looked up at Curt.

Phoebe's brother was a kind person, she knew. Yet he was an imposing figure, with his salt-and-pepper hair, horn-rimmed glasses, and business suit. He was old enough to be Spencer's grandfather, and he didn't look like the kind of grandfather who would roll around and wrestle on the floor with a little boy.

Or know that little boys like their peanut-butter-and-jelly sandwiches cut into interesting shapes.

Or know what a Happy Meal was, and how to make one when there was no McDonald's in the neighborhood.

"Spencer and I are leaving to fly back home now," Curt said. "We're going to—"

"No, we're not," Spencer cut in harshly, wrenching himself out of Jordan's embrace. "We aren't going *home!* We're going to *his* house," he told Jordan, heaving with sobs, tears streaming down his freckled cheeks. "I don't get to go home ever again."

"Oh, Spencer," Jordan said, stroking his hair, wiping her teary eyes against the shoulder of her T-shirt. There was nothing to say but, "I'm so sorry."

She looked up at Curt. "Will you have custody, then?"

He nodded. "Reno and Phoebe named me in their will. Their attorney hasn't contacted me yet, but Phoebe told me that they were going to do it back when he was born. She said that if anything happened to her and Reno, they would want Spencer to have a stable home and be with family . . ."

He trailed off, and she sensed an unspoken *but* hovering.

"You and Sue have two children, don't you?" Jordan asked him, thinking she could remind Spencer that it would be nice for him to get to know his cousins.

He nodded. "Stephen is a junior at Carnegie Mellon, and Jessica will be starting her freshman year at Ball State in Indiana in August. She just graduated from high school last week."

"So they're both grown and out of the house," Jordan said, still clasping Spencer's head against her breast. She could feel him trembling and ached to do something more to comfort him.

"Actually . . ." Curt shifted, looking uneasy. He said in a low voice, as though he could somehow keep Spencer from overhearing, "This is a difficult time for me. Sue and I have been waiting for Jess to finish school so that we . . ."

"What?" Jordan asked when he trailed off again. She

wondered if they had plans to travel now that their kids were both in college. Or maybe to sell the empty nest and get a smaller place.

But surely they would welcome Spencer into their lives anyway. He was their flesh and blood. He needed the loving family environment that his aunt and uncle could provide, and his older cousins would probably be home on vacations from school.

Curt took a deep breath. "Sue and I are separating, Jordan. A legal separation. We've already had documents drawn up."

She felt as though the wind had been knocked out of her.

It wasn't that she felt more than passing regret for Curt or his wife, whom she had met only once, at their wedding in Pittsburgh, back when she and Phoebe were in middle school. Phoebe had been allowed to bring Jordan as a guest to the wedding, and the two of them had spent the whole reception giggling about their mutual crush on the wedding band's handsome lead singer.

Back then, Jordan had been caught up in the whole romantic bride-and-groom scenario, never imagining that Curt and Sue would one day split up, as apparently they were now.

"Is it a trial separation?" she asked hopefully, thinking that maybe having custody of Spencer would draw them back together.

"No. Permanent. And it's only a matter of time before the divorce."

"I'm so sorry," Jordan managed.

"It's for the best," Curt said with a shrug. "It's actually been in the works for two years now, but we didn't want to disrupt the kids' lives. We thought we'd wait until

Jess was finished with high school and getting ready to move out. We had told the kids about our plans last week. They didn't take it well. And that was right before I found about my sister. It's been hell since then, dealing with the police, and the funeral arrangements, and wondering about Spencer, whether he was even alive . . .''

"I can only imagine," Jordan murmured sympathetically.

She looked down at Spencer. Her dismay at the news about Curt's marriage stemmed mainly from the realization that Spencer wouldn't have a stable, two-parent home after all.

Surely Phoebe had never intended to have her only child raised in a distant city by her newly divorced, middle-aged bachelor brother.

And who would be a better candidate for custody? You, of all people? she demanded of herself, feeling a familiar tug on her heartstrings. *You're single, too. You don't live in Philly, either. And you've never even been a parent.*

"Will you—will you be able to take care of him?" Jordan asked Curt, knowing she had no right to doubt his capabilities—that she was certainly in no position to judge, yet unable to help herself.

"Sure, I will," he said with a bravado that wasn't reflected in his eyes. "We'll be fine. Won't we, Spence? The two of us are going to find a neat place to live. I had already paid July rent for a condo I was going to move to, but kids aren't allowed in that building, so I'll find someplace else as soon as we get back."

"What about—what will you do with Spencer while you're at work? Will Sue be willing to—"

Curt was already shaking his head. "Sue is going back to school in August. For fashion design," he added with an expression of disdain. "She says she's through raising kids. She's done her duty. She wants to be free."

Jordan wanted to cry for Spencer's sake. Clearly, his aunt wasn't going to lavish him with the maternal love he'd lost.

"There are lots of great day-care places where we live," Curt went on. "And he'll be in school in no time— right, Spence? I'll make sure there's a full-day kindergarten in the neighborhood we move to, and if not, we'll figure something out. Look, everything is going to work out fine."

He said it as much to Spencer as to her, but she knew he wasn't so sure about that. She could hear the strain in his voice, could see the tension in his face.

"Well, I'd love to have Spencer visit me," she said, trying to muster cheerfulness. She patted the little boy's head. "Would you like that, Spencer? You can come and see me in Georgetown sometimes."

He lit up. Her spirits soared, then plummeted when Spencer asked, "Will Beau be there, too?"

"Maybe you can visit Beau, too," Jordan said, deflating.

"He talks about Beau quite a bit," Curt told her. "Are the two of you engaged, or are you just—"

"You mean Beau and me? Oh, we're not a couple," Jordan said hastily. "We're just, uh . . ."

Just what?

"Friends," came a voice behind her. "Good friends."

She spun around.

Beau stood there. His mouth was grinning, but his eyes were fixed on her with a cryptic expression.

"Beau!" Spencer flew at him, nearly knocking him off his feet. "Where have you been? I didn't think I would get to say good-bye to you!"

"Hey, I wouldn't let that happen," Beau said, scooping the child into his arms and squeezing him tight.

"What about Detective Rodgers?" Jordan asked.

"Wasn't there," Beau said simply. "He had gone out for lunch. They said he'll be back later. I'm Beau Somerville, by the way." He set Spencer down and offered his hand to Curt, who introduced himself.

"Curt has custody of Spencer," Jordan told Beau in an *isn't-that-great* tone for Spencer's benefit.

"And I'm afraid we've got a flight to catch now," Curt said, checking his watch and picking up the suitcase again. "Come on, Spence."

"No! I'm not going with you!" Spencer shrieked, cowering away from his uncle. He ducked behind Beau's legs, trying to hide. "Don't let him take me away! I want to stay with you guys! Please!"

"Spencer, it's going to be okay," Jordan said, anguish ripping through her.

It was so unfair, so terribly unfair. What would Spencer's life be like now? She was sure his uncle would try his best to raise him, but Curt was trying to pick up the pieces of his own life.

How could a little boy cope with the shattering loss of both parents when he would be plunked down in a strange environment? Stuck in a condo somewhere, and in day care, with a bachelor uncle he barely knew . . .

"I want to stay with you, Beau!" Spencer cried. "And with her." He pointed a shaking finger at Jordan.

Her heart went liquid and pooled in her throat. "Oh, Spencer . . ."

"Spencer, look at me," Beau said firmly, taking hold of the little boy's shoulders and crouching down in front of him, at eye level. "Look at me and listen carefully."

Spencer was crying.

Jordan was crying, too, silently, but unable to hold back the tidal wave of emotion a moment longer.

Curt stood by, looking helplessly stricken, as though uncertain how to handle the situation short of dragging the little boy out of the lobby kicking and screaming. Jordan prayed it wouldn't come to that, but she didn't see any way around it.

"Spencer, this isn't going to be easy," Beau said in a low, controlled voice. "It's going to be the hardest thing you've ever done. Are you listening?"

The little boy nodded miserably, his shoulders quaking with silent sobs.

"You're going to have to be braver than any boy has ever been, Spencer. Braver than you were out on that rock. Braver than a superhero, even. But I know you can do this. You're going to make me so proud of you. And Jordan, too. And your mommy and your daddy in heaven—they're going to be proud of you, too. They wanted Uncle Curt to take care of you. They knew he would give you a wonderful home and love you, Spencer. And he will."

Spencer whimpered, "But I don't want to go with him. Please don't make me go."

"It's all going to be okay. Really," Beau said. "I promise."

Spencer looked up at Jordan, who smiled through her tears.

"When Beau makes a promise, he means it, Spencer," she said shakily. "I guarantee you that he means it."

"Can I visit you?" Spencer asked.

"All the time," she said.

"Both of you?" He looked at Beau.

"Both of us," Beau pledged.

Something fluttered somewhere deep inside Jordan. She tried to quiet it, but it refused to settle.

She was going to be seeing Beau again when she got back to D.C. Even if only on occasion, for Spencer's sake . . .

"I hate to—" Curt looked at his watch, and then at Spencer. "I don't want to miss the plane," he said apologetically. "We really have to go."

"Here, fella," Beau said, reaching into his pocket. He took out a white handkerchief and held it over Spencer's nose. "Blow."

Spencer blew. Loudly. Several times.

Beau wiped the little boy's eyes, then tucked the handkerchief into Spencer's pocket. "You can borrow this in case you need it," he told Spencer. "Remember, even superheroes cry sometimes. And I'm going to need it back, you know."

"Why? Do you cry, too?" Spencer asked.

Beau nodded solemnly, squeezing his eyes shut as he pulled Spencer into a bear hug. "So you'll have to see me again. To give it back to me. Okay? Is that a deal?"

"It's a deal," Spencer said.

Beau released him.

Spencer looked at Jordan.

She knelt beside him and pulled him close. "Take care of yourself, sweetie," she whispered raggedly. "I'll be thinking of you every second."

"Bye, Jordan," the little boy said.

To her shock, he kissed her on the cheek.

Then he was gone, his small hand tucked into his uncle's as the two of them left the hotel through the wide double glass doors.

A choking sob escaped Jordan, and she fumbled in the pockets of her shorts for a tissue but found none.

She sniffled and awkwardly wiped her eyes on the short, already damp sleeve of her T-shirt.

"Thank you for what you did," she said, and looked up at Beau.

To her shock, he was weeping. Tears rolled down his face unchecked as he gazed after Spencer and Curt.

"Oh, Beau . . ." She reached out and touched his sleeve.

"He's going to be okay," Beau said, nodding, trying to get hold of himself. "I know he is. But I'm going to miss the little guy like crazy."

"So am I."

He looked at her.

Then he reached out and gently brushed away her tears with the back of his hand. "You look so sad," he said.

"My heart is breaking."

"So is mine. For him," he added.

"For him," Jordan agreed.

But it was also breaking for herself.

For all of them.

For what could never be, with Spencer—or with Beau.

"What are you doing now?" Beau asked.

She took a deep breath to compose herself. "Going upstairs to pack, remember? I have to catch my flight in a few hours."

"Want some help? I have some time to kill," Beau said. "Detective Rodgers isn't going to be back for a while."

"Sure," Jordan agreed, as though it were the most casual thing in the world to agree to have Beau come back to her room with her.

They began walking toward the elevator bank.

Beau put his arm around her.

She looked down at his hand on her shoulder, and then up at him. His face was so close that she could see the golden flecks in his eyes. She could smell the familiar, musky masculine scent of him.

Their gazes locked.

Her breath caught in her throat.

They stopped walking.

He leaned toward her.

Jordan closed her eyes.

"I have to kiss you," he said raggedly. "I promised myself that I wouldn't, but Jordan, I have to."

"You have to," she agreed in a breathless whisper.

His mouth came down to claim hers then. She was lost in the sensation of his lips caressing hers, of his tongue dipping into her mouth. Her legs went weak beneath her and she clung to his shoulders as his arms encircled her waist. He deepened the kiss, moaning low in his throat, his urgent desire blatantly, excitingly obvious when he pulled the length of her body against his.

"Let's go upstairs," he murmured, fumbling for the wall beside them, hitting the "Up" button.

She didn't protest.

He kissed her again, another passionate melding of mouths and lips and tongues.

She knew in the back of her mind that they shouldn't be doing this right here in the lobby for anyone to see. They were behaving like two lustful teenagers, yet she couldn't seem to help herself any more than Beau could.

The doors slid open with a *ding* and they stumbled inside.

As he reached for the panel of buttons, she said, "It's the third floor."

"I know. I memorized your room number."

"Were you planning this?" she asked, not caring if he had been. For once, she didn't care about anything.

"No. Maybe. Hell, I don't know. Come here." He reached for her as the doors slid closed, leaving them alone inside.

Her back was against the wall, his body pressed against her as the elevator rose with a jerk and a shudder. He kissed her hungrily, his hands cupping her face, his fingers laced in her hair.

She wanted to cry out in protest when they reached their destination and the doors opened again. She couldn't bear for him to break the exquisite contact even for a moment, but he took her hand and led her out into the deserted corridor.

"Which way?" he asked raggedly, squeezing her hand.

It took her a moment to remember. She led him down the hall, past closed doors. Up ahead she could see one that was ajar, with a maid's cart parked in front of it. She prayed that it wasn't her room. She needed to be alone with Beau behind closed doors now—and to hell with the consequences.

Right here, right now, there was only this.

Only the simmering passion between them that threatened to erupt at any moment into a full-blown inferno.

They passed the maid's cart, could hear the television blaring and tub running in the open room. There were a few more closed doors between that one and Jordan's, and both had plastic "Please Make Up Room" cards hanging around the doorknobs.

"That'll keep her busy," Beau said with a low chuckle.

Jordan nodded, fumbling in her pockets for the card

key. For a horrible moment she thought she had lost it.

"Don't tell me we're locked out," he said with a groan.

"I can't ... bingo!" She located the credit-card-shaped key and held it up, showing it to Beau.

They laughed and he took the key from her, slipping it into the electronic slot. He pulled it out. Tried the door. Nothing.

"Try again," she said urgently, desperate to be alone with him.

He did.

Nothing.

He cursed and shoved the key in again.

"Third time lucky," she said as the green light flashed and the door opened with a welcoming click.

His laugh was more of a growl as he plunked the plastic "Do Not Disturb" card on the outside knob and kicked the door closed behind them.

The room was just as she had left it: bed unmade, clothes strewn over the desk chair, half-empty water glass on the bedside table. The drapes were still drawn, leaving the room dimly lit except for a narrow shaft of light that filtered in through a crack in the curtains.

It was hardly the most romantic of settings. It couldn't compare to the other night on the deck overlooking the crashing surf. But Jordan realized that it didn't matter where they were, as long as they were together.

It didn't matter what had happened earlier, or what would happen next. Now was all that mattered, and if she closed her eyes, she could forget all the rest of it.

Beau pulled Jordan into his arms with a sweeping kiss, and the flame was ignited once more.

Lips locked, hands roaming, they found their way to

the bed. As she sank back onto the rumpled, stiffly quilted polyester bedspread, Jordan felt Beau tugging on her T-shirt. She raised her arms above her head and he pulled it off, pausing to devour the hollow of her throat with his wet, hungry mouth before reaching for the clasp of her bra.

It came open easily, the weight of her breasts spilling from the cotton cups as he pulled the bra away and tossed it recklessly aside.

She arched her back, anticipating his caress. Goose bumps prickled her flesh as first his stroking fingers and then his suckling mouth found her. She could feel the fierce tightening of her nipples in response to his caress, and she began to squirm on the bed as his fingers moved low over her belly and slipped inside the waistband of her shorts.

She raised her hips and he slid both shorts and panties down over her thighs as she went to work on his shirt, tugging it over his head. He paused to help her, then unfastened the buttons at his waist. Soon his jeans and boxer shorts sailed overboard to join the rest of their clothing in a heap on the floor.

Both naked at last, they kissed again, settling their bodies against each other in an intimately perfect fit.

Jordan could feel the ardent fluttering low in her abdomen as Beau buried his lips in the hollow beneath her ear and began to blaze a slow, passionate trail downward. Again his mouth found her taut nipples, teasing first one and then the other until she cried out softly in fervent need, opening her legs to him.

"Please, Beau," she whispered against his ear as he positioned himself above her. "Please . . . now."

He hesitated. "Open your eyes," he said hoarsely.

She did.

His gaze collided with hers, burning into her soul. His breath was coming fast and furious, matching her own.

For a long, agonizing moment, time seemed to stand still. They lay poised, staring at each other, prolonging the inevitable.

Then he sank into her with a guttural moan.

Jordan gasped at the sensation, clinging to his shoulders, exhaling his name on a shuddering sigh.

Their eyes were still locked as he began to move in an age-old, flawless rhythm, her movements soon matching his. She could feel the tension building at her core, and she knew that if he stopped what he was doing or the precise way in which he was doing it, she would, quite simply, die.

But he didn't stop.

Not when her breath began coming in high-pitched pants, or when her body began to quake violently beneath his.

She was at the brink, and then she was plunging past it, falling, spinning, reeling with one exquisite spasm after another.

She heard him call her name, felt him bucking above her, felt him pouring himself into her until he lay spent against her heaving breasts.

She reached down and touched his sweat-dampened hair, stroking his head as their passion subsided, leaving a glow of contentment in its wake.

Beau awakened to the sound of knocking, and an accented female voice calling, "Hello? Hello? Is anybody here?"

His eyes drifted open.

The instant he saw where he was—in a dimly lit hotel room, in the afternoon—he realized what had happened.

"Hmm?" Jordan stirred sleepily, naked in his arms.

"We're here!" he called to the maid. "Don't come in!"

"I have to make up the room," she called back from the corridor. He could see a triangle of light where she was holding the door open a crack. "It's past checkout time."

"We'll be out soon," Jordan called, bolting from Beau's arms and looking wildly around the room, as though trying to get her bearings.

Beau sat up, seeing their clothing strewn beside the bed.

"Then I come back in five minutes," the woman called with an exaggerated sigh, sounding disgruntled. "No longer than that, though. Or they have to charge you for another night."

Beau wanted to tell her that was fine. To go ahead and charge them for another night. It would be heaven to sink back onto the bed and pull Jordan down with him.

He looked at her, naked beside the bed. She was beautiful, tousled hair, stricken expression, and all.

"What time is it?" she asked him.

He checked his watch. "Past two."

"Two!" she echoed. "I have to get to the airport."

She began throwing things into a plastic shopping bag. Shorts. T-shirt. Sneakers. Hairbrush.

Then, as though realizing what she was doing, she began taking things out again, putting them on.

He watched her shove her arms into the straps of her bra and then hurriedly fasten it. As she pulled her

T-shirt over her head he felt a pang of disappointment. He didn't want her dressed, rushing, leaving.

He wanted her here, in his arms, languid and lusty.

"You don't have to go," he said lazily, stretching.

"Yes, I do. The other flights today are full. I'm lucky I got a seat on this one."

"You can stay here and drive back with me when I go."

She pulled on a pair of white cotton panties, shaking her head. "I can't do that."

"Why not?"

"Because I already called my partner and told him I'd be back at work tomorrow," she said.

It sounded like a lame excuse to him—and probably to her, too, he realized, seeing her pause momentarily with a faraway expression before reaching for her shorts and resuming her clothes-donning marathon.

He wanted to protest.

He longed to beg her to stay with him.

But her swift, certain movements—and her mention of the job that waited for her back in Washington— brought reality seeping into the room as vividly as the shaft of afternoon light spilling through the slightly parted curtains.

She had to go back.

He had to stay.

That was how it had to be. . . .

Unless he wanted something more.

Did he?

His thoughts whirled.

Do you? Do you want more?

Of course not, he told himself firmly. He had already decided before—several times, in fact.

He was going to move on, and so was she.

This last interlude between them had served its purpose. It had tied up loose ends, had sated his hunger for her, had been nothing more than a final good-bye.

She went to the bathroom, carrying her shopping bag. He could hear her in there, tossing toiletries into it. She closed the door. He could hear water running.

Beau got out of bed and got dressed.

He walked over to the window and pulled the draperies opened.

The room instantly filled with light, yet somehow, it didn't brighten.

Outside, the day was overcast.

He looked down at the depressing courtyard with its overgrown shrubs, plastic-webbed lounge chairs, and perfunctory, uninviting swimming pool.

He thought about what Lisa would say about this view, this room, this hotel, this town.

And what his mother would say.

That he, Beau Somerville, didn't belong in a place like this.

He considered the winding, treacherous path that had led him here, finding it—all of it—surreal.

After a long time, Jordan opened the door again.

He looked up, startled, so lost in his thoughts that he had nearly forgotten she was here.

She emerged from the bathroom, looking utterly presentable. Her hair had been brushed back into a neat ponytail, her clothing straightened, her shirt tucked in.

In her hand, she clutched the shopping bag that held her belongings.

He looked at it. "Is that everything?"

"This, and my purse. Everything else I had was at the beach house. If there's anything left—"

"I'm going to have the rental place send it to you;

don't worry," he said, and motioned at her bag of clothing. "Do you want me to drive that stuff back for you, though? Just so you don't have to carry a plastic shopping bag on the plane . . ."

She looked up, seeming interested.

He almost thought she was going to take him up on it, until he added, "I can drop it by your place when I get into town."

Her eyes clouded over. "That's okay. I've got it. It's not that big a deal."

She doesn't want to see me again, he realized.

"I'll call you for Spencer's new address and phone number," he said, needing, for some reason, to prove that this wouldn't be their last contact.

"Curt is going to move with him," she told him with a shrug. "To a condo or something . . . he doesn't know where yet."

"Oh." He took a deep breath. "I want to see Spencer, though, Jordan, if he visits you. Please let me know if he does. Okay?"

She looked directly at him for the first time since she'd left the bathroom. He saw a flicker of resentment in her gaze. "If he visits, I'll let you know."

Hell, what was wrong with her?

Didn't she want him to see Spencer?

There was a knock at the door.

"I need to get in there now," the maid's voice called. "Or else I have to get the manager up here."

"It's okay," Jordan said, walking toward the door and opening it. "We're all set."

Beau trailed her, but by the time he reached the heavyset, irritated-looking woman waiting beside the maid's cart, Jordan was already halfway down the hall.

"Jordan," he called, hurrying after her.

"I've got to run," she said over her shoulder. "I've got to get to the airport."

"Let me give you a ride there."

"It's okay. I had already arranged for a car service. He's probably waiting downstairs. I hope he hasn't left."

Before reaching the elevator bank, she shoved open the door to the stairway and gave him a little wave. "I don't have time to wait for an elevator. I'll see you, Beau."

With that, she was gone.

He stood looking after her, a hollow, desolate chill creeping over him.

This is what you wanted, he reminded himself. *Remember? A clean, easy break. No messy good-bye.*

It was for the best, he decided as he jammed the button with the "Down" arrow beside the elevator.

He told himself that if he reached the lobby and her car wasn't waiting, he would insist upon driving her to the airport.

But the elevator took a long time to come.

As it sank slowly to the first floor, he decided that he would stop her.

It was an irrational, desperate thought, and he didn't have the slightest idea how he would go about it.

He only knew that he suddenly felt as though he couldn't let her get away. As though it would be wrong to let her go.

Perhaps the biggest mistake he could possibly make.

At last, he got to the lobby and glanced toward the double glass doors through which Spencer had disappeared less than two hours ago.

He saw an airport sedan pulling away from the curb. There was a lone occupant in the backseat, the silhouette of her familiar ponytail clearly outlined.

She's riding out of your life, and you're not doing a thing to stop her, he told himself, watching the car pull out onto the street.

But he felt powerless to move.

You live in the same city, he told himself. *When you get back home, you can call her. Get in touch with her. See her, even.*

But he knew, with a certainty that chilled him to the bone, that he wouldn't.

This had been his last chance.

Somehow, he had decided in that elevator that if it was meant to be, he would find her in the lobby when the elevator doors opened.

That maybe she would even be standing there waiting for him, telling him that she couldn't leave.

Instead, she had been on her way.

And the ponytailed silhouette never turned to look back.

Obviously, it wasn't meant to be.

Chapter Fifteen

"Jordan!"

Startled, she glanced up at Jeremy Van Pragh. "Geez, do you have to yell at me?" she asked, scowling.

"Yes, apparently I do," he said, shaking his dyed blond head. "I've been nicely saying your name and it didn't work. What planet are you on?"

She shook her head, unwilling to confess the wayward path her thoughts had taken. She dragged them back to the present, to this familiar, spacious, sun-splashed catering office on the ground floor of a charming brick row house.

She gestured at the pad of paper on her desk in front of her—not that she had even glanced at it in the past fifteen minutes. "I'm just trying to figure out how many strawberries I need to buy to dip in white chocolate for the Murphy wedding next weekend. What do you need?"

"Labor Day off," Jeremy said, perching on the edge of her desk, his legs dangling in childlike fashion, swinging back and forth. "Can you handle the Tremell clambake on your own?"

"On such short notice?" She glanced at her calendar. "That's less than a week away, Jeremy!"

"I know, but Paul's boss told him he can bring me to his annual end-of-summer bash at the beach after all," Jeremy said. "I guess that a couple of Republican senators have canceled, so nobody will be scandalized if Paul shows up with me as his date."

"I'll be scandalized," Jordan said. "I was counting on you to help me with that clambake."

"Paul and I will dig the pit and lug the stuff over to the Murphys' place for you," Jeremy promised. "You can hire some other burly types to help with the shucking and cleaning. I told you, you should've replaced Amy and Rob."

Amy and Rob were the two college students they'd hired to help with the catering business over the summer. Both had left for school a few days ago. Jordan had fully intended to find replacement staff for the busy fall season, but somehow the task had managed to get away from her.

That had happened quite a bit this summer.

No longer as efficient as she had always been—especially when it came to her work—she had found herself spending much of her time lost in daydreams these past nine weeks.

Nine weeks.

Long enough for her to reassure herself that she wasn't carrying Beau's child.

At first, all she could think about was that she had been a fool to throw caution to the wind that last afternoon. The issue of protection hadn't even entered her mind—not until it was too late. Only in the cab on the way to the airport had she realized what they had done.

She had spent the next few weeks praying that she would get her period. . . .

And sometimes, late at night when loneliness enveloped her along with the darkness, she prayed—in lapses of purely irrational hope—that she wouldn't.

But she did.

And she hadn't seen or heard from Beau since she had left him in that crummy North Carolina hotel two months ago. Somehow, it seemed that her thoughts of him grew more, rather than less, prevalent as time went by.

The memories refused to fade.

She constantly found herself thinking about him, wondering where he was, what he was doing, how he had been.

She didn't even have Andrea MacDuff to ask casually about his well-being. She was back in Louisiana with her husband for the summer and wouldn't be returning to Washington until the Senate reconvened in September.

As for Spencer, he, too, was growing more prominent in her thoughts over time. Their weekly telephone conversations had become more frequent, so that at this point, hardly a day went by without her talking to him.

Spencer was still living with his aunt and uncle in their Pittsburgh home, after all. Curt had said that he and Sue had agreed to try sharing a roof for the summer, for the sake of their own children as well as for Spencer.

But he had confided yesterday that it wasn't working out. When his wife and children started college this week, he and Spencer were moving into a two-bedroom condominium in a nice complex in a residential neighborhood. Spencer would be enrolled in full-time day care as of today.

Jordan made a mental note to call him later and see how it went. She had asked Curt several times if he would bring the little boy down for a visit, but he was so busy getting his own life straightened out, as well as settling Phoebe's and Reno's legal affairs, that he hadn't had the opportunity.

She knew that Spencer had spoken to Beau over the summer, too. The child had mentioned his name in passing. It had taken all of Jordan's self-control not to ask Spencer about him—not to beg for more information.

"Earth to Jordan, come in, Jordan," Jeremy intoned, still perched on her desk.

She blinked and looked up at him. "Hmm?"

"I said, do you want a coffee? I'm going out to Starbucks for one of those sweet, frothy, fattening, slushy, caffeine drinkie-things. Can I bring you something?"

"No, thanks," Jordan murmured, absently nibbling the end of the pencil she clutched in her hand.

She thought about the package she had received from the rental agency last month. Inside the neatly wrapped package were the belongings she had left at the beach house. Not much. Just the clothes she had left in the bureau and the toiletries she'd left in the bathroom.

She had impulsively thrown away her shampoo. It wasn't even honeysuckle-scented, but she knew she would never use it again without thinking about what he'd said, or the way he'd buried his face in her hair and inhaled. . . .

"Jordan." Jeremy leaned close to her, his blue,

bespectacled gaze peering into her face. "Are you okay?"

"Sure, I'm fine."

"No, you aren't," he said, shaking his head. "You're thinking about Mr. Wonderful and Mr. Wonderful Junior again, aren't you?"

"No!"

"Yes, you are, Jordan. I can see it in your eyes. For God's sake, Jordan, why don't you just go ahead and call him?"

"I did call him. Just last night. And I'm going to call him again tonight to see how day care went."

"I wasn't talking about Junior, and you know it," Jeremy said.

She glowered at him. He glowered right back.

Jeremy knew the whole story, of course. She had filled him in on all of it as soon as she came back. She had to. The moment she had seen him, she had collapsed into his arms, sobbing. But it was one thing allowing Jeremy, her dear old pal and business partner, to comfort her. It was quite another to listen to his well-meaning but ill-conceived advice. Jeremy was a sucker for hearts-and-flowers, old-fashioned, happy-ending romance.

"Jeremy, how many times do I have to remind you? I'm not calling Beau, okay?"

"No. Not okay. You should call him."

"No!" She bit down on the pencil. So hard she tasted wood.

Ick. She tossed the pencil aside and scowled at Jeremy. "Aren't you supposed to be on your way to Starbucks?"

"I'm going," he said, rising and shaking his head. "But I think you're making a big mistake. And I'd be

willing to bet that Wonderful Senior is sitting in his
office right this very minute, mooning over you."

"Yeah, right," she muttered, going back to her straw-
berry order as Jeremy strode toward the door.

"Did you see the note I left you about the meeting
with Landry next week?" Ed asked, poking his head
into Beau's cluttered office.

"Hmm?" Startled by his partner's voice, Beau looked
up.

"Landry," Ed said. "Did you see the note? About the
meeting?"

"Saw it," Beau told him, snapping out of his reverie.
He looked down at his chaotic desktop, looking for his
date book. "I made a note of it. I'll be there."

"Good." Ed narrowed his eyes at Beau. "You okay?"

"Sure. I'm fine." Beau toyed with the computer
mouse in front of him. On the screen was the elevation
of a new office complex he was designing for a high-
profile client. He had been working on it for days, but
it wasn't coming along as quickly as he'd expected.

"How's the kid?" Ed asked, leaning against the
exposed brick wall, his arms folded across his chest.

"Spencer?" Beau exhaled through puffed cheeks.
"As well as can be expected. I talked to him yesterday.
He's starting day care today. Full time. He and his uncle
are moving to a new place, too."

"You told me."

"Did I? Sorry."

Ed flashed an understanding smile. "It's okay. I probably tell you things about my kids two or three times,
too."

But Spencer isn't my kid, Beau thought.

An image of Tyler danced into his consciousness. Seeing his son's familiar smiling face, he found himself smiling fondly, welcoming the image.

Soon it melded with another little boy's face in his mind's eye.

Spencer's face.

How Beau longed to see the child again, to scoop him into a bear hug and ease his pain.

Regular telephone conversations with Spencer—and occasionally, with his uncle—had done little to quell Beau's longing.

His wistfulness for Spencer had only deepened—along with another, far more complicated yearning that was never far from his thoughts.

Jordan.

"What's the matter?" Ed asked, watching him.

"Nothing." Beau struggled to wipe the telltale emotion from his face. "I just miss him, that's all. Spencer."

"Why don't you fly up there and visit him?"

"I don't think that would be a good idea," Beau said. "I don't want to undo what his uncle is trying to accomplish."

"Maybe it would do everyone some good if you took the little guy off his hands for a while," Ed suggested.

"I couldn't do that!" Beau protested, though the mere thought of it filled him with eager anticipation. He instantly saw himself bringing Spencer to the playground, and to the toy store, and to McDonald's for Happy Meals. He could shower the little boy with affection and gifts. He could tuck him in at night and make his breakfast in the morning, give him piggyback rides, and teach him how to ride a scooter . . .

"Why can't you do that, Beau?"

"Because the only connection I have to Spencer is

the time I spent with him during a very difficult week in his life," Beau said, dragging himself back to reality. "I'm not a relation. I never even knew his parents. His uncle has custody, and I can't go barging in someplace I don't belong."

"What about Jordan, then?" Ed asked.

"What about her?" Hearing her name, Beau fought off a shiver of unwanted feeling. "She technically has no role in Spencer's future, either."

"What about in *your* future?" Ed said quietly.

"Ed, you know I'm not looking for—"

"You don't have to be looking for it. Sometimes it just finds you," Ed told him. "And when it does, you grab it and hang on to it."

"Maybe *you* do that," Beau said stubbornly. "I don't. I like my life just the way it is."

"You live and breathe your work," Ed said, just as stubbornly. "And if you don't mind my saying so, your work hasn't been all that great these past few months. You're distracted, Beau. And until you figure out what you're going to do about that—"

"What do you want me to do about it?" Beau broke in, feeling the hot blood rising to his cheeks. "Track her down and marry her?"

"Maybe," Ed said with a maddening shrug.

With a burst of resentment, Beau thought about how easy it was for Ed to sit here and say these things. He was happily wedded to the girl he had loved half his life; he had three adoring, healthy daughters. He had everything that mattered most in the world, and he seemed to think everybody else could easily attain those things, too.

Beau cleared his throat, but his voice still emerged

hoarsely. "Hell, Ed, I'm not going to get married again, and you know it."

"I don't even think *you* know it, Beau."

With that, Ed walked out of his office, hands shoved in his pockets, whistling.

Beau glared after him, his heart pounding as though he'd just run a marathon.

Jordan shivered, rolling up her car window against the evening chill as she turned down M Street, heading home.

Labor Day had yet to arrive, and the official start of autumn was still nearly a month away, but tonight she could feel summer's end looming.

Maybe it would be easier to forget Beau and Spencer then, when fall's chilly days brought the promise of the holidays, and snow.

Snow.

She remembered Beau telling Spencer how eager he was to see snow this winter, his first away from the Deep South.

Beau.

Spencer.

Again.

Frustrated, Jordan reached out and turned on the radio. It was tuned to her favorite station.

The car filled with music. Mick Jagger singing about waiting on a friend.

Stopped at a light, Jordan listened to the familiar tune.

The Rolling Stones reminded her of Beau. They had listened to a Stones CD over and over during the endless, harrowing drive down to North Carolina that long-ago day. Not this song, but it didn't matter.

Everything, it seemed, carried her back. To him.

She reached out and jabbed the "Scan" button as the light turned. Driving forward, she heard the radio skittering from station to station, blaring snatches of familiar songs and DJs' voices.

She settled on a news station, certain that wouldn't prompt any memories of Beau and Spencer.

But as the newscaster read the weather forecast, her thoughts continued to drift back in time.

Going over everything that had happened, she tried to find something she could have done differently. Some pivotal moment when she could have gone in another direction to change the outcome.

Because, truth be told, as hard as she had tried to embrace this life she had so fleetingly left behind . . .

She could no longer deny that something was missing.

No.

That *someone* was missing.

Someone to share it with.

She was no longer content with her solo daily whirlwind of client meetings and party plans and recipe searches. It was no longer an interesting challenge to hunt down fourteen odd-sized lilac-printed tablecloths for a socialite's daughter's sweet-sixteen party, or two hundred perfect, oversized red apples for a reception for the mayor of New York. She was bored with flower arrangements and hors d'oeuvres and ice sculpture.

Bored with the work that had once felt so vital to who she was.

Yet she didn't want to be at home, either.

Her town house felt strangely empty and quiet these days. Spencer had inhabited her guest room for only a few days, yet somehow, every morning she walked by the closed door, she had to remind herself that the little boy wasn't sleeping on the other side.

She missed Spencer.

She missed Beau.

As fraught with tension and terror as those threesome days had been, she couldn't help feeling nostalgic for them.

Yet it wasn't that she wanted to go back, or that she even would if she could.

What she wanted . . .

Her impossible dream . . .

Was to go forward.

With Beau.

And Spencer.

To pick up where they had left off . . .

To make a fresh start . . .

Maybe you should start dating again, she told herself half-heartedly. *Maybe you can find your soul mate. Someone who's more right for you than Beau Somerville is. Someone steadfast and dependable and down-to-earth.*

But Beau was all of those things, she thought, shaking her head in frustration. Maybe he wasn't what she had imagined. Maybe he didn't fit the cardigan-clad, chess-playing, *Yes, dear* package.

But she couldn't help feeling as though Beau was meant to be married.

To me.

He's meant to be married to me.

Yeah, right.

And the world was meant to stop turning.

Turning down her quiet side street, Jordan tried to force her thoughts to the evening ahead—rather, what was left of it.

She would reheat the roasted red pepper, eggplant, and orzo soup she had made yesterday as an experimental recipe in preparation for a harvest luncheon she was catering. It was too heavy on the chicken stock and could have used another ingredient, maybe an herb, but it was still good. And her cupboards and fridge were pretty much bare.

Maybe she would turn on some classical music, have a glass of wine with her meal, read the latest issue of *Gourmet.*

It would be a nice, relaxing night, she promised herself as she pulled up in front of her town house.

Relaxing.

Not lonely.

But there was a disconcerting emptiness growing inside her as she got out of the car.

The streetlamps were on.

The moon was a bright, fully formed circle overhead.

The soles of her black low-heeled mules made a tapping noise on the pavement as she walked toward the house. Dangling her keys from her hand as she walked, she could hear the cicadas buzzing, and the sound of traffic nearby on the main street. The usual sounds.

Yet something was different.

She slowed her pace, looking up at her front stoop.

She felt it—the certainty that she wasn't alone—even before she saw the shadow silhouetted beside the front door.

Jordan stopped walking.

Her heart leapt into her throat.

Calacci was dead.

She knew that.

She had seen it for herself.

And Detective Rodgers kept her updated on the case

against Gisonni. His associate's incriminating testimony had virtually guaranteed that he would be spending a good, long time behind bars.

Jordan stood frozen, staring at the man on her stoop, trepidation coursing through her as her thoughts darted from one frightening possibility to another.

Gisonni could have escaped from prison.

Or sent another hit man.

Or—

"Jordan?"

The figure turned toward her.

A familiar voice carried down to where she stood.

A voice she hadn't heard in two months.

"Beau," she breathed, gaping at him as he stepped into the pool of light beside the door.

She was riveted to the spot, unable to believe he was really here. It was as though he had somehow stepped out of her fantasy and onto her doorstep.

He looked even better than she had imagined him. He was the same—broad shoulders, dark hair, handsome features—yet there was something different about his face.

She studied him as he came closer, the contrast between the old Beau and this man starkly evident in the shadowy light from the streetlight and porch lamps and from the full moon overhead.

She studied him. She couldn't put her finger on what was there that hadn't been there before. . . .

No. She couldn't do that, because that wasn't the issue. It was the opposite. She realized that something that had been there before, on Beau's face, was gone.

It was as though a veil had been lifted. His features were no longer visibly weighed by strain and sadness;

there was no longer a keep-your-distance wariness about his expression as he looked at her.

"What are you doing here?" she asked, her hushed voice laced with incredulity as he came to a stop a few feet away from her.

"Waiting for you," came the reply.

She could only stare, her thoughts careering wildly.

"Why?" she asked at last. "Did something happen?"

"Yes."

"What?" Her heart tripped over itself. Was it Spencer? Had harm come to Spencer? But how would Beau know that before she would?

"I came to my senses, Jordan," he said quietly, covering the last few feet of ground between them. "That's what happened."

He reached out and clasped her hands, both of them.

She was aware of his warm grasp, of the keys she still held pressing into her palm, of her heart beating so loudly that she was certain he could hear it.

"What do you mean, Beau?" she asked, certain she knew what he meant—and just as certain that she must be mistaken.

"I mean, my life is empty, Jordan. Without you."

Her breath caught in her throat as the meaning of those last two words sunk in.

"It's been empty for a long time," Beau went on, his voice uncustomarily husky, "but that's never felt as wrong to me as it has these last two months. I have no idea why it took me so long to figure out why."

She looked up at him, wondering if she dared to believe what he seemed to be telling her.

He brought their clasped hands up to his mouth and pressed her fingers to his lips. Their eyes met and held.

"I've missed you, Jordan."

"Beau," she said softly, "I've missed you, too. More than—more than you'll ever know."

And more than I ever wanted to admit, even to myself.

He exhaled softly, his breath a sigh of contentment in the still night air. "I'm sorry I kept pulling away from you, Jordan."

"I did the same thing."

"Believe me, it was the opposite of what I wanted to do. But for some crazy reason I thought it was the right thing to do. I thought I knew exactly why I was so drawn to you—and to Spencer, too, for that matter. I thought it must be that I was looking for a substitute for what I'd lost—"

"I thought the same thing. About you, I mean," she said in a rush, the truth spilling from her as though a tap had been opened. "Once you had told me about the plane crash—Beau, I knew that you were still troubled about what you'd been through with your wife and son . . ."

She trailed off tentatively. Yet somehow, it didn't hurt her to say those words. And they weren't met with the barren expression of grief she had grown to anticipate.

"I've had a lot to resolve," Beau told her. "And I won't pretend that it's been easy for me—or that I'm fully healed. But now I know that I can't get any further without help. Your help, Jordan."

"I'll help you." She tried to disregard a bitter shard of disappointment slicing into her heart.

All he needed was a shoulder to lean on? A sympathetic ear? How had she misunderstood what he was saying?

She looked away from his searching eyes, casting her own gaze down at her feet.

Beau gently put his hand beneath her chin and tipped her head up, forcing her to meet his gaze.

"You don't understand what I mean, Jordan," he said, his voice low. "I'm not asking you to be my therapist. And I'm not asking you to be my friend."

"You're not?"

"No."

She stared at him. Tried to deny what she saw in his eyes, but this time, she couldn't. It was plain to see.

If only he would say it aloud.

"Then . . . what are you asking me to be, Beau?" she asked in a ragged whisper.

"My wife."

His wife.

Her heart took flight, began to soar. She tried desperately to pull back, to keep her brimming emotions in check. He couldn't be saying what she thought he was saying. He couldn't be asking what she thought he was asking. Not when—

"I love you, Jordan."

She gasped.

He had said it.

Stunned, she found her voice. Echoed, "You love me?"

He nodded. "I love you. I don't know why it took me this long to figure things out, and I hope that you'll forgive me. I hope that you know those are three words I'd never use lightly."

"I know." She looked into his eyes, filled with wonder. "You love me."

"I love you." It was as though he couldn't say it enough.

And she knew she would never tire of hearing it.

"I love you, too, Beau," she said, with all her heart.

He bent his head and kissed her tenderly. If there had been the slightest ripple of doubt in her mind about his words, it was banished with his kiss. They seemed to fit perfectly together.

When he raised his head and looked down at her, they smiled.

"This is right," he said, nodding. "So incredibly right. How did we not see it before? We've wasted so much time. . . ."

"We've got nothing but time," Jordan said, tracing his jawline with her fingertips.

"You're right," Beau agreed softly, dipping his head to kiss her again. "Nothing but time."

Epilogue

It had rained during the night, but now, at eleven o'clock on Saturday morning, the June sun shone brightly and the sky was a delicate shade of blue. The notorious D.C. humidity was nowhere to be found today, and the air was pleasantly warm and breezy.

"It's perfect wedding weather," Jeremy said cheerfully, pouring himself another cup of coffee from the half-empty pot on Jordan's countertop.

Perfect wedding weather.

Once before, Jordan had heard those words.

That day, it had been Phoebe who uttered them as the two of them stood in front of a mirror in Jordan's girlhood bedroom, sunlight streaming through the window.

"It's **perfect** wedding weather, Jordan. Did you ever hear the saying, 'Happy is the bride the sun shines on'? Something like that, anyway," Phoebe had said, standing behind Jordan to adjust her billowing white illusion veil.

"I thought it was supposed to be good luck if it rains on your wedding day."

"They just say that so that brides won't feel bad about crummy weather," Phoebe had said, giving the veil a final gentle tug. "There. You look beautiful."

"You look beautiful, Jordan."

She blinked, then snapped her attention back to the present, realizing that Jeremy had spoken. He was looking at her with a fond, admiring smile.

"Thank you." She exhaled shakily and turned back to the full-length mirror on the back of the closet door to check her reflection one last time.

Her first thought was that she looked exactly as she did on any other day. Her makeup was no heavier than usual. Her hair was pulled back—all right, not in an elastic or a scrunchy, but in an ivory lace bow—but it was her typical style. Her jewelry was simple: pearl drop earrings and a matching strand.

Yes, from the neck up, she looked the pretty much the same.

From the neck down, she looked like . . .

A bride. I look like a bride.

She *was* a bride.

Again.

She shoved the slightest nagging doubt from her mind as she looked herself over, turning to the left and right with a critical eye.

The antique ivory lace dress was as far from a traditional wedding dress as you could get. It was simple yet elegant. There was no flowing train. It was ankle-length to reveal her low-heeled flapper-era shoes with wide bows.

This dress looked nothing like the wedding gown that had hung in her closet for several years.

Jordan found herself wondering idly whether someone had plucked it from the charity Dumpster shortly after she'd deposited it there last Labor Day weekend. Not that she cared. She never wanted to see that dress again.

She never wanted to think about that other wedding day again.

This was different.

"Are you ready?" Jeremy asked, setting his coffee mug in the sink and picking up his keys.

"I'm ready," she said with a smile. "Thanks for agreeing to drive me over to the church, Jeremy."

"What are friends for? As long as your father doesn't mind . . ."

"He won't mind. It's silly to make him come all the way over to Georgetown when his and Mom's hotel is right across from the church. He'll be happy just to walk me down the aisle. . . ."

Again.

Darn it! Why did the memory of the other wedding day persist?

Was this some kind of omen?

What if Beau . . . ?

No! Don't even think it! she commanded herself.

"You okay?" Jeremy asked, opening the front door for her.

"I'm fine," she said, a tremor in her voice.

Standing on the threshold, she looked around one last time.

Technically, the place was hers for another two weeks. The new occupants, Mrs. Villeroy's distant cousins, weren't moving in until the first of July. But most of Jordan's belongings were already in storage.

After she and Beau came back from their European honeymoon, she would return here only to get the last of her clothes.

Then they would head to the Delaware beach house they had rented for the summer. They had chosen Delaware because it was close enough for Beau to travel back and forth to the office on occasion, though he would mostly be working from home this summer.

And they had chosen Delaware because they wanted a fresh start. Somewhere that bore no reminders of the traumatic experiences a year ago this week.

No, they wanted to go on healing, and forgetting.

They would return to the capital area in the fall— just in time to move into their newly built three-story colonial home perched on fifty rolling acres of Virginia countryside.

Beau had designed the house, of course, with his bride in mind. It was complete with a gourmet kitchen, greenhouse, sewing room, gardens . . .

Also, of course, a sprawling playroom. A basketball hoop above the garage. And the biggest wooden jungle gym Jordan had ever seen, with swings and slides and multilevel decks covered in gaily striped awnings. It was perfect for—

"Jordan?" Jeremy prodded gently, touching her arm.

"Okay. Let's go." She smiled at him.

Then she stepped over the threshold into the bright June sunshine.

It was a beautiful day for a wedding.

Yet as they drove toward the church, Jordan found herself haunted again by memories of that other day, four years ago. . . .

"Goin' to the chapel," Phoebe had sung as the limousine headed through the familiar streets of Glen Hills. "Gonna get ma-a-a-rried . . ."

The old tune chimed in Jordan's head as Jeremy steered the car through the crowded Georgetown neighborhood. She had turned down Beau's offer of a stretch limousine. She wanted no reminders, and she wanted things to be low-key.

She might be marrying one of the wealthiest bachelors in the country, but she hadn't been looking for chauffeurs and glitz. She hadn't been looking for anything. . . .

Yet she had found the most precious, elusive thing of all.

Jeremy chattered as they drove along, mostly about the arrangements he'd made as caterer for the reception later, and about plans he had for expanding their business to include more corporate clients.

His business, now, she amended mentally.

Jordan had recently sold him her half, with only the slightest twinge of regret.

She would, after all, be busy with other things now. So busy, Beau teased, that she might not have time for him.

Smiling, she stared out the window and rested her hand—the hand upon which a colossal platinum diamond engagement ring shone—on the barely-there swell of her abdomen.

By the time they returned from Paris, she would probably be showing.

Then it wouldn't be their own special secret anymore.

It would be time to start thinking about layettes and Lamaze. About names and formula brands. Time to start sewing curtains for the nursery, and embroidering the pastel sampler she intended to hang on the wall there.

"Here we are," Jeremy said, pulling up in front of the charming white church just outside the city limits.

Yes. Here they were.

As he went around to open the door for Jordan, she saw familiar faces milling outside in the dappled shade. She saw the white runner bisecting the aisle between the open doors. She saw her father, handsome in his black tuxedo, waiting to take her arm.

Panic swelled within her.

It was just like before.

She turned away from the window, half-expecting to find Phoebe sitting next to her, saying, "Don't be nervous. It's going to be all right, Jordan."

Phoebe wasn't there.

But her voice was. It echoed in Jordan's mind.

It's going to be all right.

The words filled her with warmth. Phoebe *was* here. Jordan could feel her. In her heart, where it mattered most.

Jeremy was holding her door open.

Jordan emerged on the sidewalk, her legs nearly buckling beneath her.

Calm down. It's going to be fine.

That was then. This is now.

Now is different.

Now is Beau.

Jordan saw that the last stragglers had hastily disappeared inside the church. Moments later, after kissing her cheek and lowering her veil over her face, Jeremy trailed after them.

Now only her father remained, smiling at her through a filmy panel of illusion.

"You look beautiful, sweetheart," he said.

She nodded at him from behind her veil, unable to speak.

She took his arm.

Strains of organ music filtered out on the warm spring breeze.

Not Pachelbel's Canon in D.

This time, it was Handel's *Water Music*.

Jordan trembled, head bowed, as her father led her up the steps to the edge of the white satin runner.

The organ music faded.

There was a moment of silence.

Then came the opening strains of Handel's Wedding March.

Only then, poised in the doorway of the church, about to take the first step, did Jordan dare to look up.

It took a moment for her eyes to adjust to the dimly lit interior after the bright sunshine outside.

Then she glimpsed Spencer there, at the other end of the runner. A smile played across her lips as he made eye contact with her, grinned, and gave a cheerful wave. He looked far older than his five years, in a miniature tuxedo, his hair neatly combed to the side. Pinned to his lapel was a miniature white tea rose.

Jordan exhaled shakily, eyes searching the front of the church.

Was that—?!

Startled, she looked away—and then back again.

No. Just a trick of the light, she told herself.

For a moment, she thought she had seen Phoebe there, smiling, in her maid-of-honor dress.

Closing her eyes briefly, she heard her friend's voice again.

It's going to be all right.

Was it?

So much had happened.

Getting engaged to Beau . . .

Selling the business . . .

Planning the move . . .

And Phoebe's brother, Curt, agreeing, after a wildly successful holiday visit, to turn over custody of Spencer to Jordan and Beau.

But that was when everything had fallen into place at last.

Phoebe would have wanted it that way, Curt had said. *Spencer needs a mother. And a father. Sisters and brothers.*

Well, perhaps just one to start, Jordan thought.

She was certain there was an answering flutter in her womb.

Opening her eyes, she looked up again at the front of the church.

Where is he?

She knew that if she could just see him . . .

Where is he?

She scanned the church.

And felt a flicker of panic.

Then Andrea MacDuff, seated in the second pew on the right and wearing a large hat, moved her head.

That was when Jordan saw him.

Beau.

He was looking toward the back of the church, his chin lifted and body slightly tilted to see past the crowded pews, as if he were searching for something.

He saw her.

Their gazes collided.

He smiled.

She smiled.

That was when she knew that everything really would be all right.

And the last shred of fear evaporated.

"Here you go," her father said, giving her hand a squeeze.

"Yes," Jordan said. "Here I go."

And as the Wedding March played, she walked down the aisle toward her groom, their little boy ... and happily ever after at last.

Author's Note

If you would like to receive a current Janelle Taylor newsletter, bookmark, and descriptive flyer of past releases, send a self-addressed stamped envelope (SASE) (legal-size envelope is best for materials) to:

Janelle Taylor Newsletter #41
P.O. Box 211646
Augusta, GA 30917-1646

Reading is fun and educational, so do it often! To learn more about me and my works, check out Internet web sites at www.kensingtonbooks.com/janelletaylor, www.janelletaylor.com, and (very detailed) www.readersheart.com.

Best wishes from Janelle Taylor

Thrilling Romance from Lisa Jackson

__Twice Kissed	0-8217-6038-6	$5.99US/$7.99CAN
__Wishes	0-8217-6309-1	$5.99US/$7.99CAN
__Whispers	0-8217-6377-6	$5.99US/$7.99CAN
__Unspoken	0-8217-6402-0	$6.50US/$8.50CAN
__If She Only Knew	0-8217-6708-9	$6.50US/$8.50CAN
__Intimacies	0-8217-7054-3	$5.99US/$7.99CAN
__Hot Blooded	0-8217-6841-7	$6.99US/$8.99CAN

Call toll free **1-888-345-BOOK** to order by phone or use this coupon to order by mail.

Name_____

Address_____

City_____ State _____ Zip _____

Please send me the books I have checked above.

I am enclosing $_____

Plus postage and handling* $_____

Sales tax (in New York and Tennessee) $_____

Total amount enclosed $_____

*Add $2.50 for the first book and $.50 for each additional book.

Send check or money order (no cash or CODs) to:

Kensington Publishing Corp., 850 Third Avenue, New York, NY 10022

Prices and Numbers subject to change without notice. All orders subject to availability.

Check out our website at **www.kensingtonbooks.com**.

Discover the Magic of
Romance With

Kat Martin

__The Secret

0-8217-6798-4   **$6.99**US/**$8.99**CAN

Kat Rollins moved to Montana looking to change her life, not find
another man like Chance McLain, with a sexy smile and empty
heart. Chance can't ignore the desire he feels for her—or the suspi-
cion that somebody wants her to leave Lost Peak . . .

__Dream

0-8217-6568-X   **$6.99**US/**$8.99**CAN

Genny Austin is convinced that her nightmares are visions of another
life she lived long ago. Jack Brennan is having nightmares, too, but
his are real. In the shadows of dreams lurks a terrible truth, and only
by unlocking the past will Genny be free to love at last . . .

__Silent Rose

0-8217-6281-8   **$6.99**US/**$8.50**CAN

When best-selling author Devon James checks into a bed-and-breakfast
in Connecticut, she only hopes to put the spark back into her relationship with her fiancé. But what she experiences at the Stafford Inn
changes her life forever . . .

Call toll free **1-888-345-BOOK** to order by phone or use this
coupon to order by mail.

Name_____

Address_____

City _____ State_____ Zip_____

Please send me the books I have checked above.

I am enclosing $_____

Plus postage and handling* $_____

Sales tax (in New York and Tennessee only) $_____

Total amount enclosed $_____

*Add $2.50 for the first book and $.50 for each additional book.

Send check or money order (no cash or CODs) to: **Kensington Publishing
Corp., Dept. C.O., 850 Third Avenue, New York, NY 10022**

Prices and numbers subject to change without notice. All orders subject
to availability. Visit our website at **www.kensingtonbooks.com**.

DO YOU HAVE THE
HOHL COLLECTION?